WICKED SATYR NIGHTS

WICKED SATYR NIGHTS

THE CURSED SATYROI - BOOK ONE

REBEKAH LEWIS

CONTENTS

Chapter 1   I
Chapter 2   10
Chapter 3   30
Chapter 4   37
Chapter 5   46
Chapter 6   56
Chapter 7   69
Chapter 8   80
Chapter 9   92
Chapter 10   100
Chapter 11   129
Chapter 12   152
Chapter 13   160
Chapter 14   168
Chapter 15   176
Chapter 16   192
Chapter 17   203
Chapter 18   215
Chapter 19   223
Chapter 20   230
Bonus Scene   238

About the Author   245
Books by Rebekah Lewis   247

For Kat, Mia, and Jordy for taking time out of your busy lives to be my betas. You rock! And for Jenn, Hailey, Lana, Mel, and Dawn for being my support group and helping me pick the title of this book.

For my family: I love you.

CHAPTER 1

K at's life had become a circus. Not just because she worked with animals for a living, but because the people who meandered their way into it were bizarre. With that thought in the back of her mind, she took a seat across from the business tycoon she had never met. She straightened her posture and forced a smile on her face, even though the reason for her requested attendance was just as mysterious as the man in front of her.

Mr. Dion Bach steepled his fingers together on the glossy mahogany desk. The very picture of wealth, he wore a crisp black suit and shirt with cufflinks glistening of onyx and diamonds. His tie, however, stood out in a pop of deep burgundy, the silk of which rolled over the button line of his shirt like the richest wine. "You're probably wondering why I called you in, Dr. Silverton."

"I must say I was a little surprised when I received your phone call." More like his secretary's phone call, but Kat wasn't one to argue the small details.

With a smile that seemed more habitual than genuine, Mr. Bach opened the manila folder lying neatly in front of him. While Kat sat in the waiting room for the past thirty minutes, she'd spent the time counting the mosaic tiles on the floor and imagining what Dion Bach looked like. She'd pictured a ruddy old geezer, but that was way off. His hair was thick and tawny, closely cropped. He was attractive, about thirty, give or take, with a cleft chin, an athletic build, and skin so tan it put her Irish complexion to shame.

His bulky leather and wood chair had a high, carved back that made it look more similar to a throne than office furniture. It resided upon a raised marble slab along with the enormous wooden desk. Two Corinthian-style columns stood on either side. Small alcoves lined the shockingly white, portrait-less walls, with mythological busts displayed upon pillars. Ivy plants were placed in the corners of the room, yet the air smelled woodsy, reminiscent of evergreen. Regardless, she felt like she was in a courtroom or a museum.

Mr. Bach was the CEO of Bach Industries, a company known to invest in film, television, science, music, and just about anything which took to the elusive owner's fancy. He was wealthy, but remained out of the spotlight. He likely paid several hundred people to stay that way.

As though sensing Kat's scrutiny of him and his surroundings, he glanced up through thick, dark lashes and resumed the smile from before. It didn't meet his eyes. "I was sorry to hear of your unfortunate accident last summer. You are very lucky you had a crew member with you who scared the mountain lion away before the attack turned fatal."

He didn't waste any time. Kat nodded once, but she was used to hearing the same comments about the attack. She had grown weary of all the apologies by people who felt obligated to say something about it. Since the encounter with the cougar, she'd been the recipient of a lot of pity—not all of it genuine. Kat doubted this man was any different.

He continued, barely looking up to catch her nod. "As I understand it, you were called to the location in West Virginia to give your professional opinion to the authenticity of a supposed black panther which was sighted in the area where the cat attacked you."

"Yes, sir. We were gathering evidence in the forest when the cat came out of the bushes. Took me down between my left thigh and hip, clawed me up a bit. Luckily, we had someone in our group who was licensed to carry a firearm in case something like that did happen. He was able to run it off with a shotgun blast, so the cougar never managed to go for the kill." Had she suffered the same wounds to her throat, she'd have been dead before she registered what had her in its jaws. Kat knew she'd been extremely lucky, but it didn't help in the long run. She'd made a horrible judgment call that day, and it had cost her.

"Very fortunate indeed."

Absently, Kat found herself gazing into Mr. Bach's dark brown eyes. They were almost full black, and she couldn't distinguish where the pupil ended and the iris began. No warmth there, no welcome. Only the uncomfortable twinge of judgment made her avert her gaze and suck in a calming breath. Different from the cat in the forest, Mr. Bach's eyes seemed to hold knowledge that she was inferior to him in every way, and should he deem her unworthy, she'd be dead. Kat reached down to grasp the leather strap of her purse in a tight fist. It would be rude to bolt from an interview that could put her back to work again. Work she wanted to do, anyway. Perhaps the strain of recalling the accident was making her delusional. A sort of post-traumatic shock?

Mr. Bach cleared his throat. If he was aware of her distress, he didn't point it out. "Nevertheless, you discovered an existing population of mountain lions in an area which had not seen scientifically proven evidence of their presence in over a decade. It may not have been a black panther, but the cat was still considered a cryptid in the scientific community, was it not?"

It was. Cryptozoology was the study of creatures never proven to have existed. Yet, in some cases, the animals, or cryptids, *had* actually lived at one point, just not in the time or area the various sightings occurred. Black panthers certainly existed. Both the jaguar and leopard often bred melanistic variations rather than the familiar golden felines.

However, only a small population of wild jaguars not in captivity or owned by exotic pet owners were ever found in the United States. They were the common variety, and a far cry away from West Virginia. And that was only one location where sightings had occurred.

The scientific community generally snubbed the very idea of cryptids unless something could be substantiated, and that was rare. In most cases, the sightings were proven as hoaxes or mistaken identities. Or they were considered the results of a superstitious mind.

She let go of the purse strap and clutched both hands together in her lap to keep from fidgeting. "Yes, sir. My group got lucky." But the poor cougar was still put down afterward. Kat had been distraught. She'd begged them to catch it and take it to an animal sanctuary and not to kill it since there was evidence of a possible litter nearby. The mother cougar, considered a danger due to the attack, was hunted and shot. Kat had been furious. The four cubs were captured and taken to a nearby refuge. So far, they hadn't located the cat that fathered the young, and she hoped they never did. It didn't do much good to find an existing population if they were going to remove the entire lot of them. If humans allowed their cities to continue growing and expanding, there wouldn't be anywhere left for the animals to live outside of captivity.

"Let's jump to the chase, shall we?" Mr. Bach turned a sheet of paper over with a barely audible *swoosh* and placed it on the left side of the small stack of documents in the folder. Kat wondered what he had on her and why. He picked up the next page and studied it a moment before he spoke again. "I am invested in a series of documentaries based on popular figures of cryptozoology in the States and over the globe. The scientist I had wrangled to work one of the most anticipated segments bailed out last minute. I hoped, even though I'm fully aware this isn't the area of your expertise, that you would be willing to take on this project."

Okay, vague much? "That would depend on what the project is exactly. I'm a zoologist with a specialty in big cats. I'm not a cryptozoologist, and wouldn't know where to start with something outside of felines, so I would be little help if the project has to do with Bigfoot."

He smiled again, and this time a spark of amusement flashed in his eyes. Why did Kat feel like it was the smug look of a hunter about to go in for the kill shot?

"Ah, but that is the beauty of cryptozoology. If a creature is not an established member of the animal kingdom, has never existed in the eyes of science, how in the world could anyone become an expert on the thing? There are those with merely the knowledge of the facts at hand, those who are obsessed, and those that have a general knowledge of animal species and can use it to their advantage in seeking out clues to the *possible* existence of such a being. And that last kind of person is what I need you to be."

Being? Did he say being? Oh, Christ. It *was* Bigfoot, wasn't it? Kat looked around the room, waiting for a person to leap out, point at her, and laugh hysterically.

"Mr. Bach, I'm still not following. What exactly *is* the cryptid you want me to try to locate?"

"Oh, I didn't tell you?" He was the very picture of innocence. The type of innocence the serpent in Eden would have been if it had taken on a human figure. Those dark pits of his eyes held her reflection within them, sealing her fate.

"N-no, sir," she squeaked out, cheeks heating at her less than confident reply.

"My apologies. I have a terrible habit of getting ahead of myself." Another piece of paper was set on top of the overturned pile. He picked up the next page, glanced at it with a smirk, and placed it in front of her. He tapped it lightly with the tips of his fingers before pulling his hand away and revealing the picture printed there.

Kat stared down at it, glanced back up in disbelief, and quickly looked again. She had to have imagined it. Nope, there it was. It appeared to be a bipedal horse with scrawny stork legs, a forked tail, and bat wings. It was as though she found herself trapped in an episode of *Looney Tunes* with the word SUCKER printed across her head in all capital letters. At any second, the ground would fall out from under her.

"Pardon me, but what the hell is this thing?" She kind of wished it had been Bigfoot. At least a new species of primate walking on two legs was conceivable, even if the legends were fantastical. *This* thing was a nightmarish monster out of a storybook.

He laughed. He had a jolly, infectious laugh that made her want to join in. She began to smile foolishly, but then she remembered the horse-headed, bat-winged, demon thing and sobered up.

"That, my dear Dr. Silverton, is the most common depiction of the Jersey Devil. It's a creature that has supposedly been sighted off and on in the Pine Barrens of New Jersey for over three hundred years." With a grin, he added, "They named a hockey team after it."

Kat blinked.

"Well?" Mr. Bach's face went stoic. At least on the surface. His eyes had more of a twinkle to them than Kat appreciated. *Is he enjoying my confusion?* Kat crossed her arms and rubbed the skin exposed under the short bell sleeves of her white dress shirt. Gooseflesh met her touch, and she shivered.

"I really don't know what to say." And she didn't. Was he serious?

"Say, 'Why, yes, Mr. Bach. I will take the job.'" He examined another page in the folder. Kat inwardly groaned. *What next?*

"Bach Industries will supply film equipment, pay for hotel costs, gas, and meals. You have two to three weeks on the location to handle the project however you feel works best, beginning in two weeks' time. I would only advise you to *try* to look like you believe in at least the possibility of the creature's existence. You want to sell the footage, not make a mockery of it."

There was actually a way to make *more* of a mockery of it?

She studied felines, not crazy hybrid urban legends. There was a high chance the creature couldn't even have the precedence to exist—unless it was a freak show like the platypus, which also was said not to have existed at one point. But the platypus was tiny. This thing looked huge. And it flew!

Then again, people repeatedly reported the existence of pterosaurs in New Guinea, among other places. Either there were too many skeptics and no one took it seriously, or those creatures were really good at staying hidden even though they soared around all day, hunting whatever they made a diet of. They must have a grand ole time of causing hapless witnesses to run about in a tizzy, trying to make someone believe they saw what they saw.

Or there was that other crazy theory. The one where they don't exist and people let their imagination run wild. Kat put her money on that one. The way she saw it, animals that went extinct within the last century had a better chance of existing than something that had died out millions of years ago. And a black panther in an uncommon region could be an escaped exotic pet no one had reported. It was a small possibility, but a plausible one. Unfortunately, mistaken identity—an average cougar, a large Labrador, or a black alley cat that looked like it was a big cat from far away but really wasn't—ruled out most sightings.

Kat was a skeptic. She'd own up to it if challenged. She was a product of the stuffy scientific community, after all. Until proven, it didn't exist. Though it was fun to daydream about discovering a new or previously extinct species, she knew the chances of such a thing occurring were slim to none. People wasted their lives hunting for monsters and rarely found a single piece of compelling evidence to make it worth their while.

"If you don't mind me asking, why would you consider me for this particular project? I'm sure there are several cryptozoologists who would die for a chance like this. Not to mention how far outside of my field of expertise this is. If you're familiar with my accident, then you likely know I've had difficulty regaining my footing because of my mishap. A project like this one could ruin me, if I haven't accomplished that feat already."

"Everyone makes mistakes. You survived yours, and the majority of your problems stemmed from dealing with recovery and physical therapy rather than not having work. You've been in and out of the Florida research facilities. I've done my homework. In fact, it was while researching scientists to bring onto this project that I came across your previous work. The documentaries you did for *National Geographic* on the African leopard were phenomenal." He paused. "You blush, Dr. Silverton? Are you not used to praise?"

From a wealthy, attractive icon? Hell no, she wasn't. Though she didn't miss the fact Mr. Bach hadn't voiced concern over endangering her career by sending her out to chase urban myths.

He continued, "I figured a woman who takes her research and projects seriously would be a very nice investment into my documentary series. The fact you are accomplished in your field at only thirty-two is also a good sign. It's a bonus to have an attractive woman with beautiful red hair and bright blue eyes in front of the camera as well. Helps market to the shallow crowd and not only to those who are interested in science or the paranormal."

Because of her pale skin there was no hiding the blush that scalded her face and neck at his compliments. There was truth to what he said, but it still made her uncomfortable when people in the industry labeled her as beautiful. She was a scientist, not a movie star. Lately, the lines between the two had been thinning, even before the accident, as finding work in the current economy became more difficult than ever. She used the money from the films she'd made toward field research assignments. While she didn't mind lab work and researching from home, she preferred to be in the middle of it all. She loved being engulfed by nature. The sights, sounds, and smells...they were a wonderful escape from city life. She never thought she'd be on television, but she welcomed the opportunities when they presented themselves.

Mr. Bach put the paper down and folded his hands in front of him. "I'll let you pick your crew and your pay rate. I'll even fund the next three research expeditions of your choice as a thank you for taking on this project. I know it is rather last minute."

Wait a second? Three funded research trips? Choosing her own pay and crew? *Hellz to the yes.*

In that case... "Why, yes, Mr. Bach. I will take the job."

Even if he did give her the creeps.

CHAPTER 2

Two weeks later

"Penny for your thoughts?"

Kat glanced up from her laptop and shrieked. Recovering quickly, she hopped up and punched Rick Martinez in the shoulder. Behind him, Cindy keeled over laughing on the hotel bed.

"Ow! Lighten up." Rick rubbed his shoulder. Then he chuckled as well. "Oh, man. You shoulda seen the look on your face. You were like, 'Oh my God, the Jersey Devil is gonna get me!' and jumped about ten feet out of your chair." He dodged a second punch.

"Eat me." Kat leaned over her computer and yanked the red devil mask off Rick's face and dropped it to the floor.

"No thanks. And you better watch out, *chica*. One of these days, you're gonna say that to the wrong dude and find yourself flat on your back. Besides, I'm taken." He made a show out of planting a loud smooch on Cindy's lips and sat down across from Kat at the small round table next to the window.

"Where the hell did you get that ugly thing?" Kat sneered at the mask which peered upward like a bloodstain against ugly tan carpet.

"Gas station next door," Cindy chimed in as she tied her long brown hair into a high ponytail with a shockingly neon pink rubber band. She stretched out on the bed and then reached for the remote.

Kat snorted. "Waste of money, if you ask me."

Rick and Cindy Martinez had been married five years, and they had been working with her longer than that. Cindy was Kat's best friend, so when Cindy tagged along to "chaperone" the all-male film crew Kat used when working with *National Geographic,* she hadn't minded. Though her goal was to make sure no one took advantage of the overly trusting zoologist as they followed her around, Cindy had hit it off with Rick right away. They'd been nearly inseparable ever since. The two of them worked well together and knew the equipment. There really hadn't been any question as to who was right for the job when Kat went about organizing the trip to New Jersey.

However, she would never admit aloud that she'd only hired her two friends and no one else because the project itself embarrassed her. Oh, the ridicule she'd face in the eyes of science. Kat should've picked out a rock to hide under for when she returned to her rinky-dink apartment in Tampa. She was still trying to figure out what possessed her to tell Mr. Bach she would make the film. *Temporary insanity maybe? Over-exhaustion from having to drive to Atlanta to meet with him?*

"Learn anything new, Scully?" Rick leaned over to retrieve his mask, which was a mix between a horse face and a classical red devil. It even had the little demon horns at the top and a pointed goatee.

"Scully? Really? *X-Files* references? If that makes you Mulder, you're not a very good one. Last I checked, you considered this project to be, and I quote, 'The most atrociously stupid thing you ever agreed to do, but if you were being paid *that* much to hunt air, then you would be a fool not to jump on the crazy train before it left the station.'" Kat crossed her arms and raised a brow. Cindy snickered behind her as she flipped channels.

"Just because I don't believe in horse-faced demon bats doesn't mean I don't believe in other monsters." He reached up a tanned hand and scratched at the back of his head, mussing his short, black hair.

"Uh-huh. Name one you believe in."

Without missing a beat, Rick chucked the mask on the table in the dramatic fashion of someone dropping a football on the ground in a post-touchdown victory move. "*Chupacabra.*"

"Oh, God. Here we go again." Cindy groaned and shook her head.

Kat shared a look with her before facing Rick. "You do realize your grandmother told you those stories to prevent you from wandering off when you played outside." *El chupacabra* was a canine-like creature that supposedly sucked the blood out of goats and other small animals if they were unlucky enough to encounter it.

"That's exactly what Scully would say."

A knock at the door sounded, and her body jerked in the seat. Second time she'd jumped in surprise, and she was not amused by it. From outside, someone muttered, "Room service," and Rick strolled over to the door to see what was up. No one had placed an order, so it was with baffled surprise that Kat observed Rick accepting a bottle of wine from the hotel employee before the young woman mumbled something and turned on her heel to scamper off.

Rick placed the bottle beside Kat. It was a red wine in a frosted-over, clear bottle with a foreign label. The characters written across it seemed as though they might be Greek, but she had snoozed through foreign languages, learning what she needed to know only when she needed to know it. It could be Russian or ancient Sumerian, but she wouldn't know the difference. She was all about the animal sciences and really didn't give a crap about the human ones. They were jackasses in history, and they were jackasses in the present. Aside from a few close friends and family, Kat would rather deal with animals than humans on any given day.

"What's this?" she asked, picking up the bottle. It was cool to the touch, like it had been chilled before delivery. The rosy liquid inside swished around with movement; in the fading sunlight, it could easily pass for blood. Very thinned-out blood, anyway.

Okay, morbid much? Second time she'd compared things to blood tonight. *Get it together, Kat.*

"It's a gift from our employer. I guess it is all yours since we don't drink alcohol." The last time Rick drank was in his college days. He'd blacked out and then woken up in jail for public indecency. It seemed drunken streaking through a sorority house was frowned upon in modern society. He'd gone cold turkey ever since. When they started dating, Cindy stopped drinking as well to keep him from temptation. Kat thought it was nice seeing the support she gave him in cutting it out of her life too.

"This looks like expensive wine." Kat searched for a year marked on the bottle but only saw the foreign label. "I guess it would be rude not to drink it. I'll try a glass, well, plastic cup, rather, before bed." She'd have to see if the hotel store had a corkscrew. Although, she wasn't sure why Mr. Bach wanted her boozed up to film his documentary. Then she focused back on the computer screen where artistic renderings of the Jersey Devil awaited her attention and decided being drunk might actually help her survive the project.

Kat set the bottle aside and resumed her research. The number of police reports, urban legends, sightings, and supposed facts Mr. Bach had e-mailed her the week before still boggled her mind. She kept reading them over and over again, trying to determine the best course of action. Some of the official reports were laughable and beyond farfetched. She really had her work cut out for her and not because it was a far cry from felines. Not to mention, the reasoning for her part in the project still wasn't clear other than using her looks to sell the product. *So this is what selling out feels like, eh?* Kat shook her head. She needed the money and the funded projects. *Exactly. You sold out.*

Kat rested her face against her hand, leaning her elbow on the table, and made a real effort not to smack her forehead into her laptop repeatedly. "This thing has an origin story to coincide with the first documented sightings, and it has been seen all through the area since the eighteenth century. If it was even possible for one of these things to exist, there is no way it could have survived this long, unless it was part of a breeding population. If it came into existence the way the legend suggests, there isn't anything it could have bred with, logically, to create offspring in its image. It would have to be immortal for people to continue having sightings, and immortality is a fairy tale."

"Could be asexual reproduction," Cindy proposed.

Kat shook her head. "No. Parthenogenesis has never been proven in any mammal species. Aside from the serpentine tail, the other features of this thing come from mammals. Besides, where is the bone evidence to prove these things are even out there alive, let alone dying or reproducing?"

She was getting a massive headache. Kat didn't know how she would pull this documentary off given her own skepticism. Mr. Bach wanted believable, but she'd be lucky if she could force an authentic smile for the camera while talking about the subject. "No animal is immortal. So how is it still being sighted if not a case of mistaken identity or hoaxes?" Her question was more for herself to decipher than her companions, and she quickly scribbled it in the margin of her notebook to go back to later.

"And what was the origin of it again? You were very vague in the whole we-leave-in-two-weeks-pack-a-bag method of pulling us onto this project." Cindy had grown bored with the television and began filing her nails. She held one hand out in front of her to inspect her work. "Come to think of it, you haven't said much more on the subject itself since then."

"Yeah, because you laughed so hard when I tried to tell you about the project that you couldn't stand up. So you laid there on the floor guffawing, crying from it, and clutching your stomach like an alien would shoot out if you continued on that way. Which you did. For nearly an hour." If only she had videotaped it. One to show the grandkids.

"Well, yeah. I expected it to be the usual, not something that sounds like a bad Frankenstein's monster attempt. And who the hell uses words like guffawing?"

"Whatever. As the legend goes—"

"Hold up." Cindy jumped to her feet and grabbed the hotel keycard off table. "Let's film this so we don't have to listen to crazy talk twice while Ricardo here is trying to contain his amusement." Rick grinned like a fool as she pulled him to his feet and pushed him past the calico-patterned curtains of various greens and reds. She shoved him out the door with the keycard to collect his equipment from their room, three doors down to the right. Cindy made a shooing gesture with a wave of her hand at Rick's retreating form.

They joked with each other, but they knew the project was a wonderful opportunity for all of them. Rick had filmed some weddings here or there, but he had a hard time working for other employers. He'd encountered every issue from pushy directors to ignorant assholes who assumed he was an illegal alien when he was an American citizen, as were his parents before him. His grandparents had come to the States from Mexico in the sixties. He was born and raised in Texas, and his father had been a landowner there. Rick was full of good humor and a great husband to Cindy. On top of it all, he was an excellent cameraman who could navigate his way out of a maze using tracking skills and the sky.

Then there was Cindy. She was a true-blue Southern girl

through and through. Born and raised in Alabama, she'd moved to Florida after college and met Kat. Both had recently moved into the Tampa area, excited about warm weather and Florida beaches. She was as girly as they came. She loved pink, always had fresh-cut flowers in her house, and her fingernails were never void of color. While Rick had become the most important aspect of her life, Cindy still occasionally kicked him out for a few moments of girl time with her best friend.

Cindy flopped back on the bed, the back of one hand against her forehead, imitating a theatrical swoon. "I thought he'd never leave. He's such an attention whore."

Kat giggled. She knew Cindy was well aware Rick hadn't been part of the previous conversation. "You married him knowing he'd be in the middle of everything."

"You're right." She sat up in the middle of the bed. Her white shirt and light blue jeans stood out against the dark comforter. "What was I thinking?"

"I know exactly what you were thinking." Kat wagged her eyebrows, getting herself smacked with a pillow in response.

"Do you think we'll find the Jersey Devil? I mean, there has to be something causing all the sightings in the area. The most recent one was three weeks ago, about a twenty-minute drive away. Don't give me that look. I read your notes while you were napping in the car. I find it interesting. Hilarious, but interesting."

Kat flopped on the foot of the bed and stared at the bumpy ceiling. The hotel room had the faint smell of lemon cleaner in the air. And the chair had been uncomfortable. She rubbed her thigh where the cougar had bitten her. "Mass hysteria maybe. People wanting attention. Large owls scaring people in the dark. Teenagers chasing their friends while wearing demon costumes." She nodded toward Rick's mask. "I doubt anyone will ever find a specimen that remotely resembles the Jersey Devil. And if they do, I bet you fifty bucks it's a hoax." She had read there were a few local stops that claimed to have skeletal remains, and resigned herself to the knowledge she'd have to go take samples from them before they left town, even though she knew if the bones were legit someone would have reported it already.

"Your scar is bothering you, isn't it?"

"It still feels a little tender sometimes. I think I sat in the chair too long."

Cindy hadn't been in the woods the day of the cougar attack. She'd been in the hotel suite, cooking dinner, when she received the call from Rick and rushed to meet them at the hospital where Kat had been air-lifted. Cindy had sat with her in the hospital, held her hand, and shared her despair as the news anchor sang the praise of the animal control officials who hunted the poor cat down and ended its life for being true to its species. For defending its territory and protecting its young. She also called Kat's family to inform them of the accident, even though Kat rarely stayed in contact with them due to schedules and distance. And it was Cindy who helped her through physical therapy, always smiling and sunny even when Kat was at her lowest.

She had also been the one to argue with Kat that she wasn't selling out by doing the Jersey Devil documentary, even though Kat still believed she had. At least it would fund future fieldwork, which other scientists would understand, especially since she hadn't been able to do much more than research at home until she healed enough to walk. The cat had taken a good bite out of her leg. Since money was short due to medical bills, Kat was forced to return to the labs, but the sterile environment reminded her of the hospital. Sitting at home, pouting over her online banking account, she'd received the call from Bach Industries. When Mr. Bach offered the job to her, she'd caved so fast it was tragic.

However, Kat worried the scientific community would never let her live it down. The only reason she didn't hear smart-ass comments about her screw-up with the cougar was because she'd been badly injured. Most people knew good and well Kat had learned her lesson, and she wouldn't make the same mistake twice. As for this project, she didn't anticipate any danger aside from the damage to her reputation because the people she usually worked with didn't take cryptozoology seriously at all.

The *beep* of a keycard being swiped through the mechanized door lock had her glancing up as Rick stepped into the room carrying a camera bag, a tripod, and a microphone on a stick he referred to as a boom. When following her about as she worked, he had a handheld camera and a microphone that would be attached on her person so she didn't have to be right in front of the camera to talk. But for interior shoots, he liked to use the better equipment.

Cindy bounced off the bed and assisted him as he set up. Kat wasn't much help with the technical aspects of filming, so she left that part to the Martinezes. She just had to look pretty and sound knowledgeable while she let Rick and Cindy do the recording, editing, and all that fun stuff.

As they powered up the equipment, Kat meandered to the bathroom mirror to ensure she looked presentable for the camera. Her long coppery hair was pulled back loosely, a few strands curled down beside her face, and the rest was softly contained in an elastic band but not harshly slicked flat. Kat genuinely didn't like to wear a lot of makeup, but the camera and hotel lighting had the tendency to make her look like Casper. She powdered her face, hiding the few faint freckles that bridged across her nose. A little blush and a quick layer of lip balm finished her off.

"One day you will wish you let me do your makeup," Cindy called from the other room, and Kat smiled. Cindy could make a frog look like a princess if given cosmetics to work with.

Brushing lint off the sleeve of her dark gray cotton T-shirt, Kat wandered back into the main room. Rick had opened the curtains as far as they would go, and the setting sun allowed a small window of natural light. He positioned Kat's chair where the light would benefit the shot, and her, the best. She reclaimed her chair, sat up straight, took a deep breath, and smiled.

"Ready?"

"Just a moment." Rick angled the camera on the tripod, centering Kat in the shot. After retrieving the boom from the bed, he handed it to Cindy, and she positioned it to where the microphone would not be visible as the camera rolled. Rick hit a button on the camera. Then he nodded.

Here goes nothing.

"The Jersey Devil may very well be one of America's most notorious monsters. It makes its home in the New Jersey Pine Barrens, a densely forested area that stretches about one million acres. The origin of the legend begins in the eighteenth century, and some sources even pinpoint the exact year to be 1735. The most prominent version of the story involves a woman known as Deborah Leeds. While in the throes of birth to her thirteenth child, she cried out, 'Let this one be a devil!' Not long after the child was born, it supposedly sprouted wings and flew up the chimney, where it disappeared into the forest. In the early twentieth century, more and more reported sightings were documented, raising a panic that the creature was really lurking out in the pinelands."

Kat paused, keeping a tight grip on her facial muscles. She struggled to avoid making a face in order to continue. "The appearance of the Jersey Devil is varied at times, but more often than not, pretty standard. It has a horse-like head, a humanesque torso, and stands on two feet, which are often described as goat-like with cloven hooves. It has wings resembling those of a bat and a serpentine, forked tail."

She stopped once more and glanced down at her notes before regaining eye contact with the camera. "We're about twenty to thirty minutes away from Leeds Point, the supposed birthplace of the creature and the site of one of the most recent encounters with the cryptid. Tomorrow, we will begin our search at the ruins of the fabled birthplace. We had to obtain special permits to visit and film there, as it is not open to the public. Later in the week, we'll be placing camera traps in various sections of the Pine Barrens where locals have heard strange shrieking and where sightings have occurred. Who knows, maybe the Jersey Devil will even allow us a fleeting glimpse to prove he is alive and well so many years after his mysterious birth."

Oh, yeah. This was going to be a long two weeks.

$\sim$

THE CLAMOR OF NEARBY VOICES WOKE PAN FROM A MOST RELAXING slumber. Morning sunlight glared through the canopy of trees above, mocking him. Because the times he managed to sleep dreamlessly were few and far between, the disruption grated his nerves. He gritted his teeth at the sounds and held up a hand to shield his eyes from the bright onslaught. After adjusting, he yawned and supposed it was time to get up and occupy himself somehow. Finding a method to distract from his eternal boredom hadn't gone very well lately.

There wasn't much to do aside from playing tricks on the hapless humans. He supposed he could fall back on old habits and allow himself to be ruled by his lust as he had three thousand years ago, but he worried he wouldn't be able to stop if he did. He'd been close to mindless, living for the pleasure of it. Something he'd been able to control enough around others like him, but not entirely.

And now... Pan lived for a nice, leisurely nap. But at least he did eventually rouse, unlike so many of the other gods of olden times. Last he'd heard, most of them were just shy of comatose within their fortified realm of Mount Olympus, hoping to wake the day they had followers once more. *Idiots.* They were long forgotten, enjoyed as bedtime stories and fanciful movie characters. It amused him beyond words.

The gods had become lessons in morality, gender, religion, sexuality, and culture. Reduced to a fictional existence because the humans who told their stories had long since died. Those who remained couldn't wrap their minds around anything other than science and what their own two eyes could perceive as reality. Sure, there were several religions that believed in a higher power capable of defying the laws of science, but even those individuals would scoff when confronted with the idea of an extraordinary being and turn the other cheek. Unfortunately, those who were open-minded feared the worst from the unexplained, considering anything unheard of as unholy monsters. Demons.

Pan stretched before reaching his hand behind him to brush the moss and grass from his denim-encased backside. He'd gone through a period of nudity while living in seclusion at one point, a few centuries back. Wearing clothes served him no purpose or comfort, but rolling over on a pinecone was even less wonderful than the freedom being naked provided. In the old days, he'd covered himself in animal furs or even the light fabrics of the Greek and Roman civilizations of long past. But since arriving in North America, he'd had to adapt to new cultural trends should he wish to go among society without drawing attention to himself. The clothing over the decades changed rapidly, but he found jeans agreeable. Luckily, he could manifest his clothes, as he needed them tailor-made, so to speak. It was difficult to shop for pants that worked with hooves rather than feet. Too much length could trip him, and balance was still an issue—even for a god.

Not that anyone could see him under his cloaking glamour, but if they could, they'd see a tall man in denim and a T-shirt. If they glanced at his head or his feet, they'd believe he'd escaped from a circus sideshow. Unlike the common depiction of satyrs, his legs hadn't become scrawny appendages that could barely support his weight. Where his calves would have met with ankles and heels, they curved in the opposite direction of his knee and into thick cloven hooves. Curling along the sides of his head were two horns, like those of a ram. They were bulky and hard, the ends blunted.

Mythology painted satyrs in various different forms, but he didn't have a goatee or elongated ears. His legs were hairier than a normal man's past his knees, but looked like any other man's above mid-thigh. He didn't have a tail or any other animal-like features. In truth, he was not part animal at all, though the horns, hooves, and hairy legs might seem that way. He had been cursed into this form, and his body had grown, reshaped, and mutated into the beastly appearance. He was just malformed and horny. *Eternally horny.* The punishment for a crime he'd not meant to commit. A crime that hadn't been truly a crime. A misunderstanding really...

Fortunately for him, he was a god. He had powers at his disposal which allowed him refuge from his fate, but he always reverted to satyr form when he wasn't focused on cloaking himself in one illusion or another. He could appear as he did once, like a human, although he never was one. If scientists had been able to study the ancients, they would have categorized gods and humans in the same family in their taxonomy charts, perhaps even the same genus. The species, however, was where things would definitely differ. Gods were immortal, for the most part, and had special gifts—powers, like magic. Humans were mortal. Mundane.

The duet of yammering voices reminded Pan he had trespassers to elude. He debated wandering off in the opposite direction in order to continue enjoying the blissful solitude that was his life. Most days. He pondered if it wasn't time to find a new home as he wasn't in the mood to expel the energy it took to avoid people who hiked so far into the Pine Barrens. For them to do so meant they were looking for something. About eight times out of ten they were hunting him.

There was never a truer word of advice than, "Be careful what you wish for." Those who hunted monsters would either go home empty handed or would find way more than they were equipped to handle. Oh, and making grown men scream like little girls... *So amusing.* He became particularly proud of himself if he could make them piss their pants, but even that had started to lose its appeal.

As he turned north, intending to head deeper into the wilds, a female's whimsical laughter halted him, and his cock twitched in response. Pan rotated toward the mortals. It had taken him centuries to fight the impulse to stalk anything female until he'd seduced them and sated the limitless lust of his *Satyros* nature. In recent years, he'd even bypassed women without so much as turning his head to appreciate their voluptuous curves. He'd become so efficient at resisting that he'd been celibate for nearly three decades. He was proud of himself for mastering the desire, the arousal that ruled him. He knew the others had not been as fortunate.

But that laugh...

It was a melody of carefree wickedness, and it spoke to his soul. A temptation which beckoned him more than anything had in a very long time. The woman it belonged to could very well be his undoing.

Then again, there was also that pesky little curse which made him an insatiable, rutting sex fiend, so mostly anything about a female could, in theory, spark a reaction from him. And thirty years was a long time, especially one with his *condition.* He wondered if he was experiencing a moment of weakness.

Pan strolled toward the voices, coming across a dark-haired man holding a video camera. The man was filming a redheaded woman as she attached a video-recording device to a tree. Many people ventured into the Pine Barrens to do the same. These people were tracking wildlife, hoping to catch a photograph of something in its natural habitat. They camouflaged the camera enough so animals would move close to it and not realize they were being observed.

The woman turned and searched the area, her gaze brushing across the cluster of trees where he stood. Pan wondered if she felt him watching her and concentrated on maintaining his glamour to shield himself from view. The female was beautiful. Her hair was the perfect combination of copper and gold, as though someone had poured a chest of ancient treasures down her back where it had softened into loose, lazy ringlets. She dressed for comfort in a pair of dark blue jeans, which were tucked into a pair of brown hiking boots. Her yellow flannel shirt was unbuttoned with a lacy, white shirt beneath to softly accentuate her ample breasts. The sleeves covered her upper arms down to her elbows, leaving the rest bare except for a silver watch on her wrist.

He found himself gawking at her, entranced. Maybe he just wanted to hear her laugh again, and he imagined she did so because she was amused by something *he* had said. She'd later make wicked little sounds in the throes of passion, laughing in victory as she orgasmed astride him. All he knew was that the sound of her laugh had grabbed him by his dick and pulled him toward her like a divining rod. Pan was tempted to march out into the open, drop every illusion he held in place, and proclaim himself the one she was looking for. And he might...if only she were alone.

Pan had a weakness for redheads, but he'd learned his lesson in that regard. He needed to turn around and walk away, avoid looking back. Unfortunately, he'd never been very good at doing what was right. It was why he always ended up in the situations he found himself in. He was pretty much doomed the moment he heard her beautiful laughter.

The woman turned to her male companion and proclaimed, "That's the last of them." The man with her lowered his camera and hit a button on it while the woman spoke, "We spent the last two days talking to the locals and filming random spurts of narration. The birthplace ruins were great visual footage, but we really don't have anything to wow the viewers." She sighed. "We deserve an afternoon off. We'll check the camera traps in twenty-four hours, doing some walkthrough recording on the way to retrieve them."

The man mumbled in agreement. Pan hadn't paid him much attention before, but he studied him then. The man was of a good, solid build. What most females would find attractive. He had a Spanish look to him, but his accent was southern. Pan speculated if the male was in a relationship with the female and decided the thought didn't please him at all. He didn't know why it mattered if these two people were together or not.

Hell, scores of couples came into the Pine Barrens to fornicate. Though most of the time it was because Pan had compelled them to do so as entertainment. Sometimes watching was just as good as participating, and though he'd been celibate for so long, it didn't make him a saint. In some cases, voyeurism was much healthier considering the care, or lack thereof, humans took with their bodies in this century. He shuddered. Luckily, he couldn't catch any human diseases.

He wondered if these two would be the down and dirty, sweet and slow, or wild and acrobatic kind. With that redhead? Pan would ride her so hard into the ground there would be a crater when they were done. She'd be down and dirty, he was sure.

Curiosity getting the best of him, Pan followed behind them as they headed in the direction they had come from. Under his cloaking glamour, he could run circles around them while shrieking like a banshee, and they wouldn't bat an eye. They wouldn't see, hear, or smell him. They could stroll right through him like he was a ghost and not feel him. They damn sure couldn't taste him, though he wished the fiery-haired woman would do so.

"It's a shame we haven't found anything we can use. Cindy doesn't think we have enough to work with to stay the whole two to three weeks," the male was saying. They had another woman with them? Pan's mind went briefly into a vision of two beautiful redheads. While it was a pleasant thought, he knew the one in front of him would be enough as he studied her nicely shaped ass through the trees. He'd done the multiple partner acts, and the thrill was gone. He preferred a single partner as he could give her his undivided attention. Nevertheless, it would serve him best if he stopped thinking about all the ways he could take her. He adjusted the crotch of his pants.

She made an unladylike snort, but Pan found even that attractive. "Well, what did you expect? A bat-winged horse walking on two legs to step out and beg you to film it before showing you the location of his secret bat-horse-goat-cave?"

He halted in his tracks. There was no further question as to what they were hunting in the woods. They were looking for proof of his existence, but they didn't believe they'd find him. Yet he was close enough he could pounce on them. Pan *loved* messing with skeptics. He tried, he really did, not to do it very often, but he was never one to let such a prime opportunity pass him by. Besides, it would give him a reason to focus his energy on something other than his arousal.

All traces of his former boredom vanished. He'd put on a demonstration for her to give her a reason to continue her hunt for him. She'd have some interesting footage to show for it, but it wouldn't be enough to prove she actually found anything.

Pan mentally adjusted his cloaking glamour so he could be heard while remaining invisible. The camera would pick up the sounds, but neither it nor the two humans present would see him. Half the viewers of their footage would claim it was tampered with; the other half would come to this location seeking a repeat performance. They'd find nothing. He was never one to willingly repeat history. There was a reason he hadn't been found in several centuries.

And it would be a damned good reason not to have too much fun with the redhead.

He galloped to their left through the underbrush. He tried desperately not to laugh when the humans' eyes widened and their heads whipped around at the sound of hooves thumping as they fell heavily, hitting dirt and roots, kicking up dried leaves. His legs shook the low bushes as he tore through them with vigor.

"What the hell?" the male shouted.

Birds scattered overhead, feeling the pull of Pan's power.

"Look at those plants. It looks like a boulder tore through them. Turn your camera on!" The female pivoted and stood on tiptoes to glance behind her. Probably thinking another human was out here, not the very creature she sought.

"Cindy, is that you?" She turned back to the man. "Would she actually leave the van to pull a dumb prank like this after the attack last year?"

Pan pondered what she meant by "the attack," and experienced an urge to find the source of this aforementioned assault and harm it. The foolish male played with his toy, muttering in Spanish. Pan summoned the pair of dark wings from his alternate form, letting the leathery *whoosh, whoosh* startle his captive audience as he glided over them and into the treetops, kicking up dirt as he ascended.

He was showing off, and he found it exhilarating. A rush of warm pleasure fired through his veins, making his lips split into a grin. The need to draw attention was a trait Pan had gotten from his father. Hermes had a knack for disappearing mid-conversation or running people over upon his arrival to deliver Zeus' messages. He grimaced at the thought of his father, glad Hermes was slumbering the years away on Mount Olympus rather than being a giant pain in the ass still.

Below, the mortals frantically searched for the cause of the phantom noise, but of course they found nothing. They would flee soon, and he wasn't quite ready to lose his audience. For the finale, Pan grabbed hold of neighboring branches and shook them, bouncing lightly where he stood. Leaves rained down upon the two as they all but trembled with fear. *Ah, yeah. I still have my talent for the dramatic.*

"Tell me you're getting this on tape," the female hissed.

"I am, but I can't tell what it is. I see the branches moving, but there is nothing there."

Pan fully cloaked himself once more and fluttered down, landing directly in front of them on his hoofed feet with a soft *thud*. His wings faded into nonexistence.

Damn, the woman was stunning even when she was afraid. Pan leaned in and inhaled her scent. Her shampoo had left her hair smelling citrusy and tropical. She glanced around, eyes wide. They were pale blue, like a cloudless morning sky. Earlier, before he scared her, they had been slanted like a—

"Kat, I think it's gone," the male said. How apropos that her name was feline in nature. Pan assumed it was short for something longer. He noticed humans had the tendency to minimize their names into single syllables. Some of the satyrs who were formerly human had done so themselves. Pan reached out a hand and brushed his fingers lightly against Kat's delicate pale cheek.

She shuddered and rubbed at her face like she had felt it, even though it was impossible. Her hand went through his, but the contact sent sparks down his spine, straight to his groin.

I have to have her.

At least once.

"Let's head back to the van and make sure Cindy is okay." The male shut off his camera before making the sign of the cross over his chest.

Pan continued to admire his new female. Kat didn't wear a wedding ring, and the only jewelry she wore aside from the watch he noted earlier was a gold chain with a dainty heart hanging from it.

Pan peeked toward the man's hand and noted he was wearing a wedding band. So were they, or were they not, currently warming the same bed? He found he had to know. Perhaps Cindy, the woman purportedly sitting in the van, was his wife. It didn't matter; after noticing the ring and Kat's lack thereof, the man she traveled with became even less of a concern.

Not that he'd ever been one to begin with. *Definitely not a saint.*

"I'm not gonna argue. I feel like I'm being watched. Maybe I'm paranoid, but that was really damn weird."

"Do you think it was the creature?" The male asked as their steps became swifter while they hurried to exit the woods. Pan watched the sway of Kat's hips and ass as he followed in their wake.

"The Jersey Devil? Seriously? You just went there?"

"Well, what else could it have been?"

"A bird." She shrugged.

"An invisible bird?" The male sounded unconvinced.

"An invisible *thunder*bird." Her emphasis couldn't sound any less convincing. Pan had heard of the giant birds of prey the Native American people told tales about. Unfortunately, the only giant eagles left in existence lived on a hidden island off the coast of New Zealand, so her theory of explaining him as such was moot. He admired her effort though.

"*Pfft.* And my mother is a turkey."

Kat snorted. "I don't even want to know what kind of Thanksgiving traditions go on at your house."

"Girl, pull your head out of the gutter and put some pep in your step. Hustle."

Kat shook her head but jogged a bit faster. "I think you and I need to have a talk when we leave the Barrens. And it is gonna be about who is in charge around here."

The man chuckled and glanced over his shoulder. *Checking for monsters?* "You can be in charge all you want, but if I beat you to the van, I'm leaving your ass."

CHAPTER 3

What *was that back there?* Kat wondered for the umpteenth time as they shuffled into her hotel room. Her mind registered that they needed to film a segment to go along with the weird footage they collected while the memory was still fresh, but first they had done what any sane people would have...

They had sprinted to the van, yelling at a bewildered Cindy to start the vehicle as they threw themselves into it. Then they had sped all the way back to the hotel in order to hide, and Kat slammed the door and locked it behind them. She proceeded to close the curtains while Rick checked the ammunition in the licensed shotgun he usually kept in the van in case of emergency —like a repeat of the cougar incident.

They'd just sat down on the beds in order to collect their thoughts, Cindy calling them superstitious and accusing them of overreacting, when a knock at the door had Kat rolling over the bed like a ninja and disappearing. When had she become such a coward? Rick aimed the shotgun at the door.

A second knock. "Hello? Is everything okay in there? I'm Peter, from the room next door. I was walking back from the gas station when I saw you three running like bats out of hell."

Kat motioned to Rick to hide the gun, wondering if Peter had seen him carrying it, as she checked herself quickly in the mirror on her way to the door. Her hair was wild as usual. No helping it without a shower, blow dryer, and a straightening iron. She unlocked the door, keeping the chain latch in place, and opened it as far as it would go.

Holy hotness!

The hottie hotel neighbor from next door wore a slight frown and his brow was furrowed. He appeared to be genuinely concerned about them. Or merely perplexed. "Hold on a sec. I forgot the chain latch." She closed the door and adjusted the twins, mouthing *he's so hot* at her friends. A girl's confidence was sometimes directly proportional to how much cleavage she could use to entice a hot guy without being downright slutty about it. And for a single lady who hadn't gotten any in over a year due to little issues like, say, recovering from an animal attack, Mr. Tall, Hot, and Neighborly might be just what the doctor ordered.

Kat was still on a bit of an adrenaline rush from what happened in the woods, so her hormones were ready to jump on him and get busy. Or rather, that was what she told herself to avoid questioning her intense response to him. The events from earlier were unexplainable, at least on the surface. Even though she had cowered behind the bed when Peter knocked on the door, she had been steadily convincing herself what happened in the woods had been caused by a large bird or something out of sight. It had to be.

The Jersey Devil didn't exist. It *couldn't*.

She opened the door, smiled, and motioned for him to come inside. "Sorry to have disturbed you. We were kind of in a rush to return from filming."

Peter stepped into the room and nodded once in acknowledgement to Rick and Cindy before he turned his gaze back on her. Eye to eye too. *Oh, nope, score one for the cleavage.* Back to her eyes again. His irises were forest green, twinkling

31

mischievously, and Kat's imagination suddenly went to many different fantasy scenarios involving him, her, and his tongue trailing along where he had glimpsed moments before. She honestly couldn't remember the last time she was so turned on by only the sight of a man, fully clothed, and for some reason it didn't bother her as much as it should. *Why is that, Kat? Concentrate.* Peter's gaze dipped once more, and she lost that train of thought all together.

"Filming? Are you a movie star, then? And you didn't disturb me in the least. I was worried you were in trouble and wanted to see what I could do to help." His voice was the perfect timbre of masculine, deep enough to excite her with a slight hint of an exotic accent she couldn't quite place. Very Old World. She'd heard it before, but wasn't sure where. Perhaps in a movie or someone she spoke to recently. So instead, she observed the man before her. Peter was decked out in black jeans, equally dark shoes, and a white T-shirt with the red and black emblem for the New Jersey Devils hockey team on it.

Wait. He thought she was a movie star? *Rewind.*

"Oh, stop." She laughed and twirled a strand of her hair. *Oh, God, I'm acting like a high school girl with a crush! Get it together!* "I'm actually a zoologist. We're shooting some footage for a documentary in the Pine Barrens, but it was very sweet of you to come to our rescue." She'd leave out the part about his favorite hockey team's inspiration.

"Beautiful *and* smart. I'm pleased to meet you, Miss..." He held out a hand to her. She took it in order to shake it, but he raised her hand to his lips and lightly kissed her knuckles. She might have imagined a slight brush of his tongue as well. Her throat went dry, and she had to clear it. His gaze met hers, and there was the mischievous twinkle to them again. Peter smirked as if he knew what he was doing to her.

"Katerina, but everybody calls me Kat."

"A pleasure, Katerina." The way his soft accent lilted over her name made her shiver. "And your friends?" He scrutinized Rick, who was the perfect picture of male posturing as he stood in the background with his legs braced apart ever so much, arms crossed, and a look of wary consternation on his face as he studied Peter's flirtations. Cindy, on the other hand, appeared to be ten seconds away from ordering popcorn and a Coke and becoming thoroughly entertained.

Kat blushed, realizing her reaction to Peter was a public event. "Sorry, I'm being terribly rude. This is Cindy and her husband, Rick. They've been my partners on a lot of projects, and Rick's been my cameraman for years."

"Pleasure," Peter said, nodding toward the other two once more. Rick's scowl became more defined. Cindy beamed at Peter before hopping off the bed to put her arm through Rick's still-crossed one.

"Come on, honey. We can unload the van and see if we caught anything on camera."

Rick scoffed. "We still have to discuss what actually happened." He shot Kat a pointed glare.

"What actually happened is you spooked yourselves. Plus, I want you to myself for a while." Cindy winked at Kat and murmured a farewell to Peter as she dragged Rick out the room. He had always acted like an older brother toward Kat, intimidating men who spoke to her.

As soon as she believed they were alone, the door shot open and Kat jumped slightly as Rick wandered back into the room with exaggerated slowness and then rummaged through the closet. He retrieved his shotgun and made deliberate eye contact with Peter when he did it. The unspoken warning rang clear.

Men.

"Call me if you need me," Rick said, squeezing lightly on her shoulder before he exited the room, leaving Kat alone with the sexy stranger behind closed doors.

Peter was obviously addling her brain. She nearly forgot about the strange encounter already and it had *just* happened. She should be reviewing the footage with Rick and Cindy, not flirting with a stranger. But he was so...well...hot. Could she really be faulted for flirting a little? One time?

"Ah, alone at last," Peter said as Kat claimed one of the two chairs at the table. She raised her eyebrows at the statement as Peter seated himself in the other.

"An expression. I'm not going to attack you or anything."

Yet she secretly wanted him to. Even though she wasn't a one-night stand kind of girl, she had the inexplicable feeling she could be one that day. Her body was heavily aroused. Sure, Peter was hot, but her reaction was odd. She'd never been so fired up over a complete stranger, but if Kat told herself the truth, she kind of liked not being overcritical and reserved for a change. She wondered how her laptop would handle being shoved to the floor so she could pounce on him across the table. But then she feared that would scare him away and decided to see what happened on its own. *Ack! What is this? What is the matter with my hormones?*

Peter leaned back in his chair, relaxed as though he could be content in any setting. He cocked his head as he observed her in the way Kat did with animals in the field. It should've made her uncomfortable.

It didn't. She found herself wanting to give him a show worth seeing, but she didn't quite have the nerve to act on the impulse. So instead, she crossed her legs, gritting her teeth against the sensation the movement caused. *Definitely not a normal reaction.*

"So what brings you to the fine Fancy Pines Hotel of Jersey?" Kat would make with the small talk. Usually, she would require dinner and a few dates before *considering* sex with anyone; however, it'd been a while since her last boyfriend. She wondered if the powerful arousal was because she really, really needed something to take the edge off—not only the day, but the past year as well. Would sleeping with a stranger really be so bad in the long run?

I can't believe I am even thinking about this. At all.

Peter was so handsome she could ogle him for hours. His silky, dark hair wasn't too long, yet it wasn't short. Long enough he could probably tie it back if he wanted, but not enough to make him resemble an escapee from an 80s rock band. His olive complexion and accent seemed exotic despite the casual, down-to-earth attire. Kat's inner harlot screamed at her to stop analyzing things and toss the man on the bed before she chickened out or said something geeky and scared him away.

"Just passing through town. Thought I'd stay awhile, and it appears I made a good decision." There were crinkles around his eyes when he smiled, hinting that he must love to smile and laugh. It made him all the more attractive. "And with a celebrity at that."

"I wouldn't go as far as to say I'm a celebrity. There are maybe two households who actually know my name: my parents' and my grandparents'. But enough about me..." She trailed off as he stretched his arms over his head. His shirt rode up and revealed a set of washboard abs and a dark happy trail; her gaze couldn't go any farther due to his pants, and the table hid any evidence of said happiness. *Stupid table.* She licked her lips.

Then Kat hopped up, pacing and twisting her fingers together for something to do with them that didn't involve fondling strangers. Realizing she probably appeared unhinged, she jammed both hands into her pockets. She glanced out the corner of her eye toward Peter, hoping distance between them would help. He raised his eyebrows as he tracked her movement, and she decided he must wonder why she was acting so spastic.

A sudden thought struck her, and she went for it. Anything to break the increasingly awkward silence. "Are you thirsty? I can pour you a glass of wine. Unfortunately, it's a little warm since there isn't a fridge here." She retrieved the bottle and two plastic cups the hotel had supplied. She returned and set the bottle on the table and began to unwrap the cups.

Peter stood up so fast his chair toppled over, crashing against the heating unit under the window with a loud *crack*. He stared at her and back to the bottle of wine. His jaw was clenched, and he lost all the laid-back, casual happiness he'd previously displayed. As she was about to ask if he was okay, he smiled at her. It wasn't a full smile like earlier though. It was forced. "Sorry about that. I..." He picked up his chair and then paused after he righted it. He seemed to be concentrating on something as though it were more important than breathing. It was rather strange. Maybe Rick was right to be wary of Peter.

Just my luck that the hot man would be a loony.

"Have you ever had the feeling you forgot to do something?" he asked at last.

"Yeah. All the time." Kat set the cups down, one with the wrapper half-ripped open, and wondered if she should maybe open the door and step outside into public view.

"I didn't mean to startle you, but I have this terrible feeling about something. Maybe we can catch up later or...something."

That was a lot of "somethings." He was lying, but Kat plastered a smile on her face.

"Sure, I'd like that."

He muttered a farewell, stalked past her, and out the door. Kat peeked out through the curtains and watched him go into the room next door to hers. At least he hadn't been lying about staying at the hotel. For some reason, she half-expected him to take off in the opposite direction.

She was ever skeptical, paranoid, *and* still horny as hell.

CHAPTER 4

P an latched the door of the hotel room he "acquired" next to the female's, knowing she'd been spying on him as he mystically unlocked the door. Once more, being a god had perks. Luckily the room was vacant, or it could have been awkward. He'd taken one look at the Greek label on the wine bottle and memories flooded him like an open spigot. Still, he wouldn't have needed to read the label to know it came from Greek vineyards; it had been opened, and he could smell the tang of the vintage when she set the bottle on the table.

It couldn't possibly be the same wine he thought it was, but he knew it had been. It was too much of a coincidence. Someone had known he'd recognize it. Knew he'd remember the taste of it as if he only just taken a sip of the sweet but bitter liquid the day before. He had tasted wine of that making many times. Long before the birth of Christ. Before the Romans built their empire.

Someone knew who he was, but the important question was whom? Was his remarkably beautiful woman out to do him harm in some way? Or was she a pawn in a bigger scheme?

Too good to be true. This is why I avoid redheads.

Pan's moment of panic in her room had alarmed Katerina, and

he could have kicked himself. His human manifestation had been perilously close to slipping in front of her. Safe without humans around to witness the change, he let it fall away finally, leaving him in the form he was cursed to endure. His thick horns weighed heavily against the sides of his head. He glanced down at his deformed feet. They were nightmarish, demonic even. His ankles and lower calves had a thick pelt of fur, the same dark brown as the hair on his head. It thinned out until it was the normal amount of human hair across his thighs. His hooves were the same jet black as his horns, split down the middle.

Pan could only imagine what Katerina's reaction would have been if he'd allowed the change to come over him in front of her. The fear, the horror, the confusion. The lust he sensed coming off her in waves would have died within seconds. Very few beheld this form and desired him. No, not when he resembled the devil more than a man. A creature, a beast, an abomination. And that was only his satyr form. The other one made things a whole lot worse. His parlor tricks made people cry...and not from joy or admiration.

Katerina. Pan had known Kat was short for something, but he couldn't bring himself to shorten her beautiful name. Shortening it cheapened it. Everything about her deserved to be savored. *And someone else knows it too. Why else send her with that wine to bait me?*

His jeans were too tight against his arousal, throbbing in need of the woman next door, and he cursed himself because he'd known all he needed to do was make a move to have her. She had been willing, but he'd sat there waiting for her to make a move on him. Pan hadn't been able to help himself. Her desire and confusion were evident, and he wanted to see which won out. It had gone so well until she showed him the wine.

Fool, the wine saved you. The element of surprise is gone, and now it is a matter of finding out what she is up to.

As Pan leaned against the cool, metallic door, he unfastened his pants, gripped his penis, and then stroked it. Katerina had been all but ready to strip naked for him. He'd seen it in her eyes. He could have claimed her mouth with his and had her on the spot. And now there he was, reduced to masturbation because his curse had finally run the course of allowing him any sort of reprieve. She was his undoing. She could be his destruction.

He wanted her anyway.

He handled himself a little tighter, roughly, as he berated his lack of control. The *clop* of his left hoof hitting the door as his body jerked would have sickened him in the past, but he barely heard it. He'd long come to terms with the fact he would forever be beastly in form—a physical manifestation of the lecherous nature of men.

Gods, he could detect her arousal through the thin hotel walls. He jerked again, so close to release. Pan stroked faster with his right hand and braced his left against the wall beside him, adjacent to the door. With a lift of his head, he spotted the air vent that likely connected with the ventilation to her room. Combined with his enhanced senses...

A low moan sounded from next door. Was she doing the same as he was, caressing herself while imagining his tongue on her? He closed his eyes, letting his mind paint a picture. *Katerina lay on the bed, pants and shoes kicked off and forgotten on the tan carpet below. She had one hand under her shirt, cupping her breast. The other rubbing slow, lazy circles around her clit.*

She was a true redhead.

He came, hard. He muted his shout as he spilled over his hand and onto the carpet, which contained gods knew what else from previous patrons of the hotel.

Making his way through the dark room, twin to the one next door, Pan washed off at the sink. He adamantly avoided his reflection. Afterward, he grabbed tissues and cleaned up his mess on the carpet as much as he could, flushing it down the toilet when he finished.

He wanted nothing more than to have fucked Katerina the

entire night through. Her eyes had begun to dilate as soon as she saw him. He'd watched her gaze peruse over his body multiple times. It was a reaction he'd only seen when he or one of the other Arcadians played their panpipes to entice a woman to want a satyr for sex. But he hadn't been playing, nor had he heard the flutes nearby. Maybe it had to do with the wine. *The red hair, the musical laughter, the wine.* He'd expected his past to stay where he left it, not to find him again.

Had the wine been any other wine, Pan was sure he would have humored her by accepting a glass as she used hers to lower her inhibitions. They would have spent the night fucking like animals on every available surface of the room. But it hadn't been any other wine, it had been...

He shook his head. Maybe his lust for the woman was distracting him too much to look at the bigger picture. He should be focusing on the mystery of the wine being present there, but he was hardening once more. If he kept it up, he'd have an eternal case of carpel tunnel by the morning. The best thing to do was try to ignore it. Unfortunately, because of the curse, ignoring it wouldn't make it go away. It had never been gone; he'd merely distracted himself so he couldn't think about the need. So, doing it again shouldn't be too difficult.

Pan picked up the remote and flicked the television on, making himself comfortable on the double bed closest to the bathroom. As people on the screen came to life, bickering with each other, his thoughts immediately reverted back to Katerina. He'd nearly revealed the monster beneath the surface. That wouldn't work very well in seducing her—which he still planned to do—unless she was into that sort of thing.

She's not going to open her legs for a man with hooves.

It was no use. How utterly frustrating it was to not be able to refocus his thoughts on anything other than sex. Thirty years of fighting it, lost in one day. *Tragic.*

He stopped flipping channels when he came to some movie

about the Greek gods and Perseus. It was fairly recent, considering the special effects, but way too modernized. At least they had one fact right in the film: Perseus *was* a selfish prick. Pan turned the television off.

There was no choice but to remain near Katerina and wait to see if someone from his past decided to show themselves or make a move against him. Although, his weirdness probably ruined his shot of bedding her with his human glamour. As far as the wine was concerned, if Katerina was planted here to seduce him, the best way to avoid a trap was to not take the bait. Having his wicked satyr way with her was most definitely taking the bait.

"And that is why they call it temptation, my son." His father's voice bombarded his memories. He'd said it the last time Pan saw him, not long after the curse. As much as he hated to take any advice from Hermes, it would be in his best interest to remember that Katerina was a temptation he needed to avoid.

Pan wanted her, but he'd wait until he discovered her true intentions. She was hunting him, well...hunting his other form. He would not walk willingly into a trap.

"WHATEVER IT WAS, WE NEVER MANAGED TO GET A LOOK AT IT. WE heard movement, wings flapping as a large animal took flight, and then the trees started to shake. More than likely it was a bird. There's a good chance if there is a big animal in that area, the camera traps will catch something worthwhile. Maybe we will even find some animal tracks to make casts from or other physical evidence. Tomorrow, when we pick up the cameras, we'll see. After the encounter yesterday, we didn't want to hang around and endanger ourselves."

Rick shut off the camera and placed it on the extra bed which was covered by the gaudy maroon, gold, and green tribal print comforter. There had to be a secret hotel catalogue for finding the most hideous comforters on the planet. *Fugly Hotels Unlimited.*

"You're not even going to say anything about it?" Cindy finally pushed, taking the seat opposite of Kat.

"Anything about what?"

"You can sit there, batting your eyelashes and looking as oblivious as the days are long, but you know what?" Cindy crossed her arms and glared at her. "You totally got it on with that guy, didn't you?" She smiled, silently begging for juicy tidbits.

"Please say you didn't jump in bed with some creepy dude you just met," Rick added.

"He wasn't creepy," Kat mumbled. He was a bit creepy, but she didn't want to admit it to Rick. "And no, we didn't hop in the bed, but there were sparks. Definite sparks." Until she scared him away.

At first, she worried he'd been a fruit basket, and she was lucky to have gotten through meeting him without being slobbered on. Then she remembered how badly she wanted him to...okay, not to slobber on her, but to put his mouth on certain areas. His weird reaction had followed the wine's appearance. Perhaps he was in AA and the reminder set something off. That didn't necessarily make him a bad person, but it was a history she would need to know before moving further with him. If that is what she even wanted.

For God's sake, Kat, you're in town for a few weeks. Not the time to shop for dates.

"Why would you say he's creepy?" Kat asked with a frown.

Rick rolled his eyes. "Well, for starters, there was nobody walking over from the store next door when we got here."

"Maybe he hadn't walked out the door yet," Cindy offered as she twisted open a bottle of bright blue nail polish. She'd been sitting Indian-style in the chair, but she shifted to rest one foot at the end. With her chin against her knee, she began beautifying her naked toenails.

Rick countered, "The whole front of the store is glass. There was no one even there, but the clerk who was reading a newspaper behind the counter."

Cindy scoffed. "Seriously, who is that observant?"

"I didn't want to be arrested for carrying a gun into the hotel. I was checking for witnesses."

"Oh, because that doesn't sound sketchy at all. If anyone has anything to be guilty for, obviously it's you since you were, 'checking for witnesses.' Damn, Ricardo!"

"I was still on edge from the weirdness in the woods."

"Of course you were. There was nothing on the footage but moving tree limbs and grass. It was some big, dumb animal you didn't see, or it was the wind. Like I said earlier, you spooked yourselves."

Kat sighed and opened her laptop, removing herself from the married couple's conversation. She'd brought it with her to Rick's room because she didn't trust herself to try to work being next door to the new distraction. She'd never come so hard from masturbation in her life, but the things her fantasy Peter could do with his tongue, his hands, his penis... Her hormones really, really liked good ol' Peter. And they really, really, *really* wanted to get intimate with Peter's peter.

"You might not have seen him," she cut into the conversation. "Peter was a perfect gentleman. He didn't do anything *untoward* with me." Except get crazy weird at the last second, but he didn't seem like he'd hurt her.

Rick snorted.

Kat waited for the super slow Wi-Fi connection to figure out that it should do something other than nothing. "You're just jealous of all Peter's yummy muscles."

"I have my own muscles."

Cindy snickered. "Had. Then you got married. I mourn their loss every day."

"So that's why you always have flowers in the house?" Kat offered.

Cindy pointed her nail polish applicator at her. "Exactly. I live in the funeral parlor of lost abs." At this, Rick sputtered indignantly.

Kat connected to Google and searched for recent Jersey Devil sightings. There were a few here and there. All varied. "The Jersey Devil was on my roof." *Yeah, and you saw him while you were watching* Supernatural *on television and freaked yourself out.* "The Jersey Devil scared my dog, I didn't see it, but poor Sparky was wigging out." *Because poor Sparky opened his mouth and told you, "It was him! I saw him; I know it!"*

She honestly didn't remember being as skeptical before the accident with the cougar. Kat hadn't admitted it, even to herself, but a small thrill of excitement had followed her into the woods the day they hunted one of the elusive black panthers locals claimed were prowling about. When she'd accepted the invitation to be the zoological expert in the investigation, it was something different. An adventure.

A throb in her thigh brought her back to reality. When the black panther turned out to be a territorial, ordinary cougar...reality had paid her a visit. She'd gotten her wake-up call back to the world of scientific fact, and all fiction had to be pushed aside. She looked forward to studying real cats, even cougars, in the wild once more. The one that attacked her had been acting on instinct. It had been *her* fault she'd been attacked, not the cougar's. Kat should've been more careful, but she hadn't paid close enough attention to the signs, and she'd suffered the consequences for it. One mishap shouldn't prevent her from pursuing her passion forever.

After she finished hunting the Jersey Devil, she would immerse herself back into her work. Perhaps she'd start with cougars to prove the attack wouldn't keep her down. A smile teased the edge of her lips at the thought.

Cindy twisted the lid back on her nail polish and set it on the table. "I heard there's lots of weird shit in the Pine Barrens. The clerk in the lobby was telling me about all these urban legends in the area. Creepy dirt roads in the middle of the woods, secluded towns, and stuff. Maybe we should check some out. It could provide filler if we can't find any better footage to use."

Kat turned back to her computer screen and ran an Internet search for strange places in the Pine Barrens, and when the links popped up, all the words seemed to blur together. She stared at the screen while her thoughts remained in the past and future, avoiding the present. "Maybe. I mean, nothing can be weirder than this afternoon, can it?"

CHAPTER 5

Moonlight flooded the dirt path with subtle illumination, making the dense fog eerier as it curled around the trees. It made visibility difficult for more than a few feet. In most instances, nighttime strolls through the forest filled Pan with a sense of tranquility. However, making sure Katerina didn't find herself into serious trouble was becoming exhausting. For the sole purpose of entertainment value, she and her friends had been traversing through dangerous areas of the Pine Barrens with the intent of running into something scary. Well, if Pan were not around, they likely would. People who lived in those areas were not fans of trespassers wandering around with cameras.

Even worse, it had been three days since he met the woman, yet no one had dared reveal themselves as the reason for placing her there. To top it all, Pan still had not bedded Katerina. Not because he couldn't, but because he didn't want to be underhanded in his methods. He could have acted as an incubus and taken her while she slept. She would have remembered it only as a dream, so he could have knocked on the door after Katerina consumed the wine and taken advantage of her. Pan could have played her music on his panpipes. The music would have acted as an aphrodisiac, making her burn to have him inside her.

Too easy. Too desperate. She tempted him harder than anyone since Syrinx, perhaps more so. Which was why Pan had made as little contact with her as possible since Wednesday, but he'd spied on her regardless.

Not knowing what else to do for material—the camera traps they set had only picked up deer and raccoons, big surprise there —Katerina and her posse had taken to exploring a few other local legends while they were in town. There were many places in the Pine Barrens bordering on the strange and unusual, and nearly all of them were dangerous after dark. Tonight, they took a great risk in hiking dirt roads through privately owned property lines so far into the woods that, if anything were to happen, they would not be discovered for days or weeks, if at all. The road they currently ambled down was known as the hunting grounds of a serial rapist of the past.

The fog had thickened enough to conceal them without his help. Or it would have if Katerina hadn't decided to wear a lime-green sweater with light blue jeans. She was a beacon of color proclaiming, *I'm a victim, take me now!* Sure, it would keep her from being run over by a car, but did she have to prance around all vulnerable?

He palmed himself, wishing once more that he had given into the easy route despite knowing he'd hate himself for it later. Blue balls were becoming a fashion statement instead of a condition, and he didn't wear them with pride. He wondered how Katerina would feel knowing a naked satyr followed her around through the woods, keeping her hidden from anyone who could do her harm. And he *was* currently walking the dirt road in all his naked glory. The discomfort had gotten so bad that clothing irritated him. Not like he could offend anyone when he was invisible anyway.

Would Katerina be appalled by his body?

Thoughts of his affliction, as they often did, put him in a foul mood. He supposed it was a side effect of the curse itself. He fidgeted from hoof to hoof as he waited for Katerina to cease talking to the camera Rick aimed at her.

Pan crossed his arms and glared at everyone, but at no one in particular. When that did nothing to enhance his mood, he perused the area around the group of humans, unable to see far enough through the fog to determine if any threat loomed in the distance. If he had hackles, they'd be raised. Was Katerina so desperate to catch a monster on film that she'd risk her life to do it? The residents of the area were known to chase people through the woods in their pickup trucks, to threaten them with firearms, and sometimes people weren't seen again. On the other hand, the crazy inhabitants and stories surrounding the location were what made the Pine Barrens a superb place to blend in and stay hidden.

The group moved on, soon coming to another halt. The more he followed behind the filmmakers, the more he grinded his teeth together and felt the urge to do...something. Katerina droned on and on about the local stories. Rick mentioned night vision cameras to which Cindy mumbled an inaudible reply. Soon after that, the fog provided a great ambiance for their footage as it gave the location a supernatural atmosphere without having to use infrared. Cindy carried a bulky flashlight with a wide, bright beam that could double as a searchlight. Pan made sure the light wasn't seen by the residents.

Accident. Waiting. To. Happen.

None of them truly believed in the stories of the Jersey Devil, despite being shaken by his earlier display. Traipsing about in the daytime, hunting for creatures was one thing; willingly venturing into dangerous territories at night, with one gun—which was left in the truck as the humans were worried about the state laws on firearms being an issue—was beyond stupidity. A gun would not keep them safe if they didn't have it with them. Pan was more than willing to give them the footage they craved by proving how reckless they were.

The need to act on a buried instinct, to take pleasure in what he wanted, damn all the consequences, became more difficult to deny by the minute. It was too late to stomp it back down. Pan knew, even before he made his move, he was making a terrible mistake. His impulsiveness had gotten Syrinx killed, and he'd lived with regret every damned day for centuries, but he was beyond reason. He'd fought his nature so long he barely recognized his own actions when he finally gave in.

There wasn't time to think about the repercussions. Katerina wanted a demonic creature to jump out at her, well, her wish was his demand. Pan dropped all the glamour he had around him and transformed into the nightmarish Jersey Devil. Dark wings sprang from his back as a long, serpentine tail slithered behind him, forked at the end. His face protruded into a snout that, if it could be compared to any living creature, was a mixture of goat and horse in appearance. He let out an inhuman growl from where he hovered behind Katerina, Rick, and Cindy. The humans stopped dead in their tracks, and he mused that they knew running from a wild animal would incite the beast to attack.

They were right. Pan longed for Katerina to run. He craved the exhilaration in the chase, in the pursuit of that which he craved most of all. The hunt, the glorious chase, would thrill him in ways it shouldn't. His breathing deepened as the anticipation mounted.

Rick's hand went for the weapon he belatedly realized was not slung over his shoulder. Cursing under his breath, Rick started to turn when Katerina glanced over her shoulder at Pan. Her eyes widened in disbelief, and she looked away again with clipped breaths she didn't seem to be able to take in fully. Pan heard her heartbeat increase to a rapid pace.

Katerina rasped out to her companions, "We have to run for the van. Now." She didn't give them a chance to agree or argue. She took off.

Rick and Cindy, encouraged by her action, did the same. The van remained a good distance away, but the faint outline of the solid white vehicle was barely distinguishable in the glow of Cindy's light. Unfortunately for Katerina, she didn't realize how much Pan had denied himself the simple pleasure of the chase. Honestly, he shouldn't have been as excited as he was in that moment, as it alone would horrify Katerina if she noticed. This glamour was beyond atrocious, and his desire would be obnoxiously evident.

Pan flapped his leathery wings, gaining air. He then swooped down in front of Rick, shielding himself from being filmed as he did. The footage would show no visible evidence to make believers out of the humans who would view it. As with the first time he'd toyed with them, he knew sound effects could be easily added from an unseen location, so he wasn't worried about being heard.

Cindy noticed the threat to her husband and shined light in Pan's eyes, hoping to blind him. He couldn't blame her for not knowing he wasn't a meager animal to be deterred by such a feeble attempt. His eyes adjusted easily to any location and most levels of brightness or darkness. But since he was going for dramatic...

Pan used his wing to slap the spotlight out of her hands, and it skidded across the dirt road with a loud clatter. The light flickered once, twice, dimmed, and finally went dead. The moon proved bright enough to outline the individuals present, but offered little more than that. Cindy took a few steps back and tripped, landing hard on her ass. She immediately scrambled backward, attempting to regain her footing while placing distance between them.

Rick stepped in front of his wife, shielding her. He hadn't turned off the camera, but he slowly set it down, probably hoping the beast before him was too stupid to realize what a camera was. Keeping his hands out in nonthreatening gesture, Rick cautiously stood up and then began to back away. He remained between Pan and Cindy. How very noble.

Pan smiled, though in this form it likely appeared as a snarl. Lifting off from the ground, he knocked Rick over, which caused Cindy to tumble back down in effect. Neither concerned him. They weren't his prey.

He closed his eyes and inhaled sharply, citrus and female filled his senses. *Katerina.* She was afraid, but her fear would be short lived. He'd make it up to her.

With a gust of air, he glided upward, flapping his wings every so often as he gained altitude. The trees made it difficult, but he maneuvered through them like he'd been born to fly. He dipped under a low branch as he descended toward Katerina.

She dropped to the ground as he flew over her head, dodging him. Adrenaline shot through his system, almost as invigorating as an orgasm in itself. He was pleased she wasn't to be caught easily. The hunt made the capture so much more satisfying.

Katerina was almost to the van when he landed on the top of the vehicle and perched in front of her like a gargoyle, crouched with one hand on the edge of the roof. Pan folded his wings and towered above her as he leered, sizing her up. She stared up at him, mouth open in a scream that provided no sound. Pan watched as a tear streaked down her face, and it impacted him like a sucker punch to the gut.

She was terrified of him and would never want him now. He'd only deluded himself. However, if he gave up and let her go, she'd flee the area and give up her film. She *should* leave the area. It was the best thing for her to do. The only thing that would keep her safe from his lecherous thoughts.

No. She is mine.

The last time he'd felt a strong connection to someone, he'd let her slip through his fingers and into the path of harm before he could see if anything more could have blossomed between them. He'd been so scared of consequences for his actions that he hadn't manned up in time to act. Not again. Fuck waiting to see why she was there. He wasn't allowing her to leave, and he damned sure wouldn't stand by as something happened to her because of any association she had with him.

Never again.

His wings unfurled as he used the leverage of the van to push into a dive, the strength and force of his body knocking the vehicle sideways in the road. Katerina screamed, finding her voice at last, as he landed directly in front of her on hoofed feet. He intimidated her with his size, fearsome appearance, and blatant nudity. She scrambled backward in the dirt like a crab, rolling over into a crawl as she forced herself to her feet. When she attempted to run, the fog hindered her by concealing the line of trees beyond her field of vision.

Katerina crashed into a tree, turned, and caught the impact with her back and an "*oomph*." He took the opportunity to crowd her in, blocking any escape with his body. Trapping her against the pine tree, he buried his snout between her neck and shoulder. The scent of fear came off her in waves, mixed with the distinct hint of oranges. Her breathing was heavy, choked with sobs, and leaving smoky clouds in the crisp October air, containing the scent of the wine she'd been drinking the last few days. It had been made to linger and affect its drinker long after consuming it.

The wine was most definitely a message to him. *She* was a message to him. One he should study before sampling. Avoid sampling. A warning; one he should heed. No matter how many times he tried to convince himself of what he should do, the more he longed to do the opposite.

It's too late.

Pan dragged her bodily to his chest with one arm; the other dipped down to catch behind her knees in order to lift her. She was too shocked to react. With Katerina in his arms, he tore off the ground and into the trees. A beast with his beauty. Her terrified scream echoed in the night and shattered his soul.

~

KAT'S THROAT BURNED AND HER SCREAMS GREW HOARSE AS THE
Jersey Devil—*the Jersey Fucking Devil*—snatched her off the ground
and flew into the air. She had been too stunned to believe what
was happening at first. An animalistic growl had cut through the
silence somewhere behind her, and her first thought had been
that she'd screwed up a second time and couldn't be lucky enough
to live through a brutal attack twice.

She'd expected a bear or a bobcat behind her, not a mythical
monster! The creature was supposed to be a superstition; it wasn't
supposed to be real. Everything about it didn't add up to a real
creature, yet she couldn't come up with any reasonable
explanation for what happened or what was currently carrying
her over the Pine Barrens like a fat, juicy grub being hauled to a
nest full of squawking baby birds by their mother. Not an image
that helped pacify her nerves in the least.

When he'd backed her against the tree, she hadn't moved,
hadn't fought. The creature had sported an enormous erection,
which was wedged against her hip at the moment. More
disturbingly, many aspects of the creature, from its shoulders
down to its thighs, looked human. Its penis resembled a human
penis, and that freaked her out more than anything else. It was
scientifically impossible for anything human to breed with an
animal and create offspring, but this thing was a genetic
clusterfuck on two legs.

*I'm being kidnapped by the Jersey Devil. Probably about to get raped
and then eaten.*

Maybe not in that order.

Hell no.

A glimpse below proved they were flying miles above the tops
of the tall pines that gave the Barrens its name, but she squirmed
and kicked, hell, she put in a good, hard blood-drawing bite for
good measure. She'd rather a swift plummet to her death than a

prolonged death by violation. Her sick mind painted vivid, detailed scenarios involving what was in store for her when they landed. It would drink her blood like wine to wash down the meat it stripped from her bones, using said bones as toothpicks when it was finished. If she made it out of New Jersey alive, she was throwing away every horror movie she owned.

The creature only wrapped his arms around her tighter with a grunt and a growl to demonstrate its displeasure at her actions. All she was left with from her exertion was a coppery taste in her mouth and a closer encounter with the part of him she wanted to be farthest away from. Well, second part of him. She'd prefer to be far away from his pointed teeth as well. Nevertheless, the erection pressing into her side reminded her that he was most definitely a warm-blooded male, no matter the species.

Abruptly, the creature descended into the fog and trees. Kat shrieked at the sudden downward motion and tightened her arms around her captor. When she realized what she had done, she immediately tried to wiggle out of the monster's grasp, but could not pry herself loose.

JD, she decided to call him in an attempt to calm herself somewhat in order to be brave, landed in front of a long unused marble fountain full of leaves and branches rather than water. The figure in the middle was of a woman, draped in a sheet or a toga-style dress. The stone woman had long, curled hair, and one of her hands dipped into the area where water should have been. Her expression appeared so sad, lost even. The oddity of seeing it momentarily made Kat forget her current circumstances. *What a peculiar thing to find in the middle of the woods.*

Then the creature carried her past the fountain and into the dark shadow of some large structure looming ahead. She shoved against JD's chest, attempting to force the creature to drop her. It was futile as the monster retained its death grip.

As JD carried her onward, the curtain of fog revealed the shape to be an old house. Not quite a mansion, it appeared to be an oversized two-story building in dire need of repair from what small amount of detail she could discern in the gloom. The closer the beast carried her, the more details she could make out. Windows were broken, and graffiti covered the walls. The beast paused on the front steps, giving Kat time to see THE DEVIL'S LAIR scrawled in vivid red letters over the front door, clearly visible even in the darkness. It might as well have read, "*Abandon all hope ye who enter here*." Nothing good could result in going inside.

The door creaked open of its own accord. Like anything creepier had been necessary.

"Please," Kat pleaded, drawing the Jersey Devil's crimson glowing eyes to hers. "Don't do this. Let me go. I won't tell anyone I saw you. I'll go home. I'll burn the footage we took. Just please, don't hurt me. Don't take me in there."

JD glanced away from her and exhaled loudly. As Kat flirted with the possibility the creature had understood her and would maybe concede to her wishes, it took a step forward. Then another. Before her mind could fully register the hopelessness of her situation, they were inside. The door slammed behind them, and the world was bathed in darkness.

CHAPTER 6

The situation looked bad. Pan's arousal had calmed itself—mostly—but it was still at attention in her presence. He'd run off with her to a dark, secluded place. To somewhere no one could hear her scream. His home.

It looked worse than bad.

Pan carried Katerina up the grand staircase and swung a left on the landing, toward his bedroom. He'd bespelled the interior of the house to appear to humans as too hazardous for trespassing. He lifted the illusion for Katerina. While much of the inside really did need work done, it wasn't beyond suitable to live in. The outside appeared worse by far, but it kept squatters from taking up residence in his home while he was away. Aside from some graffiti and smashed windows, most trespassers stayed clear.

Inside the bedroom was a king-size bed. Regrettably, it was a little dusty from disuse, so Pan turned and flapped a wing in its direction. Katerina sneezed as the dust went airborne before settling in new homes throughout the room. He could see well enough in the dark to catch the annoyed glare she cast his way. Better anger than fear, he supposed.

He dropped his precious cargo onto the dark emerald

comforter turned black by the lack of lighting. Pan had deposited her a little less delicately than he meant to, and she bounced upon impact, giving a faint squeak. Afterward, he lit the candles in the candelabra that rested on the dresser across from the bed with matches he retrieved from the top drawer. The glow illuminated the room, though the shadows in the corners seemed even more ominous due to the flickering flames.

The room seemed bare, he supposed. Having learned a few style methods from the Spartans, there wasn't much in terms of decoration. He had a bed and a chest of drawers, mostly empty. There was a modest nightstand to the right of the bed, and the tall bookcase against the far wall was the only piece of furniture he really utilized at all. It was filled with several classics, contemporary novels, and books on the history and folklore of the ages. Pan was well-read, despite spending most of his time in the woods. It helped him acclimate to the times and cultures and to live a life other than his own for a brief time. Even the gods needed escapism, and he'd always been the black sheep of the family who hadn't wanted to live amongst the Olympians.

He watched Katerina blink against the light before she scanned the room in open-mouthed wonderment at where the infamous Jersey Devil had brought her. Then an expression of horror washed over her face as she recalled her predicament. He could see the precise moment Katerina realized she was in his bedroom, in his bed, and what that could possibly mean for her. He hadn't considered that when he chose this room for her. If he'd been digging a hole in the dirt since he revealed himself to Katerina, Rick, and Cindy, he'd be six-feet deep and still digging.

She leaped off the bed and attempted to rush past him to the hall. He stretched out his wings and let the eight-foot span intimidate her, denying her passage. The room was barely big enough for him to pull such a stunt.

This is getting old.

She turned her back to him and slinked toward the bed,

appearing so defeated that he actually felt like an ass. Pan reverted to his basic satyr form, but kept the wings. "Katerina, desist from the feeble escape attempts. You'll only exhaust yourself, and I'll just keep catching you and bringing you back here." He bit back a laugh as she nearly toppled over, spinning to face him.

Katerina took in his familiar features and then those that were new to her—his horns, wings, and finally his hooves—and she sputtered. She rubbed her eyes and stared at his feet again before her gaze traveled upward, searching his face for an explanation. Pan wondered if she would find one there. Truthfully, with the gawking his satyr appearance brought out in people, he never expected much in the way of acceptance. *Humans are too easily spooked.*

"P-Peter? You're the Jersey Devil? How is this even possible?" Katerina backed into the chest of drawers. It made an unattractive noise as it scooted a few inches behind her. She placed her hands on the object to steady it and herself.

Pan shrugged. He willed away the wings and stepped toward her. Katerina scrambled to the bookshelf, grabbed a heavy hardback copy of Homer's *The Odyssey*, and wielded it like a weapon. "Stay right there." Katerina waved the book at him, using both hands to grasp it. She reminded him of a woman trying to scare a rodent away with a broom.

Arms crossed, he stated, "That's an antique edition." Pages were already starting to deteriorate. In five to ten years, it would crumble, maybe sooner.

Clearly, he'd said the wrong thing because she hurled the book at him. He dodged it but didn't react in time to miss the brick titled *Moby Dick* as it followed. It struck him in the shoulder with a *thump*, and he laughed. Katerina seemed to take a personal affront to his amusement and began chucking literature at him more fervently.

Pan took a few hits on his way to her, but he managed to snag her wrist and drag her away from her artillery supply. Katerina yanked her hand out of his grasp and bared her teeth. *Feisty wench.*

"Damn it, stop," he said through clenched teeth of his own. "I'm not going to harm you. Calm down."

She punched him in the face. The impact a sudden flare of soreness that spread hotly from his cheek to his neck as his head whipped to the side.

Katerina immediately cradled her hand against her chest and bit her lip. The punch hadn't really hurt *him.* It had shocked him, yet he understood what drove her to it. He'd abducted and toyed with her. He deserved to be the target of her fury.

Katerina turned from him and sank onto the end of the bed, rubbing lightly at her knuckles. She didn't retain eye contact afterward, but she seemed to find the floorboards intriguing. "Could you please put on a pair of pants or something? If you aren't going to hurt me, I would assume you aren't planning on using...that." She finally looked back at him, gaze brushing over his penis before she looked away just as quickly.

His cock appreciated any and all attention, and was so flattered by her quick peek, that it stirred. No matter that it wasn't the time for it. Pan observed the reddening of her cheeks. It wouldn't have been perceptible to a mortal's eye in the low lighting.

Pan resumed his human glamour, sporting dark blue jeans, a black T-shirt, and no shoes.

"What are you?" Katerina asked, eyes widening as his form changed.

He could've answered her, but he wanted to lighten the mood. "That hurts. Here I thought we were upon an era where everyone was accepted for who and what they are."

She glared.

"Fine." He leaned back against the wall and re-crossed his arms. "I'm a satyr." He figured the god bit might be overkill if he started there. Anyone with knowledge of mythology could see his satyr form and come to terms with that far easier than they could handle that Olympians really existed. She'd think he was full of himself rather than believe he was an actual deity. Pan almost missed the good ole days where humans were honored by being in their presence.

When she didn't reply to his revelation, he prodded, "Well?"

"Sorry. You were speaking crazy. I had a hard time following."

He glowered. "If you would like me to do another demonstration..." He knew his eyes started to glow red as though he were about to go full Jersey Devil on her.

"No!" She cleared her throat. "Please, no. Sarcasm is my coping mechanism. I can't help myself."

He calmed. "I forgive you. However, I'm aware you were a skeptic before this evening. While seeing is believing in your line of work, I can practically hear your mind churning out petty excuses to explain what you deem impossible. Let me assure you, there were no tricks of light, smoke, and mirrors, or being knocked out and dreaming it all. I *am* one of the *Satyroi*, an immortal race of satyrs, and I can amplify my appearance into that which has been commonly referred to as the Jersey Devil."

"Immor...immortal?" Her voice cracked. "This is all too much." Katerina put her head in her hands as she leaned over her lap, attempting to curl into a ball. Her breaths came a bit heavier as she began hyperventilating. He inched toward her, wanting to help, but she held out her hand without lifting her head, motioning for him to stay put.

"I can't deal with this right now."

"I understand." Pan opened the top drawer of the dresser and retrieved his panpipes. He could have manifested them easily, but some notion of normality would be better for the time being. "I've frightened and upset you, and for that I truly am sorry. I'm known to be impulsive and don't quite think things through as I should. It's my flaw."

"Really? *That's* your flaw?" Katerina had glanced up when he'd opened the drawer. She eyed the panpipes warily. "What are you gonna do with that?"

"This?" He held the pipes into the light. There were seven reed shoots, all different lengths in size, bound together with leather from shortest to tallest. "I am going to play you a lullaby. You grow weary and need to rest. Your mind will manage better after it has recovered from tonight."

But he didn't play them yet. He frowned at her, still puzzled by her appearance in the Pine Barrens and his life. "You may have many questions, but then I do too. The most important being, why are you here?"

"Gee. I don't know," she said flatly. "Maybe because my mother and my father got it on. The sperm found the egg, and *voilà!* Nine months later and you have me, rosy cherub cheeks and all."

Pan instantly regretted ever wishing to meet someone who could be more of a smartass than himself—or worse, his father. Hermes infuriated even the most patient of men. Katerina had the same quick wit.

"I meant, why are you in the Pine Barrens looking for the Jersey Devil?"

"I told you the other day that I'm filming a documentary. Many a person has done it before. He...you...are kind of famous. Don't let it go to your head. By the way, do you kidnap every person who searches for proof of your existence? Is this how you welcome them?"

"No. Only you received the joy of meeting me, but whoever sent you here suspected as much."

"What are you talking about? I don't see how my being here means anyone has nefarious purposes other than entertaining viewers with the unknown." Katerina was breathing normally again, her panic dissolving into confusion, and if he wasn't mistaken, annoyance.

"That may be true, but usually Greek wine is not a common preference shared by your average American cryptozoologist."

Katerina huffed, and Pan half expected her to stomp a foot. She didn't though. "I'm not a cryptozoologist." She sniffed haughtily. "I'm a zoologist. No *crypto* prefix attached to it. I only happen to be doing a documentary on a cryptid... Wait...wine? This is about... Of course."

She perked up as she thought about whatever had prompted her epiphany. "That is what must have set you off and sent you running. You saw the wine bottle and recognized it. What does it mean to you?"

How charming. She attempted to turn the tables on him. Not happening, at least not yet. Pan wasn't revealing anything more about himself until he knew for sure if she was in on some grand scheme or not. "Nuh-uh. You get answers once I am satisfied with yours. Who gave you the wine?"

"My boss sent it. He's some wealthy guy who randomly wanted me to do this documentary despite it being outside of my field." She frowned as her words registered to her own ears, and then she veered off the subject slightly. "I study big cats, not cryptids. I wouldn't have even taken this job if the money wasn't so good. Does my selling out for cash satisfy your curiosity?"

"Maybe." He scratched at his chin. "Who hired you?" He wouldn't let her off the hook.

"Does it really matter?"

Pan considered her words. *Where that particular wine is involved, yes.* "It matters more than you know. If it is who I think it is, then your life could be in danger the longer you protect him by not telling me the truth."

Her gaze sought answers from his expression, and Pan struggled to keep it blank. Katerina appeared affected by the softening of his tone and the meaning behind his words. Whatever she saw cross his face must have driven home the fact he needed to know that information. Not just to appease his curiosity, but because her future depended on it. She couldn't escape him, and if she had any survival instincts at all, she'd cooperate.

"His name is Dion Bach. I don't know much about him other than he's really rich and owns a powerful compa—um...what's so funny?"

Pan sniggered. Then he cackled so hard he doubled over.

"Of all...the...stupid...names!" He gasped for breath, sobered a little, and then fell into more guffaws, sliding to the floor, clasping his side with his free hand. "He's *oh* so...so subtle!"

"Do you care to share with the class? Or should I just leave? Here, I'll see myself out." She ambled toward the hall without hesitation.

Pan willed the door shut with a *bang*. He stood, relieved of his amusement. "You will do no such thing. I was overcome by the wonderful dramatic irony. He is *such* a blasted Greek. If you knew anything about him, the name is a dead giveaway."

"The irony of what!"

"Patience, woman." That only seemed to infuriate her more, so he quickly explained, "Greek wine. Dion. Bach. You didn't find a connection in this at all?"

"Should I have?"

He threw his hands up. "Dionysus! Bacchus! That mother fu—"

"Whoa, whoa, whoa. Dionysus? As in the god of wine?"

"Ding, ding! We have a winner. It's painfully obvious now, isn't it?" He grinned.

"Actually, it just took things from boatloads of crazy to delusionally insane in the matter of seconds. Remind me never to come back to Jersey."

So she didn't believe the god of wine purposely sent her into the woods to find a satyr and wayward god that he hates with a passion?

That's fair.

"How is it irony?"

Pan blinked. "What?"

"If his name is obvious it wouldn't be irony."

"Dramatic irony, like in a play. The audience knows that which the characters do not. Greeks used it all the time."

Katerina didn't seem convinced. She muttered something under her breath about it not being ironic, and he let it slide. Unfortunately, he was weighted down with the implications of Dionysus rigging a "documentary" on him and didn't have the energy to explain why a god would trouble himself or debate elements of literature and drama.

Pan lifted the panpipes to his lips. Katerina glanced around with wide eyes, as though seeking another escape route. As he played his melody, her lids grew heavy.

"Don't want. To...sleep," she murmured as she drifted off, breathing deeply.

Pan played to her a while longer, enjoying the foreign sensation of making music for someone else and not because he was bored or needed them for sex. When he finished his tune, he placed the pipes into his back pocket, untucked the covers from under Katerina, and drew them over her. He made sure she seemed comfortable against the pillow, and then he took the candelabra with him on his way out the door.

Once he made his way back downstairs, he finally allowed himself to worry about the consequences to his actions. Katerina would need food and require use of the restroom which had been in disrepair for years. He would need to run out and snag supplies while she slept and begin renovating his house for company.

A KNOCK SOUNDED AT THE DOOR, DISTRACTING DION FROM THE two blondes in his bed. He'd told Pavlo not to disturb him unless it was an emergency or unless something happened in Jersey. As much as he mourned prying the tag team of skilled mouths away from his dick, Dion sat up and told the women to play with each other until he returned. He heard them giggling as he made his way across the elaborate bedroom to the set of double doors.

The knocking repeated, louder this time. "I'm coming, Pavlo. For gods' sake, this better be good." He opened the doors wide to reveal a fair-haired man with brown eyes, about five-eight in height. Two horns jutted straight upward from the top of his cranium, the physical characteristic of the Boeotian satyrs. Not one to be abashed by the display behind him nor his current nudity, Dion waited for Pavlo to explain why a disturbance at two o'clock in the morning was called for.

"I bring news, sir. Pan has abducted the girl." Always straight to the point. That's why Dion liked him.

"Splendid." He turned to his guests. "Ladies, try not to wear yourselves out. I shall return shortly." Grabbing his silk robe from the hook beside the door, Dion slipped it on. He followed Pavlo down the stairs to the study on the first floor.

"Tell me everything," Dion began, but then he noticed the phone was laying face up on the desk, the light on the charging unit indicated the line was on hold. He arched a brow and waited for Pavlo to explain.

"Cynthia Martinez is on the line, sir. She is demanding your presence in New Jersey." Pavlo stood straight and tall, hands at his side. Dion didn't offer Pavlo a seat but sat down himself, placing the phone to his ear, and taking it off hold.

"Dion Bach speaking."

The woman on the other end had been crying. He heard her sniffle and take a breath. "I am so sorry to disturb you..."

"Not at all. Mrs. Martinez, was it? Whatever is the matter?" He feigned complete obliviousness.

Another sniffle. "It's Kat. That thing... That thing took her. It's real! It's really real, Mr. Bach. The Jersey Devil flew off with Katerina Silverton." She sobbed heavily through the phone.

Dion's grin felt so wide his face could have been cleaved in half. But, of course, he was all sincerity and compassion on the phone. It wouldn't do at all to let his contentment color his words. "Wait, slow down. Did you say someone attacked Dr. Silverton?" He mimicked a shocked expression for Pavlo's benefit, which was met with a contrary roll of the eyes. That bastard Pan never could pass up the opportunity to fuck a redhead. It was almost *too* easy. Everything was falling into place. He hadn't expected the dimwit to abscond with her though. But Dion could work with that.

More sobs muffled Cindy's voice. "Yes. It had wings and horns, oh, and the tail! It was awful. And we can't find her. It took her. There is no telling how far into the Pine Barrens it went or if she's even still alive..."

"Have you contacted the local authorities?"

"Of course. We called them first. They had to send someone to get us because the thing knocked over our van. They didn't believe our story. Our footage had sounds but not visual proof. It stood directly in front of the camera but didn't show on the film, so it lacks credibility. They think we are attempting an elaborate hoax, and they threatened to arrest us if they discovered that was the case." She blew her nose.

"Don't worry about the film, Mrs. Martinez. What's important is finding Dr. Silverton alive and well. For her sake, do not alert the media or her family. We don't want to raise a panic, not yet. There will be a gag order faxed to the hotel for you and your husband to sign within the hour. I will catch a flight first thing in the morning to New Jersey. Perhaps I can help influence the police to make a serious effort in searching for her." Because money could buy cooperation. Not that he would really involve the police. "If we can't locate her within the week, the gag order will be lifted, and we will bring in the media to help with the search. I am only issuing it to keep the press and fanatics out of the way in finding her."

"Thank you. I understand the reasoning. I am so sorry to have disturbed you so late."

After a few more encouraging words to the woman, he finally

got her to hang up. He curled his lip at the mock sympathy. Then he chortled. Pavlo cracked a ghost of a smile.

"This is excellent." Dion went to the wine rack in the corner of the room and chose a choice bottle. After popping the cork, he poured a glass without offering any to the other man. It wasn't that he was being rude, but Pavlo always rejected the offer. Ever since the ordeal with Syrinx...well, the other man had been more closed off. Yet he remained with Dion anyway. He could have followed Pan regardless of his appearance. All the Arcadians had curled horns. Pan had offered to take the Boeotians with him that wished to go. Surprisingly, none had.

"Yes, sir. Your plan seems to be working as you anticipated."

"Indeed. I cannot wait to see the outcome." He took a sip of his drink. "Call Melancton. Tell him it is time to reveal Pan's location to Silenus."

Pavlo cringed and then nodded. Dion knew he had a history with Silenus, much like Pan did. It was part of the reason there was a middleman having to pass the word down the line. Dion had noticed, of all the Boeotian satyrs, Melancton was the only one Pavlo trusted. Even though Pavlo had remained with Dion of his own freewill, he didn't particularly seem to enjoy his company. But Dion paid him well and kept him living comfortably throughout the centuries as a personal assistant. He could leave if he wanted to, but he would not be welcomed back. Dion was sure that was why he stayed. Why they all did. Loyalty brought them benefits they wouldn't survive in the modern era without.

"Also, we fly to New Jersey in the morning. Make the arrangements, will you? Oh, and fax those gag orders to the hotel we drafted in case Pan acted out, and then call the police station and warn them to keep it under wraps as well." It was a command, not a request. Dion would simply flash himself to the airport in Atlantic City once the other satyrs landed. He had provided them a way to change to human form during the day. A gift Dion much like Pan had given the Arcadian satyrs when they followed him to the other god's homeland.

Pavlo nodded once more, bowed, and left the room.

Finishing his glass of wine, Dion then made his way back up the stairs to his bedroom. As he entered, one of his women screamed in the throes of an orgasm, compliments of the other's tongue.

"Don't think that means you're finished for the night, my dear." Dion stripped back out of the robe and tossed it to the floor before climbing into the deep red, nearly violet, silk sheets. He plunged his cock into the wet folds of the blonde who had climaxed seconds ago. The other female he positioned to where he could lick her at the same time.

The god of debauchery was a title he'd oft heard in reference to him. If he had to be a god of anything, there was nothing better, and he damn sure lived up to the hype.

CHAPTER 7

Mornings sucked. Kat opened her eyes, and the events from the previous night assaulted her memory and she groaned. Peter was sitting on top of the chest of drawers, hands resting on the wooden edge of the piece of furniture visible between his denim-clad thighs. He arched a brow and smirked as she became aware of him.

"It wasn't a nightmare, was it?" Her fear wasn't with her anymore. Instead, she felt the pull of sadness gripping her heartstrings. What would happen to her? *Cindy and Rick must be freaking out. Oh God, I've been so focused on myself that I've not given them a bit of thought.*

"I'm 'fraid not, vixen. I owe you explanations, and now that you slept off your denial and panic, you might be able to handle it." He snorted. "You know the word 'panic' is derived from the god Pan's enjoyment of hiding in bushes and startling trespassers as they wandered through the Arcadian forests?"

Ugh, Greek gods again? She didn't know why he found his comment so amusing. Why encourage him? However, she couldn't prevent herself from asking, "Vixen?"

Peter released a great sigh, probably because she wasn't biting at his baited hook. Was he disappointed she'd asked about that and not his strange Pan comment?

"Your hair and your spirit. Reminds me of a fox because of the color and your cunningness..." He scrunched up his nose. "Is cunningness a word? Anyway, you're female, ergo, vixen. I would have thought the comparison would be straightforward."

He pushed himself off the chest of drawers, the muscles in his arms flexing as he did so, and onto the floor. He landed lightly on his bare feet—the toed variety, not the hoofed ones. He was dressed in only a pair of jeans. If he was attempting to entice her with those scrumptious abs and the thick, corded muscle that led into the waistband of his jeans, well... Then she should probably be deeply ashamed that it kind of worked, and that made her increasingly uncomfortable.

As strange as the whole situation was, her body still reacted to his. Not as strongly as it had the first time, but the arousal was there, beneath the surface. Too afraid to notice it the night before, it had reared its head once more. Her reaction was beginning to concern her. It couldn't be natural, yet it didn't feel wrong.

I'm losing my mind.

Peter held a hand toward her, and she warily accepted it. He pulled her to her feet and led her into the hall. Kat half-expected human hands holding elaborate candelabras to extend from the walls, moving with them as they passed, like in *The Phantom of the Opera*. Except Peter would turn around, half demon-faced, and proclaim he was the devil of New Jersey rather than the Opera Ghost.

Then he did turn around and gave her a reassuring smile and her stomach fluttered. She told herself it was fear, but she wasn't exactly sure. Why did she feel things she shouldn't with this man?

Leaves and debris littered the upstairs floor, blown in from the broken windows that lined the path. She could smell the pines and also something else. *Bacon?* Kat fidgeted, hating to have to ask the question she needed to ask. "Um, which way is the bathroom?"

Momentarily startled, Peter opened a door not far from the room they'd exited. "I apologize. I nearly forgot."

Light poured through the small window at the back of the room he revealed, made brighter by the dirty white floors and walls. The porcelain tub was old, with the lion claw feet at the bottom lifting it off the floor. The enamel of the sink was cracked down the center, and the toilet looked like it hadn't been used in years. A bucket of water sat next to it on the floor and an unopened package of toilet paper beside it.

"Do you not use the bathroom?"

He shrugged. "I do, but not as often since I don't need to eat regularly like humans. My body doesn't produce waste unless I eat or drink daily. And I haven't been really living here much lately. I move around from place to place."

She didn't think she'd ever had a stranger conversation. He'd considered himself not human, yet he looked perfectly human at the moment. Nothing like the creature she'd seen the night before. She shuddered involuntarily. "A satyr thing?"

"Not quite. I believe I'm one of a kind among them."

Kat waited to see if he would elaborate, but he pointed to the water pail instead. "As I haven't been living here frequently, the utilities are not turned on. About ten years ago, the plumbing was updated, but if I turn it back on, the company will trace it, and I find I'm not in the mood for more visitors. I poured water in the toilet last night, but in case more is needed for flushing, I have provided more. There is a well behind the house. I'll be happy to carry the bucket up the stairs for you when you have need of it."

Kat guessed Peter had been quite spontaneous with the kidnapping if he hadn't even turned the utilities on to accommodate her. Or maybe she was giving him too much credit and he was only playing nice to get in her pants, and then he'd kill her afterward. Therefore, utilities were not necessary in the grand scheme of things. It *was* a secluded spot in the woods. The chances of surviving his little fiasco were looking worse by the minute.

After ushering him out of the room, Kat practically flew to the window to judge her chances of climbing outside. Her heart sank. Not only would her hips not fit through that frame, but she would have to drop all the way down where a wicked looking tree stump twisted out of the ground. She slinked back to the toilet and did her business. Then she washed her hands and face with the freshly unwrapped bar of soap using the bucket of water. Since the shower was obviously out of the question with no running water, and filling it full of lukewarm well water to bathe in would be quite the hassle, she made do with a quick rinse with the water she had. She'd refill the toilet tank the next time she came up here. And she figured Peter telling her where to find the water meant he wasn't going to hold her hand as she moved about the house. Or at least she hoped so because convincing him she wouldn't run provided an opportunity to, well, run.

When she exited the bathroom and joined him at the top of the stairs, Peter picked her up. Kat stiffened, and he explained that the stairs, like most of the house, were in need of repair and dangerous. She didn't question why he thought putting two people's weight into one would be any safer but went with it. If they fell through, he'd be a cushion to land on.

Kat observed her surroundings as they descended. The banister was thick and solid wood. It had seen better days. The windows on the first floor were all cracked or broken in. In fact, the only one she'd seen still intact was in the bedroom Peter had taken her to the night before. More leaves were scattered around the first floor. Dense cobwebs hung in all the corners and from the unused light fixtures. Dirty, dusty sheets draped what little furniture remained in the house. There were no pictures on the walls, and other than the room upstairs and the things she noticed crawling through some of the webs, no signs of life existed within.

Peter returned Kat to her feet and reclaimed her hand. Wordlessly, he led her through the next doorway, brushing the cobwebs aside to allow her entry. After she passed through a short, dark corridor, they entered a wide, spacious kitchen and dining area. It had been scrubbed clean. Two plates of eggs and bacon were placed on opposite ends of the long dining room table, which could seat about sixteen people. Along with the food, there were utensils and glasses of orange juice. The food smelled delicious, and glancing at the dish in the center of the table, she saw there was enough for second helpings. He'd cooked for her.

Kat's mouth watered. She glanced at Peter, seeking an explanation.

"I cleaned it while you slept. Went into town..." He narrowed his eyes. Kat's first thought was there must be a town nearby or he must have a car, which meant getting away wasn't as futile as she'd assumed. "I flew."

So much for hoping.

She gestured at the food. "I thought you didn't have utilities." Like electricity or gas.

"I don't. I cooked over a small fire in the yard. Like campers do these days—how people cooked in the past. The juice isn't cold, but it is freshly squeezed.

Kat decided the thought of Peter gently squeezing the oranges, coaxing the juice from them, was more than she could deal with imagining at the moment. Her filthy mind imagined his hands squeezing her breasts, causing her feminine juices to...well... Since her mind was too easily influenced, she'd throw away her romance novels when she made it home too.

PAN LED KATERINA TO THE TABLE, PULLED OUT THE CHAIR FOR HER, and pushed it in when she was seated. He then took his time strutting to his own chair and sat down, instantly regretting that he'd placed himself at the opposite end rather than next to her. Yet he'd hoped she may appreciate a little space while she came to know him.

He picked up his fork and peeked through his lashes at her. Katerina sat, hands in her lap, scrutinizing him. Pan put his fork down, the clank of silver against the stoneware echoing in the large room. "Aren't you going to eat?"

Her stomach growled in response, making her cheeks pinken. "How do I know it's not poisoned?"

"If I wanted to kill you, Katerina, you'd be dead already." This answer seemed to placate her enough. Why would he go through the trouble of cooking only to murder her later? Pan watched as she frowned at her plate and stabbed a fluffy, yellow piece of scrambled egg with a fork before she lifted it off the plate. She sniffed it, turning her blue gaze toward him. She popped the food into her mouth and chewed. Closing her eyes, she sighed.

Damned curse. Surely, he wouldn't have been turned on by a woman eating scrambled eggs without it. *Surely.*

Satisfied his woman wouldn't starve to death on his watch, Pan ate his own breakfast. The flavors hit his tongue and he stifled a groan. When was the last time he'd eaten a cooked meal rather than fruit or vegetation? He didn't have to eat daily to stay alive, but being around humans made him feel awkward if he wasn't mimicking their actions to blend in. Otherwise, he could go weeks without a single bite to eat. Pan enjoyed food though, and bacon was delicious.

Taking a sip of orange juice, he began wondering how to explain his existence to a human. He'd never had to. Before the curse, gods were accepted by the mortals. The human women and nymphs he'd bedded had known who he was, what he was, and had accepted him for it. After the curse, things became...more difficult. There'd not been a choice in honesty with the human women he'd slept with since then. Pan kept his illusion of human form firmly in place, or did as far as *they* knew, and left them directly afterward. Still, he hated hiding any aspect of himself.

Meanwhile, Katerina nibbled a piece of crispy bacon, and examined him silently. Neither one said a word. It was... *Awkward.*

A morning after without the benefit of sex the night before. *A damned shame, that.*

He took another swig of juice and cleared his throat as he returned the glass to the table. Katerina made eye contact with him and quirked a brow. He wasn't sure if she was simply curious about what he had to say or chastising him for interrupting the meal she finally began enjoying. She had stopped struggling to escape, but she wasn't happy with him. Her slight frown, in addition, revealed she still viewed the ordeal through skeptical eyes. Pan had seen it before with those who wouldn't accept the truth though they'd stood directly in front of him.

Beating around the bush wasn't going to help his cause. Katerina needed to *see* it. She needed to observe the truth to accept it. As harsh as it was, Pan needed his true nature exposed to her in order to convince her she'd not dreamed it. Satyrs were very real; *he* was real.

Despite what she saw last night, he'd been sheltering her by staying in human form this morning. He let go of his human appearance only enough to manifest his horns, feeling them curl from the sides of his head, the thick appendages impressive and large like a proud ram's.

Katerina narrowed her eyes into slits. From denial to anger? She had liked *Peter*. But Pan had taken away her option of normality when he stopped pretending to be an average human male. He would've probably gotten farther with her as a man than as himself. As a satyr. Pan scowled at the realization. Perfect human Peter was good enough, but monstrous Pan was not. Yet, for some reason, he didn't like the idea of deceiving her. So he wouldn't.

"I guess it's high time I introduce myself. Properly this time."

He waited for Katerina to comment, but she didn't. She merely watched him, observing, drinking in the scene as calmly as she did her orange juice. At least, he assumed that was the facade she attempted to put forward. Her hand shook when it lifted her glass.

"Long ago, the humans accepted there were higher powers living among them. In ancient Greece, these beings were known as the Olympian gods, descendants of the Titans before them. I was once one of their own, though I did not reside with the rest of the pantheon in their kingdom. Instead, I chose the wilds of the Arcadian forests as my home. Being a nature deity, this wasn't considered odd by my people. So I lived in the wilderness, amusing myself with the nymphs and becoming a protector, of sorts, to the creatures of the forest. I became the patron god of herdsmen and shepherds, and Arcadia—and soon after, all of Greece—came to know me by my given name," he paused for the drama of it. "Which is Pan."

Katerina's eyes widened slightly. Then she snorted and followed it with peals of laughter, reminiscent of his display when he'd told her she was working for Dionysus. She clutched her stomach with one hand and covered her mouth with the other in an attempt to contain herself. But she couldn't. It only made her start laughing anew when she'd open her eyes and see him there, a muscle twitching in his jaw.

He began to understand her chagrin from his reaction the night before, but it didn't make him any less irritated now. This was different than learning her boss was a drunken god. He was trying to tell her things he'd not shared in since the Olympians became irrelevant outside of legend, and how did she handle these great revelations? Like he'd told her a grand joke. When she nearly toppled from her chair due to the strength of her amusement, his pride ignited indignation.

"What in the name of the gods is so funny?"

"I'm s-sorry." More cackles. She breathed heavily. "I just can't believe you th-think you're a Greek god." Tears streamed down her cheeks, and she giggled more. "Suddenly your belief that Mr. Bach is Dionysus is making more sense. You're insane!"

She was the very definition of infuriating. It didn't matter that Pan was aware the stress of the situation could be the real culprit behind her hysterical laughter. There was a very real chance she was not insulting him of her on volition, but it didn't matter. He didn't like being laughed at unless he had done something worthy of laughter. It was a trait ingrained in Olympian blood; offending a god had consequences, no matter how unintentional the slight had been. Pan would have to put Katerina in her place, but he wouldn't punish her. No, he had never been one of the truly brutal among his kind.

Pan went full-on satyr, standing up and abandoning the illusion he'd decided to keep in order to protect her sensitive, human modesty. He didn't think she was aware he'd moved until she opened her eyes, panting from laughter, hunched over on the arm of the chair. Her face was level with his arousal—even her laughter could not diminish his need for her. In fact, her ability to do the opposite of what he'd expected only made him want her more.

Katerina regained her composure and sat ramrod straight in her chair, staring ahead of her rather than at him. "I'm sorry," she muttered under her breath, wiping at the remnants of her tears of merriment.

Pan invaded her space. His cockhead lightly brushed against her arm. Sadly, her sleeve prevented contact, but it was enough to make her visibly swallow in trepidation. Sex was not something he used for intimidation, but he could not think of any other way to bring her to heel after her hysterical laughter. Katerina was safe from him, but she needed to understand she was not the alpha wolf in the room.

"I find it fascinating you still think I'm making things up, yet you have seen me in my true form. Is this something you see often? Can this be explained away with your science and research?" He lifted a leg and wiggled his cloven hoof. She flicked her gaze toward it and back away again.

Katerina didn't move a muscle after that. She didn't even blink, though she still stared everywhere but at him. Her cheeks reddened more by the second, and her jaw was clenched. She had the nerve to be angry? After she'd laughed at *him?*

"Look at me." He kneeled, grabbing her chin and gently forcing her to obey. "Back in ancient times, your laughter would have been considered an insult to the gods. I was never one who cared so much about what the humans thought, but even I have limits. I am one of the few who never took a mortal life by my own hand. But had I been, I'd have punished you severely for such disrespect. You'd do well to understand how lucky you are that you are in *my* care and not one of theirs. Dionysus would have abused you in ways your nightmares would not comprehend for such a slight. Remember that next time you wish to compare me to your precious *Mr. Bach.*"

She glared at him as he stood. "If you wave your dick in my face one more time, I swear to God, I will bite it off."

Such fire! Pan controlled the urge to laugh at her boast and leveled his face with hers. "I was cursed, along with twenty-three other men, over a misunderstanding with another god. He thought *I* had insulted him. And so *I* was punished. I realized what was about to occur as it happened. I even tried to fight it, prevent it. I attempted to counter the curse, but it backfired. Because I refused to live among the gods, I never quite got the full handle on my abilities, and I never regretted it more than in that moment. The curse affected every man present and resulted in the creation of the *Satyroi* race I mentioned last night. Despite how I look, I am not really a hybrid of man and beast."

He took a few steps back and resumed the guise of the Jersey Devil. Wings, tail, and glowing red eyes amplified his horrid features, creating a truly demonic facade. "This," he said through sharp, gritted teeth, "is what I was meant to look like if the curse had struck full force. Because of my abilities, I can call it forward.

Sometimes, when I lose control of my anger, it happens on its own."

Katerina gasped, her horror apparent in her wide eyes. At least she was over the blatant denial.

Pan returned to his human glamour, dressed in jeans. He wished he could remain in this form at all times, but he couldn't. The horns never really bothered him. The hairy, hoofed legs did. "Luckily for me, the horns and hooves aren't quite as extreme as the chaotic mixture of appendages belonging to the Jersey Devil. And I can still take a human form, thank the gods."

He crossed his arms and spoke before she could comment, "So before you find amusement in my plight, before you doubt all you have seen, know the reason this happened was because I made love to the wrong woman at the wrong time. A woman, who was promised to another. Because of my mistake, several people were forced to unjustly endure the consequences of *my* actions. And I have to live with that knowledge every damn day."

Pan turned on his heel and stormed across the room. He slammed through the front doors as he headed into the open courtyard beyond them. Realizing he had no idea what he was doing, why he took Katerina, and what he would do with her, he went to the one place on the property that was sure to distract him from his newest problem by ambushing him with mistakes of his past. The truth was, no matter how badly he wanted Katerina, she would never have him. But he couldn't convince himself to let her go. For the first time in a very long time, Pan felt truly lost.

CHAPTER 8

K at hesitated on the doorstep of the dilapidated house and spied on Peter—she couldn't accept his claims of being the god Pan—as he picked up debris, removing it from the marble fountain. She bit her lip and shifted from one foot to the other and exhaled in a huff. If Peter had wanted to harm her, he would have. He'd said as much himself. While he'd frightened her and left the Martinezes in an upheaval of distress, he hadn't injured anyone.

Cindy and Rick have probably called the military in already.

Basically, she had two options of survival since Peter had promised to catch her if she ran away, and she was sure he could, given his wings and unnatural abilities. The first option was to fight him and be uncooperative, which could lead to his giving up and leaving her alone with no food...or merely offing her when she irritated him one time too many. The second was to at least listen to what he had to say. Maybe if she was complaisant, he would realize he was being idiotic and let her go.

She could then get away or at least send someone to help him. Though she wasn't sure she wouldn't be the one committed to an institution if she told anyone about a man in the woods who was a satyr, a Greek god, *and* the legendary Jersey Devil all in one. Hell, just thinking it sounded insane.

She didn't like the idea of giving in, but she wouldn't surrender and die. She'd survived a cougar attack, and if she could do that, she could survive playing house with a satyr...as long as he kept his pants on. First and foremost, she needed more information. He'd only given her the short version earlier. She still had questions, and she knew some of the answers he had wouldn't please her. Hiding from the truth was a cowardly approach, and Peter was clearly something supernatural in nature, even though the idea of ancient gods existing in real life was a concept she wasn't ready to accept. What did that mean about other religions? She was a Christian. She believed there was, and has always been, one true God. Was Pan's existence confirmation of a higher power, or did it contradict everything in her faith? Furthermore, if she accepted everything in the Bible, why could she not accept the idea of satyrs and curses?

Maybe because blind faith is much easier than witnessing magic firsthand.

Kat fidgeted, completely conflicted about faith, about her circumstances, about everything. Peter wasn't paying attention to her, so if she sneaked around the back of the house, she could easily make a break for it. Freedom was so close she could taste it, but it had a bitter taste.

Kat had seen the look in his eyes and the hurt when she'd laughed. He was baring the truth of his existence to her, and anyone living with an affliction that had them walking on hooves like an animal rather than feet like a man had to be a bit sensitive about it.

She wondered why he didn't stay in his human form all the time. He'd said it was a curse, so maybe holding the human appearance was difficult for him to maintain. Maybe he hadn't kidnapped her for nefarious purposes at all.

Maybe he just needed a friend.

With a deep breath, she closed her eyes in a silent prayer, and took a step forward. And then another. She fell into a steady gait that eventually brought her face-to-face with Peter, who paused as he bent to retrieve another handful of debris. Kat stood tall, hands clasped in front of her. Peter straightened as well and crossed his arms again, a stance he seemed to favor—he tended to fall back on the intimidating male posturing. Let him. Men liked to pretend they had the upper hand. It made them feel in control and balanced. She'd allow it...for a while. After she had her answers, she might knock him off-balance a bit with her inner smartass. He deserved it.

"I'm not going to apologize for not taking you seriously before." She held up a hand when he parted his lips in preparation of rebuttal. "You kidnapped me, terrified my friends, and are currently jeopardizing my job. I have every right to be pissed off at you. I told you once that my fallback is sarcasm, and you know I'm a skeptic. So if you don't like it, you can take me to the nearest town. I'm out here right now for answers. You"—she pointed at him for emphasis—"are going to open up and let the words spill from you like viscera."

Peter snorted and then motioned for Kat to take a seat on the edge of the fountain. She complied, and then rested her arms on her thighs. He pulled the panpipes he'd played the night before out of his back pocket and sat them on the lip of the fountain as he joined her. She noted that he must be able to reclaim what was in his pockets before or after he shifted forms. Good trick.

"Okay. So...you're the Jersey Devil, but also a satyr out of Greek mythology. I, um, guess that makes 'mythology' improper terminology, as it implies it isn't real..." Kat shook her head, refocusing on the topic. She was already rambling on. "And Peter isn't your real name."

"No." He didn't specify if he was referring to her comment about mythology or his name. She chose to go with the second option and continued that aspect of the conversation. She wasn't quite ready for the mythology part, as it made her world a scarier place than she wanted it to be.

"As I told you before, my name is Pan."

And the mythology part refused to go away. She wanted to deny it, to keep calling him Peter to keep her sanity.

"But I thought Pan was, uh, *is* a demigod?" Knowing she wasn't handling the conversation well, she looked down at the glaringly obvious set of *pan*pipes and recalled his quip about the origins of the word *panic*. He'd tried to hint it to her, but she'd ignored the signs. He had told her his name over the breakfast table, and she'd laughed in his face. And her occupation was based on her ability to observe. Shameful.

"More like god. Minus the demi. My father, you may have heard of Hermes, never told me who my mother was. Many women claimed they were she, but it was always a lie. Hermes took great pride in relating the story of my origin to the human storytellers, ensuring I was known as only half a god, as it protected the identity of the woman who birthed me, even from *me*. Unfortunately, the majority of the tales that survived were his embellishments." Smirking, he added, "He stopped that shit when I spread my own version where he wasn't my father. He didn't appreciate that very much."

Of course. His father would be one of the most well-known figures in the tales of the ancient Greeks. One of the ones who had a whole freaking planet named after their Roman title. "I take it you two aren't close."

"With that prick? *Pfft.*" He looked appalled. "Last time I saw him was after the curse when he'd found nothing other than amusement in my plight. Sure, he'd tried to be fatherly at the time, but it was too little, too late."

Daddy issues. Also noted. It always goes back to parent issues with men suffering from some ordeal. Violent men. Drunken men. Men with hooves for feet. Perhaps she should find a better group of men to classify him in because Peter...

"Wait a second. Seriously?"

Pan arched a brow. "Are you questioning whether I'm not really best friends with my asshole father or that he is, in fact, a prick?"

"No! Your name." Kat almost smacked herself in the forehead for not seeing it before.

"What about it?"

She shot him her best unamused glare. "Peter. You told me your name was *Peter*, but your name is really *Pan*. Did you seriously roll with the name Peter Pan?"

He flashed her a devastating grin befitting of Puck, and considering that comparison, she decided she wouldn't be surprised if the two were one in the same. But that smile... Her mouth went a bit dry. Damn the man, er, god/satyr/humanoid being was sexy.

"Don't knock it. It's a classic. Besides, Barrie and I go way back. He got his inspiration for that book from me, you know."

"Are you taking credit for a character that lives and behaves as an eternally immature child?"

"You wound me. Peter Pan played one of these." He picked up the panpipes. "He was named after me, and he was pretty clever. He always outsmarted the pirates."

"He also tried to attach his shadow to his foot using a bar of soap," Kat replied in a flat tone.

"You're just a, what is the term the cool kids say these days? Hater."

"Whatever. Is that the name you use if you have to go into a town or a city? Peter Pan?"

"Hell no. Draws the wrong kind of attention. The name on my illegally created identity is Peter Panic." The corner of his lips twitched as he attempted to keep a straight face.

"Um..."

"What?" Pan waved the panpipes around. "I'm a musician."

Her face met the palm of her hand. "I bet you invented the term 'panic' to create a legacy to yourself in human language."

"I admit to nothing."

Unsure how else to respond to his easygoing banter, she snickered. His gaze heated, and she choked. As he dropped eye contact to stare at her mouth, her lips suddenly felt sticky and dry. Kat had an uncontrollable urge to moisten them with her tongue. She'd read enough romance novels to know the man *always* considered such a move as invitation. As though her body had a mind of its own, it urged her to invite him, but in her mind, she wasn't sure it was such a good idea.

The dampness between her legs mocked her brain and its objections. She knew getting it on with Pan was wrong, but she grew a little wetter as she imagined allowing it to occur. *Traitor. You're mad at him. Stay mad!*

He's a god. A freaking god wants you bad!

Ugh. She was ashamed even her thoughts could be so shallow. It didn't matter that he was a god, if he really was. Or sexy as all hell, even with the freakish satyr legs... *What does that say about me anyway?* She glanced away, covering her mouth with her hand in a motion to scratch the opposite cheek. While her lips were covered, she licked them to dampen them again.

Ha ha! Because I'm sneaky.

The movement broke Pan's focus, and he closed his eyes. Could he be fighting his response to her as strongly as she was?

"I enjoyed that." When Kat didn't respond, he elaborated, "The conversation. You have a quick wit and the most beautiful laugh I have ever heard. Musical even."

"Oh, uh...thanks." How does anyone respond to something like that? Drop trou?

Her lady parts were totally down with that idea. She was back to feeling the way she did at the hotel when she met him, wanting him terribly, but not understanding the ferocity of her lust. And his junk looked human enough. It was the knees down that looked wrong. *Maybe if he wore pants...*

She mentally slapped herself out of it. Kat knew she should continue being mad at Pan, but she wasn't an angry sort of person. She hated to admit it, but they kind of got along pretty well when they joked and teased.

I can't get Stockholm syndrome overnight, can I?

"I suppose I should explain why I took you." Pan fidgeted with the panpipes. "I heard your laugh the day I made that ruckus in the woods for your camera. I was moving on to another area when you and your friend showed up. Then you laughed." His emerald eyes sparkled. "It seeped into me, grabbing hold. I wanted you desperately. More than anyone before you." He peered over his shoulder to the face of the statue. His skin paled slightly and sadness seemed to overcome his features. "More than her..."

Before Kat had a chance to ask about whom the statue depicted or even comment over why one did not simply kidnap people based on their pretty laughs, Pan turned away from the stone woman. "I hadn't even seen you yet and I wanted you. At first, I believed it had to do with the curse. If you know anything about satyrs, I am sure you've heard we are most often seen chasing the nymphs and women around because we are lascivious beasts. Sadly, in the first century of the curse's hold, it was true. Over time, we have managed to recognize when our urges are out of control, and we take to seclusion, or at least I do. So it was very possible my reaction was because I'd denied myself for nearly thirty years."

He'd been celibate for thirty years? Kat shuddered at the thought. She'd assumed going one year had been terrible. Life didn't revolve around sex, but where was the fun in that? Although, she had also never been forced to have it due to a curse. She couldn't begin to understand what he'd gone through. Realizing her train of thought was becoming sympathetic toward him, she shook her head to clear it.

"Then you made a retort about the Jersey Devil, and I wanted to play with you. Make you believe in the unknown. Give you hope that you were not hunting a fantasy." He smiled. "Impulsiveness has always been a burden I live with. As you've noticed, I have the tendency to act before thinking things through."

"You hadn't planned on kidnapping me?"

Pan shook his head. "I almost lost my hold on this form when I was in your hotel room and you produced Dionysus' wine, which is why I shot out of there like my ass was on fire. I apologize for that. I wanted to believe Dionysus had nothing to do with you being here, but there were too many coincidental factors at play."

Kat nodded. "At first I thought you were a super-weirdo. Then I worried you didn't like me, or I was, uh—" She almost revealed she'd been ready to jump his bones so hard the hotel quaked. "I don't think I would have reacted very well to a satyr standing in my room."

However, the way he'd revealed it had been about a hundred times worse.

The wind blew cool air in their direction. Kat rubbed her arms through her sweater. It was a chilly autumn day.

"I stayed away as much as I could, trying to come up with a way to be less awkward and approach you again after the previous mishap, but I kept expecting Dionysus or someone else unsavory to show up. They never did. So I promised myself I wouldn't seduce you until I knew for sure you weren't in cahoots with anyone."

Kat wondered who he meant by someone else, and her eyebrows rose when he'd implied he'd seduce her as though he'd succeed.

"Then you went out at night in bad areas of the Pine Barrens," Pan continued. "Wearing bright colors and being reckless. I thought you wanted a monster to find you since you behaved as such, so I became that monster and granted your wish."

He put his head in his hands, tugging at his dark hair. "Once I had a hold of you, I couldn't think of what to do. If I let you go, you'd have left New Jersey and disappeared. I can't flash myself to other locations like I could before the curse, and flying with a cloaking glamour expels a lot of energy. Chasing you across state lines may not have worked in my favor, so I brought you here."

She almost felt sorry for him. Almost. He'd scared the hell out of her. If he'd eased her into the fact he was more than human, showed her gradually, she may have been able to deal with it better. Accept it. And, yeah, she might have even thrown caution to the wind and slept with him had things ended differently.

There was no telling what would happen anymore. She desired him, strongly, but having sex with him wouldn't do more than make him believe he hadn't done anything wrong because he would be getting what he'd wanted from the start. Just because he apologized didn't mean the actions were erased. Not to mention the idea of having sex with a satyr was...weird. Not horrid, but strange. And having seen him as the full-fledged JD, sort of terrifying.

What she wanted was to make contact with Cindy and Rick, but doubted Pan had a phone. No utilities led to no landline, and who would he be talking to on a cell phone? She knew asking would bring nothing but failure, so she placed the wish on the backburner. Not to mention, she needed to know more before she brought anyone she cared about back to his attention. She would worry more about her friends later.

Instead, she focused on what information he was willing to give her currently. "This was your home once, wasn't it?" The thought had crossed her mind several times. The bedroom, the graffiti on the walls, and his reaction to the fountain. The woman immortalized in marble must have been a great love of his.

"Yes. I built this house in 1697. The forest was dense and uninhibited by colonists for the most part. At least in this section. Native tribes knew I lived in these woods, but having seen me in my true form as I built the house from the foundation up, they knew I was more than a man. It was because I was a creature of nature that they showed me no ill will. I returned the favor likewise."

"So you weren't the thirteenth child of the Jersey Devil legend?" Kat joked.

"Unfortunately, no. The legend of the Jersey Devil was created by superstitious men and women, using the names of neighbors they disliked." He cocked his head to the side." However, I'm sure Hermes would have loved that version of my supposed origin."

"Seriously, though. How did the Jersey Devil arrive in New Jersey?"

"Are you asking because you genuinely want to know, or because you are paid to seek out answers regarding me?" he teased.

"I want to know. I mean, I did find you..."

"I *let* you find me, but that is beside the point. In actuality, my coming to be the Jersey Devil was an accident. I had lured a woman into the woods through the song of my panpipes. Because my human form is retained by illusion, in the middle of things, well...illusions can falter when you stop concentrating on them. We were caught by a group of drunken adolescent boys. The woman, I regret I never asked her name, didn't see my satyr form as I was taking her from behind." He laughed. "Don't give me that look. If they can't see the horns or the hooves, they can't be horrified by the sight of them, and I don't have to explain myself or placate them. Anyway, the woman was very, uh, vocal and drew the attention of the boys."

"Then what happened?"

"The boys saw what I was and thought a woman who would lower herself to a monster would be open for a round with all of them. They attempted to kill me and rape her."

Kat gasped. The story had not gone how she expected at all. It was terrible. Pan furrowed his brows as he retold the events. She could tell he was still infuriated by the actions of those men.

"In my anger, I manifested the form immortalized today as the Jersey Devil for the first time. Later, I was able to study it, learn how I achieved the form, and realized it was how I was meant to have been changed by the curse. I'd frightened the boys so badly that half of them pissed themselves. They ran away, screaming and crying like small children. The woman fainted under the duress." He added softly, "I played her a song to forget the whole evening ever happened and took her home."

"Let me guess. Tales of your existence were spread in a state of panic and skepticism?"

Pan winked. "Yup. And occasionally I would hop out and scare someone new to keep Jersey on its toes. Old habits never die and all that."

"If you don't mind me asking..." Kat stood up and stretched. Sitting for long periods of time sometimes cramped her scarred leg. "How did your house become so rundown?"

With a shrug, Pan said, "I've been spending days, and then months, sometimes years, wandering around the woods. On occasion, I travel into other states, losing track of time. I'll live in town for a while, catch up on the current literature and films. Keeps me from feeling too old. I had the electricity and modern plumbing installed sometime in the late 1990s when I came back from exploring the Pacific Coast. The men who came out thought it was strange to have such a large house out in the woods no one knew about. I played them a song to forget; I'm not one for many visitors. They have the information in their systems somewhere, but no one from the electric or water companies remember this house until they have reason to come here. As to the current state of the place, I just never got around to repairing the building since then or paying the bills." He shrugged. "I cast an illusion over it using the panpipes when I am not around. Humans will stumble upon it, some spend a night here and leave, but they cannot find the house again after."

That explained the graffiti. Someone must have suspected.

"And the woman in the fountain?" Kat gestured back at the figure.

He sighed. "She is a long story."

"Well, I am a captive audience. Emphasis on captive."

He rolled his eyes playfully. "It's a story I can't really tell you. Syrinx"—he gestured to the woman—"is the start, middle, and end to how the curse of the *Satyroi* came into being. The only way to really tell the story is to show you."

"Can you do that?"

"Why, woman, must you constantly doubt me? I'm a god. Of course I can." He stood and put the panpipes back in his pocket. He gestured to the pile of leaves in the empty structure. "Now help me clear this rubbish, and I will play the song of my memories for you."

"Song? As in an actual song?"

"Doubting again. Remember the conversation in which I am a musician? Less questions. More clearing." He grabbed two armfuls of leaves and tossed them outside of the fountain, not seeming to care where they ended up.

Kat bit her tongue, on the verge of retorting that he should just swoosh it all away with his wings like he had the night before with the dust, but then she remembered the hurt in his eyes when he had glanced up at the statue. He needed to do this by hand. Guilt perhaps? She'd give him this boon.

CHAPTER 9

"Tell me where that asshole is hiding," Silenus demanded as soon as Dion stepped out of the bathroom stall. He had flashed to one of the men's restrooms at the airport in Atlantic City, one of the few areas where surveillance was not an issue. Pavlo, Melancton, and Silenus were waiting on him, having arrived not too long beforehand from private jets owned by Bach Industries.

"I'll tell you where he is once I am sure of the location and the timing is right. I know he's in the area, but you cannot act out. Not yet. There are certain events that must take place before you can confront him." Dion pushed past Silenus, noting the rage in the man's icy glare. He'd promised the satyr revenge thousands of years ago, but had never let him take it. Soon he would.

Silenus had been forty-two when he'd become a satyr. He was the oldest, in terms of human years, and it showed in the gray at his temples and facial hair. When in satyr form, his pelted legs were also sprinkled with gray. Silenus was the only satyr with the characteristic goatee the classical depictions favored, at least that Dion knew about—he didn't particularly keep tabs on the Arcadians' grooming habits.

Furthermore, Dion was aware Silenus rarely sported a human glamour anymore, but it was hard to focus on magic when one's very core was seething hatred. Hatred for Pan. Hatred for Dion. It had gotten old centuries ago. He had festered into an infectious cyst of violent rage waiting to erupt.

The fool had been spotted by mortals so many times, it was a wonder it took Dion so damn long to figure out he could pinpoint Pan's location through urban legends. Silenus had been the cause of "goatman" legends in at least five states that he knew of, reported to have attacked people with his axe and frighten people on bridges.

Even though Dion hadn't allowed Silenus to go after Pan, he knew the crotchety old goat had searched anyway. It was nearly time to see what would happen when the two of them met once again. Of course, Pan could always kill Silenus, which would not necessarily be a bad thing as the Boeotian had lost his usefulness a long time ago. This could be his defining moment, or his final.

Either result would be...interesting. Pan refused to take a life, but Dion secretly hoped he would falter in his ways. He would relish in Pan's regret for the rest of eternity. Corrupting that sap would be glorious in its own right. Though he supposed it was cruel of him to not care which satyr killed the other in the long run. *Oh, well... Things happen.*

Melancton cracked the restroom door open and peered out, his long raven hair shining in the glow of the fluorescents. "We do not have much time until the humans realize no one authorized this facility to be closed from the public."

"Facility? Stop being so stuffy, Melancton."

Melancton turned and bowed his head, a subtle glimmer of defiance quickly masked in his expression. "I will try to appease your wishes, sir." When he lifted his head, his light violet eyes scanned the area for signs of threats, even though they were both aware there were none. Habits were hard things to break, and while Dion knew Melancton loathed him, the satyr remained loyal. He had his reasons.

"Appease," Dion repeated under his breath and rolled his eyes.

Dion and Melancton exited the bathroom, and then headed in the direction of the luggage carousels to collect the items brought with them for their stay. They didn't need a lot, but to keep up appearances, they all had luggage. The only thing not with them was Silenus' axe, which had been FedExed to the hotel to avoid getting it past airport security, and also to remove the temptation for the satyr to use it on anyone.

Pavlo stomped into stride beside Dion a few seconds later and bit out, "Where's the car?"

Silenus seemed a bit smug when he finally emerged from the restroom. Obviously, he'd said something to rile Pavlo. It was like working with a bunch of children always picking on each other. Melancton was charged with keeping a leash on Silenus until Dion approved a confrontation with Pan. But it seemed he'd have to worry about an altercation between Pavlo and the elder satyr in the meantime. Given their past with Syrinx, there was no surprise.

About an hour or so later, the taxi that took them to meet with the Martinezes came to a stop outside of the Fancy Pines Hotel. Dion had sat in the front with the driver. He tried not to laugh as he recalled glancing over his shoulder during the silent drive through Jersey. Melancton had sat between Pavlo and Silenus, all of them looking pissed to no end. Hell, they still did. Arms crossed, Pavlo and Silenus had stared out the opposite windows. Only Melancton had met his gaze dead on.

Currently, Pavlo remained with Dion while the other two stalked off toward the woods. Silenus would be scouting for Pan, he knew. Melancton's job was to rein him in until it was time. Assuming Silenus tracked him that quickly.

The original plan had been to confine Silenus to a hotel room, but the strain between him and Pavlo could become an issue. Dion's nerves were starting to get frazzled, and when his nerves were frazzled, people died bloody. He didn't want to kill a satyr before his plan was seen through. So he'd let Silenus hunt Pan through the Pine Barrens to calm his own temper as much as Pavlo's.

"Come. Let's get the formalities taken care of and out of the way."

Not saying a word, Pavlo followed Dion to room nine. A brief knock on the door, and a Latino man with a grim expression answered.

"Mr. Martinez?" Dion asked, despite knowing full well he was looking at Ricardo Martinez. He'd done extensive research when Katerina Silverton had sent the names and information on her two crew members. He'd been pleased the crew ended up so small. The fewer mortals he had to bring into this, the better.

Rick held out his hand, and Dion shook it. "You must be Mr. Bach. Sorry to have to meet under such dire circumstances." He peered over Dion's shoulder.

"Ah, this is my personal assistant, Pavlo."

Rick held his hand out and shook Pavlo's hand as well before motioning them inside the cramped hotel room. Dion supposed he could have upgraded them to a suite like he had booked for himself since he was paying for the Martinezes' stay in New Jersey. He dismissed the thought. He didn't know these people well enough, and they didn't drink alcohol, let alone wine. He found it disturbing. They were not his people, and he only rewarded those who belonged in his circle of people.

"This is my wife, Cindy." Rick held his wife's hand as everyone said their pleasantries. The married couple took a seat on the bed and left the chairs to their guests.

Dion listened, expressionless, as Rick relayed the turn of events from the previous evening. Cindy played the film footage for them. While there were sounds of growling, wings flapping, and screaming, only the humans were ever seen in the footage. They hadn't even managed to film Dr. Silverton flying away. That would have been some quality television, not that he'd ever really planned on broadcasting it.

"As I told you over the phone, we've only gone to the police," Cindy began. "But they think it is a joke and won't cooperate with us. They looked around, did a report on our vehicle, but since they didn't find any evidence of a 'monster attack,' they threatened to charge us with falsifying information if we don't come clean with what they call 'what really happened.'" She made air quotes.

Rick patted her shoulder.

"I'll speak to them this afternoon. Perhaps I can convince them to cooperate," Dion told them. He had no intention of speaking to the police or involving more humans, but placating those involved would ensure they didn't become a problem.

"While I'm here, do you happen to have any wine? I find myself rather parched after the long flight." He knew they didn't, but he was curious as to whether or not Katerina Silverton had consumed the wine he'd sent over. He really hoped she had.

Rick shook his head. "Cindy and I do not drink, but Kat enjoyed the wine you sent. I believe she finished it all, though."

Excellent. Everything was falling into place.

"We have some cola if you don't mind that kind of drink. Or water," Cindy offered.

"No worries. I was just hoping for something a little stronger, and I've always had a fondness for wine." He stood up and buttoned his suit jacket. "Had I known I'd be placing your friend in danger, I wouldn't have asked her on to the assignment."

Dion's apparent concern for Katerina Silverton seemed to win them over. But there was only so much of this facade he could take. Pavlo excused himself to check in to the hotel. He would be back with the hotel keys, and Dion would be able to extract himself in order to determine how to proceed to the next phase of his little experiment.

~

PAN PICKED OUT THE LAST LEAF, AND ALL THAT REMAINED AT THE bottom of the fountain pool was dirt and grime. Not wanting to waste time heading back up to the house, he summoned the broom and dustpan from the closet in the front hallway and began to sweep. He may not have been able to transport himself around as he did before the curse, but he could still move objects over a short distance with the limited telekinesis he'd retained.

Katerina watched him, a curious expression on her face. He couldn't tell if her slight frown was due to worry over her current circumstances, the magically appearing cleaning supplies, or for him. Pan really hoped she didn't pity him, because if she did at the present, revealing his past would be painful for them both. Experiencing it again as the feature presentation, start to finish, was going to suck horribly.

After Pan removed the loose dirt from the fountain, he tossed the broom and dustpan beside the pile of leaves. Having fixated his energy doing something hands on helped him prepare for the onslaught of memories, but he had to start soon before he changed his mind and didn't go through with it. Pan dropped to his knees and rubbed his hands together, looking at the ground around him, contemplating how best to go about filling the fountain with water.

"Now what?" Katerina paced, wringing her hands. Barely looking up at her, Pan put his hand to the ground and concentrated. The well water came from a creek not too far beyond the trees to the right of the house. He focused on the water there, putting all he had into calling it to him. Had he been a water god, no real effort would be necessary, but telekinesis worked better on solid objects more so than billions of molecules of water. As it was, he half-expected to have a nosebleed by the time he finished.

The earth trembled beneath his hand, bending. A small furrow formed in the ground, and suddenly water flowed past and over his hand, up the side of the marble and into the fountain pool. Physics were a joke when one had otherworldly abilities.

"Nice trick, Moses. I would say why don't you let your people go, but since you won't let me leave, it would fall on deaf ears."

Pan chuckled. She could claim sarcasm as a language of its own. But even though she sounded bored and unimpressed, the awe was written all over her face. She was riveted by the unnatural flow of water. "Moses didn't enslave anybody. The pharaoh did."

"Details."

The pool would only hold about a foot and a half of water, and he stopped the flow once it reached that point. Pan stood up and wiped his hands on his thighs. The pool wasn't as clear as he'd like it to be, but it was enough to cast a reasonable reflection. It would do. He motioned for Katerina to step forward, and she did so with some hesitation.

"Find a comfortable position where you can see into the water. You may be sitting for a while." He resisted the urge to pick the leaves out of her curled hair. The appearance made her look wild, like a nymph, though she wasn't one. She sat on the ground, legs curled to her side, laying both arms crossed on the lip of the fountain. She laid her head on her arms and gazed into the water.

"I'm not going to like what I see, am I?" She didn't turn to look at him, but she watched his reflection when she spoke.

"No, Katerina." Pan lifted his pipes to the level of his mouth. "You're not. I'm ashamed for my part in the memories you're about to see. Know that, when you see them. Try not to hate me for what I have done, and for what I didn't do. For what I allowed to occur when I could have prevented it."

He began to play, conjuring his memories and letting them

pour from a melody in a series of notes invisible to the naked eye, yet soft and seductive to the ear. It coursed through him and out like blood from a wound. It had threatened to bleed from him for years, and Pan feared he wouldn't be able to stop it even if he wanted to. As the murky water churned and formed the images that haunted his mind, he closed his eyes and just played, lost in his song.

CHAPTER 10

Mount Kithairon, Greece, 1123 B.C.

The tangled bodies writhed in the firelight. They moved out of sync with each other but maintained the illusion of one impenetrable whole, like ants defending a disturbed mound. Every so often a head would surface for air or to drink from the ever-plentiful wine. A delicate nymph would escape and prance away, laughing; a male form, erect and eager for the chase, never far behind.

Most were stripped of their garments, leaving several lengths of cloth littered through the grass and abandoned in the neighboring trees. Some merely lifted the ends of their chitons—too impatient to proceed with unwrapping their clothing—in order to plunge into the next willing body. The heat from the exertion and proximity to the bonfire only soaked the fabric to their flesh, hindering more than hiding. Many were so far gone in their cups they no longer cared who they pounded into, regardless of their sex, as long as they found the pleasure that made life worth living. Once they found it, they'd start all over again, often exchanging partners for another.

The scent of wine and sweat, musky, damp, mixed in with the tang of the soil they rutted upon, permeated the night air. Bitter drafts of smoke coupled with the crackle of the dancing flame on the outskirts of the outdoor temple of trees, rock, and dirt.

Moaning chorused with grunts of satisfaction. The whimpers of need urged on the triumphant cries. Moistened slaps of flesh sounded over and over in response. The cacophony of sounds varied in pitch and made up the notes for a song primitive in nature. Instinct. To find solace through pleasure. To give into temptation, living for the moment. That. One. Fucking. Blissful. Moment!

Or several if it was done just right.

Sensory overload. Intense satisfaction rolling like waves. The heat of it, buried beneath the perspiring flesh; thrusting, arching up to meet them. Brutal pushing and pulling, groping hands seeking purchase. Finding leverage in the earth, bracing themselves for the next onslaught upon their bodies. Greeting it with glorious relish.

Pan threw his head back and laughed as he came, fisting the mane of the dark-haired beauty as she took him with her mouth. She released his member and licked up his torso, around the indentions of muscle, and captured the sweat that ran like salted tears, not from the heat of the fire, as gods did not react to changes in climate, but from the exertion. She groaned as another male rocked between her thighs, and she groped handfuls of Pan's backside as she reached her own climax. Pan pushed his drenched hair out of his eyes and pried himself from the woman's grasp. Weaving in and out of the labyrinth of jumbled limbs, he made his way to a flat boulder with a clear view of the night sky and the landscape beyond the mountain. The grunting behind him continued, not disrupted by his departure in the least.

He crossed his ankles and reclined back, hands behind his head. His still semi-hard penis stretched upward against his belly. The stars above were hundreds of jewels thrown against a dark cloth. Their beauty had always distracted Pan from his endless existence. He'd been alive for so many years he'd stopped counting. And while every now and then the star pattern would shift, they remained, for the most part, a constant in his life. Always there when he needed an escape. *Always there.*

Someone clamped a hand on his shoulder, startling him from his reverie. "My friend, why do you hide away from the crowd?" Dionysus smiled widely, his pearly white teeth contrasted against his tan skin and sandy hair. Behind him, the shadows of the rutting humans undulated through the firelight, a great beast through the trees. "I bring you the best wine you could ever have the pleasure of tasting, the most beautiful nymphs of the mountains, forests, and rivers, and still you sit alone and stare at stars. Does my hospitality bore you?"

Pan chuckled. "I've already sampled your nymphs this evening. Twice. And you know I cannot get drunk on wine."

"Twice you say? I'm amazed you didn't wear them all out."

"It's near impossible to exhaust a nymph."

"And here I thought I wasn't doing it right."

Both gods laughed heartily at the jest. Dionysus conjured a golden goblet, more advanced in design than humans of the period were accustomed to. He filled it with deep red wine and handed it to Pan. "If you aren't going to enjoy the pleasures of flesh any longer, at least do me the honor of drinking my wine. I can't have you looking neglected over here—I have a reputation to uphold. You'll drive the crowds away." He flashed away without waiting for a response and reappeared where he'd erected a dais composed of rocks and upraised earth, standing tall and commanding attention. Having no structured temples to his name, Dionysus had fashioned his own to preside over his followers.

Pan turned back to the stars. Dionysus had the habit of giving speeches about how he was honored by mortals' love for him. How, as long as they continued to pay tribute and worship at his altars, he would continue sharing his wine and women and allowing his renowned orgies to come to their cities and villages. The humans may have cared, but Pan did not. He only participated because he had nothing better to do. Very little held his attention aside from lust and fun, and becoming a member of Dionysus' circle of debauchers was the last thing on his mind. He was merely in the area that night. And, well, an orgy promised a good time.

Zoning in and out of the present, hearing only bits here or there in the background, Pan enjoyed his blissful solitude. Varied cries of ecstasy would pull him from his thoughts with a sudden increase of volume that became soft whimpers after hitting their crescendos. Somewhere through the muffled moans, Dionysus droned on about how his faithful follower, Silenus, an old drunkard from Thebes, did him a great honor in allowing him first rights to his new bride.

Pan didn't catch the poor girl's name, but he didn't envy the woman having to bed the wine god in front of his worshipers. If she was lucky, they'd be busy with another orgy, and she'd only have to deal with Dionysus' pawing and insensitive nature for a few minutes. Pan decided not to bear witness to it either way. Traditions of the gods and Greeks alike could be cruel or unreasonable. He hadn't been back to Mount Olympus for nearly two hundred years, partly because the ways of his people often angered him.

You poor girl, whoever you are.

Bored and feeling the first pulses of a headache from the exuberant noises, Pan flashed away to a secluded area near the Asopos River. It began on the mountain and flowed in the direction of Thebes and Plataea. He waded into the cool water and washed the night's actions from his body. When he drifted back to the river's bank, he sprawled out on the soft grass to dry. Before he could think too much about anything, he drifted to sleep, watching the reeds protruding from the water's glossy surface as they swayed in the gentle breeze. Hearing the whisper of the wind across them as though they were a soft lullaby subtly warning him of what was to come.

~

GIGGLING BROUGHT PAN BACK INTO CONSCIOUSNESS. HE stretched, not wanting to rise just yet, and rolled over on his back. He slid his palm down his torso as he did, making him well aware something else had indeed arisen while he slumbered.

More giggles.

As he tilted his head upward, Pan cracked his eyes open. He viewed three women watching him appreciatively, and they covered their mouths as they snickered. The two dark-haired ones were nymphs and were as naked as he. The one with red hair was human, and she wore a sheer, coppery peplos—a single piece of fabric pinned over the shoulders with a leather cord around the waist. It fell to her ankles but was so thin it didn't actually cover what lay beneath it, despite the extra fold of material over her breasts. Her rosy nipples were beaded, and her secret curls were the same fiery shade as the ones on her head. She had eyes as brilliantly blue as the Aegean Sea which sparkled with interest as they lighted upon him.

The dark-haired nymphs were forgotten in an instant. There was only one who caught his eye. Pan knew he would have her before Helios rode the sun chariot to the highest point in the sky. He had never wanted a woman more, especially not a mere human who could only be enjoyed for a short period of time. Mortality was short-lived, after all.

He bolted upright, and the women fled, chortling as they scattered in various directions. If it was a chase they wanted, a chase they would get, but there was only one who would be caught. Pan fell into pursuit, hardly registered the sting of stones and twigs beneath his bare feet. He didn't need to worry about them due to his healing factor being nearly immediate. He took running leaps over clumps of the underbrush and limestone rocks that littered the base of the mountain and swung beneath low branches like the large, orange apes he'd seen when visiting an island off the coast of the far eastern lands.

Pan pursued the woman into a clearing where the sunlight seemed too bright, too close. Her hair glistened like Dionysus' favored wine poured over molten gold, and it spilled past her hips in waves. She peeked over her shoulder and yelped when she realized Pan would reach her in a few short strides. Her awareness made the anticipation zing through his blood.

He pounced, and then he rolled with her tucked against him in order to catch the impact himself. Allowing his hands the freedom to wander over his newly captured prize, he groaned when her backside rubbed against his groin. Pan turned her over on her stomach, and then he pinned her down. He placed his mouth beside her ear and whispered, "Caught you."

She shivered, but she didn't fight him off. Instead, she reached her hand back and gripped his length, hesitantly at first like she wasn't sure what to do with it once she'd touched it. Pan reached between them and showed her how he liked to be stroked. She caught on quickly.

When he was on the brink, he rolled back over, breaking the contact. He wasn't ready to be finished off before he tasted her. She turned, accepting his kiss while he settled between her thighs. Pan reached a hand under her clothing and she jumped at the contact.

"Virgin?" he rasped out as he licked the delicate structure of her collarbone, enjoying how her skin held a rosy blush to it as she became aroused. He brought both his hands back to her hips, willing to move a bit slower for her benefit.

She nodded.

"What's your name?" Pan bit her earlobe and licked it lightly to ease the sting. She jerked against his lap.

"Syrinx." Her delicate voice lilted over the syllables. *Sear-inks.* She attempted to grasp his cock a second time, but Pan wouldn't allow it. He pushed her arms over her head and held her hands captive there.

"I'm not done getting to know you, Syrinx. Please keep your hands to yourself until we are further acquainted." He was able to secure both her wrists in his left hand while he reached down and unfastened the fibula brooches holding her clothing together over the shoulders.

"W-what..." She shivered as he tongued one sensitive, puckered nipple through the thin fabric. "...do I call you?"

"You don't know me, then?" He used his right hand and his teeth to untie the cord at her waist. He peeled the layer of fabric from her skin, freeing her from its confinement. "My name is Pan." He released her hands to run his over the bared flesh of her thighs, and leaned back to view the treasure hidden between them.

"Ah, I have heard tales of your prowess through the forests and mountains where I've traveled. They say Arcadia is where you call home. You are a long way from there, are you not?"

"You've heard all good things, I hope. Arcadia's not too terribly far away. I needed a change of scenery, and I come to find the current view beautiful, indeed."

Before she could respond, he parted her folds and took exceedingly long, leisurely licks at the core of her. She twitched and shook beneath his hands, gripping his hair, pulling a bit too roughly with one hand while the other fondled her own breast. He inserted a finger, then two, mimicking the act of lovemaking, and finally a third, preparing her for him.

She moaned, unable to answer coherently. After several minutes, she came against his mouth, writhing and panting. Syrinx shuddered so hard Pan had to hold her body down, as if it would float away otherwise. He crawled up her body, held his cock at her entrance, and she urged him on with the lifting of her hips and he dove in, shoving all the way through her maidenhead. The sting would fade faster the quicker it was done. He hated causing her pain, but slowness prolonged the process.

Syrinx winced and tears formed in her eyes, but she did not push him away. Pan kissed her, seeking to distract her from the intrusion as he remained motionless. The worst of it was over, and now he needed the passion to overcome the discomfort. He hummed softly to her, focused on relieving her pain rather than how good it felt to be nestled within her. It seemed to work; at least he thought so, since Syrinx wiggled as though she, too, could no longer stand the torment from the lack of motion.

Following her cue, he pulled back, almost completely out, and drove back in. The strokes were slow and precise, but she was tight, wet, and an exquisitely beautiful woman. Control was lost to him in no time at all, and his thrusts became quicker, primitive. Pan felt himself tense up and a rapture so strong coursed through him as he came in powerful bursts within her, bringing Syrinx to a second peak. Her skin seeming to glow as his seed filled her. His power hummed within him and he closed his eyes to call it back.

"Syrinx, no!" One of the dark-haired nymphs dropped to her knees at the edge of the clearing, gawking. "Do you realize what you have just done?"

Pan sat up, staring from one female to the next. What was he missing?

"Klytie!" Syrinx scrambled out from under Pan, struggling to dress herself. Klytie winced at the smear of blood that graced Syrinx's thigh.

"He's not going to be pleased," Klytie murmured as the other nymph joined her.

"Who's not going to be pleased? What—"

"Syrinx impaled herself upon the nature god's heavy spear."

"Oh, that's bad..."

"Klytie, Daphne, you aren't being helpful." Syrinx pulled the leather cord at her waist into a knot with a dramatic tug and glared at the nymphs.

"Can somebody please explain to me what in the name of the gods is going on here?" Pan asked.

The one referred to as Daphne replied, "Syrinx was promised by Silenus to Dionysus in an act of loyalty." She nodded, as though the motion made the remark an official order.

"So?" Pan urged, but then he slapped a hand to his forehead as muffled phrases of Dionysus' announcement the night before came to his mind. Syrinx was the woman whose virginity Silenus was offering to Dionysus as tribute before he took her to be his bride. The virginity Pan had just taken from her.

Fuck.

"*So,*" Klytie repeated in a clipped tone, ignoring the startled look on his face, "she was to be presented and mounted beneath the full moon this evening. But she's defiled herself upon you. This could result in her death."

"You three were the ones who woke me with your enticing giggling and twitching your rear ends in my direction, seeking my attention."

Daphne coughed delicately against her fist. "You were supposed to go for Klytie or myself. See how we are naked?" She motioned to her nude form. "Yes, we were pretty obvious about it." Though she teased, there was a strange tone to her voice. Almost like she was relieved he hadn't gone after her. When she met his gaze, her expression was sad.

Of course it is. Dionysus is going to blame her and Klytie for letting me near Syrinx. Why wouldn't she be upset?

"Just like a male to go for the only one unavailable," Klytie mumbled.

"Why did it take you this long to realize I hadn't captured either of you and Syrinx was no longer in your group?"

"That damned Apollo." Daphne huffed, shaking her fist toward the sky in the direction of Olympus.

Before Pan could ask what Apollo had to do with anything, Klytie cut in. "He desires Daphne and me, and he believes we are his property until he declares otherwise." So much for their supposed availability. All three of them had been off limits. If a god had his eye set on a female, it was wise to stay out of their way until they lost interest. But why would Syrinx purposely throw her virginity at him? She never tried to stop him; she'd urged him on. Initiated it even.

"Which will be for eternity, because Apollo is selfish and greedy." Daphne remarked. "He flashed us to the gates of Olympus —couldn't even make the effort to come to us—in order to explain in detail what being 'his' meant. Like we're simpleminded." She snorted. "I'll have my way with whomever I so choose. He can turn his pretty blond head in another direction if he doesn't like it."

Pan stared at her. If Apollo heard such open vehemence he could very well kill her for it. Daphne was either very brave or very foolish.

"Apparently, Apollo objected to the thought of us sullying ourselves with your..." Klytie trailed off as she stared at his manhood and sighed wistfully. "Would have been worth his anger, I think."

They were all addled in the brain.

At last, the nymphs ceased their chatter, and Pan was able to direct his attention toward Syrinx, who had listened to the conversation in silence. She seemed different somehow. Surely he hadn't impregnated her. He'd never done so with a human before and figured he wasn't capable of it at that point—he wasn't exactly chaste. "Why would you allow me to take your virginity if you knew it was promised to another?"

Morosely, Syrinx lowered her gaze and her delicate upper lip curled to one side. "I am to be given to a god, against my will in front of a group of onlookers, and afterward I am promised to be the wife of a drunken idiot who is already nearing old age. I wanted one time with someone who knew what they were doing, and who may have the common decency to take care and not hurt me the first time through. You met all the requirements."

She met his stare, looking both fierce and worried at the same time. "I may have been dishonest with you, as I knew who you were from the very start. And while I played along with Klytie and Daphne in waking you, I desired you for myself as much as they did." She lifted her chin a little higher. Pan found her defiance incredibly appealing, and wanted nothing more than to have her again, with or without the nymphs present.

Klytie groaned. "And now we all will be punished due to your impulsiveness, child. Come. We must get you cleaned up and redressed. Hopefully Dionysus will be too caught up in your beauty to notice something amiss." One should hope. Unfortunately, the god of wine rarely was taken unaware and had a keen sense of observation. Even Pan couldn't pull one over on him, and he'd attempted to fool the god on several occasions, all in good fun. Something told him Dionysus wouldn't be amused this time.

Syrinx curled her lip, and Pan couldn't help but cringe at the thought of Dionysus hovering over her. If only circumstances were different. What he would have given to claim her as his own, to take her back to his home in the Arcadian forests and enjoy her every day, every night.

He was at a loss as he watched the nymphs cart Syrinx away with them. Pan couldn't approach Dionysus about it, as bringing the situation to light would only endanger Syrinx, and he couldn't stand the thought of her being harmed. The only way to avoid it would be to hide her and hope Dionysus never found out. But if he did, and Dionysus discovered what happened, he could go into a rage. It was said Dionysus became as unpredictable and unstable as the effects of his wine on mortal men. If that was the case, Pan wasn't sure what would happen as a result of his wrath.

~

THE REMAINDER OF THE DAY WAS SPENT IN THE CLEARING, contemplating all that had transpired and the various consequences that could arise from it. He kept reliving the morning in his mind, wondering how he could have seen the truth and stopped himself from falling into the trap laid out for him. That was what virginity was: a trap. If a beautiful female was still a maid and throwing herself at a man, there was a good reason. Pan should have known. He probably *had* known, but he had been too busy thinking with his dick.

By the time he snapped out of his thoughts, all he knew for certain was he still wanted Syrinx. He barely registered night had fallen until he heard the distant voices from the mountain. Reality crashed down upon him, forcing him to become aware he'd chased Syrinx near the site of Dionysus' makeshift temple. Like he really needed to add further insult to the other god.

The responsible thing to do was to attend, if only to ensure Syrinx wasn't harmed if the truth came out. If Dionysus didn't notice, then there was no harm. If he did...

Pan wondered if there was some way he could put a stop to the whole event without revealing the slight in the process. There wasn't, unfortunately. Dionysus would never turn away from the opportunity to take the virginity of a woman and then plaster her with wine. Sometimes he shared her with the entire group that came to witness the action.

He faltered. Maybe it wouldn't come to that, considering she was promised to Silenus, but he would stop them if it progressed past Dionysus. There was no way to prevent the Olympian from doing what he was promised, not without revealing the reasoning and causing more trouble for everyone involved. That didn't mean he couldn't be there to save her if something terrible did occur.

Pan paused when the glow of a fire revealed the location of the site through the thicket of trees. The whole reason he'd left Olympus was to distance himself from the egotistical gods that lived there. His father had not approved of the decision, and had called Pan selfish to seclude himself away in Arcadia. Sometimes he grew lonely, and it was such an instance that drew him to Kithairon and Dionysus' orgy the night before. Now an innocent woman was in a perilous situation because he'd not followed his one truest desire and steered clear.

I don't know what to do to make this right.

Hesitating didn't give him the answers he sought, and stealing Syrinx would place her in a lifetime of danger. Not acting wasn't any better. There was no easy way to solve it. All paths led to peril for the mortal woman, and it wasn't good enough. Pan braced himself anyway, and marched toward the firelight, head held high.

The crowd was infinitely smaller that evening. For once, no women were present, which was surprising. *Did all the nymphs run off?* Nearly two dozen men stood or reclined with kylixes of wine, conversing and smiling, waiting for the ceremony to end so they could partake in another night of gratification. No one seemed to find anything amiss and continued consuming the rich liquid in the name of their patron god.

He had heard rumors that Dionysus favored one circle of followers above all others, and perhaps these were those men, though he couldn't be sure. Soldiers, scholars, even a prince was present. Then again, he'd also heard about six or seven different origin stories regarding his own parentage, so he didn't hold everything he'd heard in passing as truth.

"Pan?" A familiar voice questioned to his left, drawing his attention from the man of royal birth conversing with one of the guards flanking him. Turning, Pan saw double and he blinked. Ariston laughed at the reaction and pushed his twin forward. "I take it you were unaware my brother and I shared the same face. We get that rather often."

Ariston and his twin both had the same long, golden hair and sapphire eyes. Even their build was identical: strong and athletic. Try as he might, Pan couldn't find a distinguishing feature to tell them apart aside from their clothing—Ariston's sandals were well-worn in comparison to his twin's. The brother looked Pan up and down with a scowl, reminding him he hadn't clothed himself after his encounter with Syrinx, and he was, so far, the only nude male present. He shrugged. Nudity didn't bother him in the least, nor did it seem to draw a critical eye from anyone else. Only Ariston's brother seemed opposed to it. Nevertheless, he conjured a chiton as he didn't want to draw too much attention to himself when Dionysus arrived.

"So you're the god my *dear* brother calls a friend?" Bitterness colored Ariston's brother's words. Pan wondered if the man merely disliked him on sight or if there was bad blood between the twins. Perhaps he took issue with the gods in general. The best option would be to ignore it, as he already made a mess of things earlier and didn't need to stir up more unnecessary trouble.

He tried to be cordial. "I was unaware Ariston had a brother at all. What is your name, *mortal*?" Still, he couldn't help himself. The words hit their mark, and the man curled his perfectly formed upper lip.

"Surely you've heard of me, though you have never seen my face. Ariston never mentions me because he loathes living in my shadow."

"Narcissus! How wonderful to meet you. Seen any good reflections lately? And by the way, I have seen your face. Many times. If I knew Ariston had such a burden to bear, sharing his face, I would have taken him far, far away from here to escape." As anticipated, the barb was dead on.

Ariston quickly disguised an outburst of laughter with a fit of coughs, earning an icy glare from his brother, who stomped past Pan, shoving him hard on his way by. Strong resolve for a mortal to push a god, as most would have killed him for it. Pan was sorely tempted, but the only thing that kept him from smiting the human on the spot was Syrinx. It would not do to infuriate Dionysus right away.

"Never a dull moment when you're around. Don't mind Adonis. He's angry with me because he was practically a love slave to Aphrodite for several fortnights now—I lose count how long—and when she discovered he had a twin, she wanted a matching set. I refused, and she discarded him because she couldn't have her way." Ariston leaned back against a tree trunk and observed his brother's retreating form with a frown. "He was too attached to her, I think."

So that was the infamous Adonis. Goddesses and nymphs had been whispering about the mortal's physical perfection in awe for about as long as Ariston had said Adonis had been with Aphrodite. Pan would bet those same people were not aware he had a twin either. "Aphrodite tends to do that to men. Why did you bring him here of all places?"

Ariston sighed. "I'd mentioned it to him, mostly in passing. As a way to bring him out among other people again. Instead of moving on, he's hoping to make Aphrodite jealous by showering himself with nymphs. He said I owed it to him to come along and participate in order to doubly irritate the goddess."

"Is he not afraid Aphrodite will retaliate with hostility?" Pan observed as Adonis spoke to the tall, dark-haired man Pan had met the night before as he was arriving, and the man was rushing off in a hurry. Melancton, if he remembered the name correctly, was a warrior; he still wore his leathered armor. There were several scars on the man's arms, including a jagged one down the inside of his left forearm. Adonis motioned around to the small crowd, probably questioning where the nymphs were. Melancton shrugged and moved on, his eyes scanning the trees as though expecting someone.

"He's not exactly thinking with the head upon his shoulders at the moment. If Aphrodite arrives to murder us both, I am counting on you to protect me." When Pan snorted, Ariston interrupted, "I'm serious. I will give a blood oath to serve you for the remainder of my days if I have to. I don't want to die over a foolish man's indignity about being turned out of a goddess' bed, even if that man is my flesh and blood."

The conversation never made it any further. Dionysus appeared on his earthen dais and greeted his followers. "I'm sure you may have noticed the lack of female companions." Murmurs throughout the crowd of men assented that, yes, they had noticed. "Do not fret. They will come after the ceremony. I forbade the nymphs' entrance to this area until the tribute has been paid." In short, no one had sex until Dionysus was through with Syrinx.

He droned on and on about how Syrinx, promised bride of Silenus, was given the "honor" of sacrificing her virginity to a god. What honor was there in being forced to have sex as entertainment for men, by men? Pan had learned through the whispers around him that Syrinx's brother, Pavlo of Thebes, had offered her as a wife to Silenus in order to gain access to the depravity of Dionysus' wild nights. And in turn, Silenus had promised Dionysus he could be the first to bed his beautiful bride-to-be.

Pan was sickened by the lot of them. Nobody at all seemed to spare a thought for Syrinx, as virgins were offered to gods all the time as a sign of respect. He'd lost count of the number offered up to Apollo on a regular basis.

Dionysus snapped his fingers. Klytie and Daphne, both dressed in white, appeared as though they'd stepped out of the trees themselves. Syrinx followed behind them, eyes downcast as she lifted the hem of her peplos to avoid stepping on it. Silenus leered at her as a jackal would a juicy piece of meat. With his enhanced vision, Pan spied multiple nymphs shy of the tree line. When a mortal male turned in their direction, the nymphs disappeared into trees or seemed to shrink into the forms of flowers to stay hidden, fearing Dionysus' displeasure at their disobedience. They came to watch.

Pan gritted his teeth as Syrinx spread herself upon the flat surface of the limestone boulder he had lounged on the night before. The crowd waited on baited breath, some men more excited than others about watching a woman having sex on the uncomfortable surface with a male who likely wouldn't even bother to ensure she was wet and willing before shoving his prick inside her. His narrow-eyed glare caught Syrinx's gaze and her lips parted, like she hadn't expected to see him there. She quickly glanced away.

Disgusted, Pan couldn't watch. He'd run out of time to save Syrinx from her fate, as Dionysus was a much older, much more powerful deity than him. Pan didn't even know what all he could manage with his magic, had not taken Hermes and Zeus seriously when they'd demanded he remain in Olympus and experiment rather than galloping into the mortal world unaware of his own strengths. Never before had he regretted his decision of leaving Olympus, but he did now.

Where a few men around him looked intrigued by the display on the boulder, others, like Ariston, appeared uncomfortable. Many—like Melancton, the prince, and the guards with him him —refused to watch and waited for the act to be over with. Syrinx's brother, who didn't resemble his sister at all with his light coloring, dark eyes, and short stature, stared at the ground, arms crossed, dejected. Pan wondered if Pavlo hadn't known he would be forced to witness the act, and he probably hadn't anticipated Silenus sharing her, let alone publicly. Honestly, Pan hoped this night haunted the man forever.

Caught between the desire to leave, wanting to flash to her side and rescue her, and knowing all he could do was watch as the event unfolded before him, Pan felt his heart breaking for Syrinx. He'd just met her, but he'd been a dreamer. He'd foolishly hoped to have some great affair, lasting years, possibly even her whole lifetime, before he ceased enjoying her. Perhaps he was no better than Apollo or Dionysus in his possessiveness, and he really was the same as the other Olympians, despite his departure from their realm at a young age. He'd been selfish, full of himself, and had taken without thought of consequence.

Torn fabric drew his attention back to the scene before him. Dionysus ripped Syrinx's peplos straight down the front and was practically salivating at her breasts. Syrinx, gods protect her, focused above her on the stars. Pan's heart clenched. The stars were there for her too. The constant that never faltered.

Dionysus stiffened suddenly, sitting up as he peered down at the girl with a fierce expression mixed with surprise. Pan took a step forward. He should probably interfere before it went any farther, but Ariston grabbed hold of his arm and shook his head. He didn't have to speak to tell him it was a bad idea to disrupt a Dionysian ceremony. Not when the god in question could hurt the woman at his mercy.

Frowning, Dionysus leaned in and sniffed Syrinx's neck and backed away as though burned. He removed himself from the rock and, almost comically, gawked at Syrinx, the others, and back again. With a brisk shake of his head, he bellowed, "This is no human virgin. I have been deceived. She is a nymph, and she's given her virtue to another!"

Syrinx clutched the ripped material to her chest, covering herself as best she could. Tears ran down her face, and Pan felt like the lowest of villains to ever live. It was all his fault, and he was powerless to stop it from escalating. He should have run off with her, faced Dionysus, and fought for her. Murdered Silenus and Pavlo for their role in her fate. He'd not known his powers, true, but he'd not even tried. Instead, he continued to make excuse after excuse not to do a thing to help her.

You're doing it even now.

"She is impure," Dionysus announced, and whirled on Syrinx. "You little whore." She flinched. "Who defiled you? Who would dare?" When she didn't answer, he turned on Klytie and Daphne, both watching the scene with ashen faces.

Suddenly it dawned on Pan what Dionysus had said before. Syrinx was a nymph? But how? She had been human that morning. He scrutinized Daphne and Klytie and opened his sense. Definitely nymphs, and...interestingly, Daphne was immortal. Someone had given her ambrosia.

Then he turned his senses toward Syrinx. That morning everything about her had been human. But now, the same aura of magic surrounded her as Klytie—one that didn't exist that morning. She was a nymph, without a doubt. Pan wondered if that was the difference he had noted when he feared he'd gotten her with child. He hadn't figured it out because he already sensed the other nymphs. Did he somehow turn Syrinx into a nymph with his seed? Had it happened before? His mind reeled.

It was possible he had tapped into a power he hadn't realized he possessed. He lived in the forests of Arcadia, which were inhabited with many nymphs, so he had a natural affinity for them. But for a mere human to become one after being intimate with him...it had to be something he'd done. Nothing else made sense.

"Who did it?" Dionysus shouted, his face molten. He was so livid with the fury and the humiliation of being tricked that the ground he walked on quivered beneath him. The nymphs didn't answer his question. Instead, they swore Syrinx had been pure and human that morning when they'd attended her. But the god was no fool.

Dionysus grabbed Klytie by the throat as he glared down at Daphne. He smiled cruelly and stomped his foot, opening a chasm which split the ground wide for several feet. "You will tell me," he told Daphne, "or you will be next." He dropped Klytie into the pit. The ground sealed itself immediately, cutting off the nymph's scream and leaving only silence in her wake. A blue-violet hyacinth sprung into bloom within seconds, marking the death of a nymph by her body becoming one with nature indefinitely. Pan had seen it happen before, and because of Klytie's death there, hyacinths would always grow in that spot no matter how many times the roots were removed.

Daphne shrieked and collapsed, and then she dug at the earth with her hands, raking through the soil, refusing to believe Klytie was dead. Dionysus lifted her by her hair, and yanked her to her feet to face him. "Tell me!"

"It was Pan," Daphne wailed, pointing. The onlookers parted out of the scorching path of Dionysus' wrath, all staring at Pan in shock. Ariston gaped at him. Men he met briefly before, Silas and Orestes, looked startled. While other men he'd never met spoke incoherently to each other, shaking their heads and driving home the shame. Pavlo glared daggers at him, attempting murder with a look, projecting the blame on Pan. Silenus sneered, but then everyone knew the drunkard enjoyed altercations and considered them entertaining. Even Melancton frowned at him, but he seemed agitated too, though it was hard to tell.

"You dare to defy my will?" Dionysus let the nymph go and took several steps in Pan's direction. The humans present moved farther aside, leaving the two gods in the middle. They circled around to witness the drama unfolding, the audience to the making of a Greek tragedy.

Pan could deny having knowledge of Syrinx's identity when he took her, but then it would be apparent she'd deliberately disobeyed Dionysus' wishes.

"Nothing to say for yourself?"

There was no use in trying to remain civil. Dionysus had already murdered an innocent female for no reason, and it was unacceptable. Pan wanted to keep Syrinx and Daphne out of harm's way if he could. Past Dionysus, he saw Daphne crying on Melancton's shoulder. Behind him, Syrinx sat, half hidden on the other side of the boulder, forgotten for the moment.

Pan was often considered a trickster, but he'd always avoided confrontation if possible. He'd never killed for the sake of it, and hadn't ever taken a human or immortal life. They weren't his to take. He killed animals for food on the rare occasions he ate, but found no purpose in hunting for any other reason. Dionysus had demonstrated with Klytie that there was no life he found valuable except for his own. So he decided if Dionysus wanted to go down the, I'm-a-powerful-god path, then so would he. Pan smiled, knowing it would only piss Dionysus off, and it did.

"If you want to cover the facts here, *old friend*, I am a nature god."

"What relevance does that make?"

"You are the god of wine and excess. I am a god of nature. Nymphs are nature spirits, and therefore fall under my protection, or possession, should I deem it necessary to offer it." His smile grew wider the redder the other god's face became. "She was human until I spilled my seed in her. I made her a nymph. I believe that makes her mine in every way." He couldn't help himself and added, "Having sex with me gave her magical abilities and enhanced stamina. I am *that* good."

He had no idea how he turned Syrinx into a nymph, but the other god didn't need to know that. And Pan wished he'd thought about his role in the balance of power sooner. Not wanting to cause a rift between their somewhat of a friendship—neither really liked the other very much, though they were cordial in the past—he'd not considered the fact that the nymphs were not Dionysus' to give. Not until then.

True, most nymphs felt inclined to do as Dionysus asked of them because their kind had nursed him to health after the Titan queen, Rhea, brought him back to life. He'd been torn to pieces and proclaimed dead at a young age. As traumatic as that had to have been, Pan had never heard of an instance of violence being used against nymphs by the wine god, but he had murdered Klytie right in front of him and the others. Everything would change because of that one action.

Pan never cared about his powers or what he was "the god of" before. Poseidon had claimed the whole blasted ocean.

Hades had named the underworld after himself. Pan should have been protecting the nymphs who lived in his forests, but he hadn't. Instead, he ran about fucking anyone he could and humming songs to help the herdsmen with their work. Playing pranks on innocent mortals amused him, and he had no worries except for dreading the next time Hermes would show up and aggravate him. He hadn't grown into his role in the hierarchy of the immortal gods, and perhaps if he had, tonight could have been avoided. But what could have been wouldn't fix the present.

Dionysus took advantage of his distraction, and if Pan had blinked, it would have been too late. He raised his hands to the heavens, and the sound of his voice echoed through the trees. "Let it be known the god Pan will from this day become the lecherous beast he is in his heart—"

Pan quickly raised his arms out in front of him like a shield. Impulsively, he yelled back, "Let this curse begot upon me reverse back upon the one who spoke it!" His exclamation drowned out the rest of Dionysus' words. But as their voices overlapped, the air crackled with an electric charge and the sulfuric smell of Hades was detectable in the air. It felt like they had shot Zeus' lightning bolts at each other, and the force of the power meeting between them ricocheted outward in every direction.

The invisible blast struck him in the gut and the ground vanished from under him. Seconds later, he landed on his back, ten feet away from where he'd been. He thought he'd countered Dionysus' curse effectively, but the victory was short-lived. Within seconds, his head and legs felt like the bones within were trying to escape his skin. Glancing up, he saw his counterattack had knocked Dionysus over as well. The wine god peeled himself off the ground, dazed. All around them, the men present were groaning and gripping their heads. Syrinx and Daphne stood outside the circle of men, watching in horror at what continued to transpire.

Pan touched his scalp, and his hand hit something rock solid that didn't belong there. *Horns.*

He had horns like an animal would have spiraling out from the side of his head. The others had them too. Some curled like Pan's, and some men had two straight, sharp horns shooting up off the top of their heads. Strangely, all of the ones with straight horns were behind Dionysus. It looked as though the men behind Pan received the same curse as he did, but when Pan had attempted to block it, what struck the other god also hit the men behind Dionysus.

Yet Dionysus himself appeared to be unaffected.

Pan's legs itched. He reached to scratch them and was startled to discover a small creature lying on top of his leg. No... There wasn't a creature at all.

His gaze shot down. Dark, coarse fur sprouted along the lower portion of his legs. It thinned to the normal amount when it reached his thighs. Around him, shocked outbursts alerted him he wasn't the only one experiencing the deformity. Suddenly his bones snapped and reformed below his knees. He bit his tongue, tasting metallic blood, to keep from crying out like the mortals. His toes shriveled and disappeared into his flesh with ten sick *pops.* The balls of his feet hardened and grew darker until black hooves remained. Then they split down the center, becoming cloven like a goat's.

Dionysus laughed. "Well, this is an unforeseen twist. Now you shall all look like the animals you are for eternity, and you can thank Pan for it since his counter-curse failed to do more than curse everyone." He brushed off his golden Olympian robe as though he'd merely gotten a little dust on himself in the event.

"Dionysus." Silenus stumbled toward him on wobbly legs, attempting to walk on the hooves, but not quite having the hang of it. He'd dragged Syrinx out from behind the rocks and struggled to keep his balance and his hold on her at the same time. When he shoved her in front of Dionysus, she stumbled and ran toward the trees. Silenus garbled a stream of obscenities and searched the area around him. He smiled as his gaze fell on something beside the rocks.

Pan followed his line of sight. One of the warriors present had removed his armor and laid a spear down beside it when they'd arrived. He must have been fresh from battle or on his way when he'd arrived here, but Pan didn't have time to ponder any further. In slow motion, he could only watch as Silenus leaned down and gripped the spear. He stood up straight and threw it.

It struck true.

"No!"

Syrinx staggered, staining the green grass red upon her collapse. Pan didn't remember moving, but he cradled her in his arms as best he could as she shuddered. The spear had caught her in the middle of her back, and she lay against his chest, facing him. The old man had surprisingly accurate aim, and Pan realized he'd underestimated the fool on many occasions. He wouldn't again...if he lived long enough for there to be a next time.

He wasn't sure what to do about the spearhead. If Pan were to remove it from Syrinx's back, the wound would bleed out swiftly. But to leave it in meant she'd suffer longer. Once more, he was left in a position that didn't benefit Syrinx either way, and he was at a loss. He searched for a cure he would never find as he perused the grass and rocks in his immediate vicinity. Pan couldn't heal a mortal wound; it wasn't the same as stopping pain.

Of course! *Her pain.* He could stop her from feeling it.

Pan focused on her wound and hummed, concentrating to remove her agony. If it worked, he couldn't tell. Syrinx caressed his face, and then she coughed. Blood dribbled out the side of her mouth, a harbinger of her time reaching its finality. "T-take me to...w-water..." Her breathing was erratic. Then she shuddered, gurgled wetly, and didn't make a further sound. Her eyes stared at him, but she didn't blink. The pupils lost their focus, dilating one final time as death took hold.

Oh gods, no! She couldn't die when he'd just found her. There could have been a way around this. He could have saved her, and they could have taken to the wilderness together. But now they never would. She'd belong to the Elysian Fields, and her body would belong to nature. Pan hugged her limp body close, but he refused to give into the sadness overtaking him in front of this crowd, especially not in front of Silenus or Dionysus. Through dampened eyes, he glared at the onlookers as he realized what Syrinx had meant by wanting to be taken to water.

Her body hadn't formed a flower like Klytie's had but remained cold in his arms. She would only seek water in death if she had been a water nymph. She must have instinctively known. "I'll take you to the river. Don't fret." The words were a mere whisper, a breath against her cheek. He'd take her to where he first saw her.

"I guess this serves as adequate punishment," Dionysus said from somewhere out of sight. As though death was even necessary! The other god had willed a curse upon him which hadn't gone the way it had been intended, but he still sought out punishment for being denied a virgin's blood upon his cock.

For the first time since Pan had been born to this world, there was murder in his heart. He'd start with Silenus for striking the death blow. He'd grab the man by his horns and split him in two, rip one out of his dead skull, and slice Dionysus open to spill his entrails. He'd rip the god asunder for the second time, but there would be no nymphs to nurture him back to health. Pan was preparing to make good on his fantasy when Pavlo leaped upon Silenus and began pummeling the older, taller man into the ground. Pavlo thought to rob Pan of his revenge? He delicately placed Syrinx on the ground and stood, fingers curled as though they were claws.

A flash of golden light was prelude to a gust of energy which sent Pan on his ass again. Apollo stood in the middle of the circle of newly distorted men, searching for something, disdainful at the deformities upon those he saw. Everything from his posture to his chin to his dramatically arched brows screamed of pure arrogance. Hair and eyes the color of the purest gold, his skin taking on a similar hue as well, the god was considered one of the most beautiful in creation. Even more so than the rumors of the mortal Adonis, who presently appeared so distraught over his pointy horns that he hadn't moved from the ground and continued to touch their tips in disbelief.

Apollo's gaze landed on Daphne, and he held out his hand. "Come to me."

Daphne had once again taken her place beside Melancton, clinging to him as though seeking comfort or perhaps giving it. The man didn't seem to mind and actually had one arm in front of the nymph in an effort to shield her from Apollo. Daphne didn't move on command, and the god exhaled impatiently.

"Now."

She hesitated at the order, but then Daphne pushed her way through the circle of men and took Apollo's hand. Despite her earlier annoyance toward him, something like relief crossed her features. Apollo provided a means to escape the tragedy upon Kithairon, but when she glanced back to Melancton, the expression turned bleak.

"Where is Klytie?" Apollo asked, still taking in the scene, bewildered at the sight but not in the least bit concerned. Pan noted Dionysus had crept into the shadows and promptly flashed away. The nymphs in the shelter of trees no longer cared if they were seen as they poked their heads out to study the horned men and the golden god among them.

Daphne burst into tears and pointed to the hyacinth that grew in the place of the other nymph. Apollo beheld her grief-stricken face, the flower, and then Daphne again. It dawned on him slowly, as though he hadn't remotely considered such a thing would happen unless he was the one to command it.

Overhead, a shadow had cast itself over the moon, darkening

the night sky, leaving a sliver of pale light at the edge. Those who were superstitious cowered at the sight, considering it an omen of doom. And perhaps it was—darkness overtaking something of beauty, like death consuming a young maid who hadn't yet lived her full life.

"Who did it?" Dionysus' earlier demand was repeated, this time by yet another vengeful god. Unlike then, Daphne told him everything. Apollo narrowed his eyes at Pan as he listened to the story, nodding once or twice. The moon was completely shrouded in shadow when Apollo spoke again, "Dionysus has scampered away with his tail between his legs, but know this..."

Pan could see the pleading faces of the bystanders in the darkness, begging for release from Dionysus' wrath, not realizing Apollo was a much crueler god. He hid it well with beauty, but underneath that golden facade, he was as vicious as they came. And when the air crackled once more with energy, Pan realized Apollo had not changed in the slightest.

"From this day forth, you are known to all as the *Satyroi*: men forced to walk this world forever in a partially beastlike form. Women will fear you upon the sight of your ugliness. Nymphs will abhor you and will be always hidden from your sight. And you will live your lives consumed by a raging lust that can never be sated."

Daphne made a startled noise and said something to Apollo, who grunted as he considered her words. He then cocked his head to the side and nodded once.

"There is, of course, a way to relieve yourselves from this curse, for I am a merciful god."

Pan barely kept himself from snorting.

Apollo raised a hand to gesture above him to the shadowed moon. "On the night of the Satyr Moon you were made into monsters, so it shall be under a Satyr Moon you can be changed back. As the nymphs shall be hidden from your sight once my decree is complete, the chances of redemption are not in your favor. Only a nymph can break your curse. A nymph must find you of her own free will, seek you out, allow you to see her, and accept you into her body under no guise of a human form. Should this happen, you will become a mortal again, fully restored to your human state to live out a mortal life, as you were meant to."

Nobody commented, but the expressions on everyone's faces made it clear. They were all doomed. Dionysus had cursed them, but Apollo had laid out a sentence.

Apollo turned to Pan. "Or immortal, if that be the case. However, should you have sex with a nymph before the Satyr Moon, you will be stuck in this form eternally, as the nature of the curse would have consumed you too completely to be saved." He smiled, looking pleased with himself for his cleverness in preventing any of them from ever breaking the wretched curse. Merciful indeed.

"As for Dionysus, for his slight, he shall be cast out of Olympus. Never again to step foot within the realm of the gods. Punishment for attempting to do so will be instant death." He glanced at the *Satyroi*, sneering. "Do not think I have granted you only ill will. I've made you immortal. It's a gift not given to many."

Apollo and Daphne vanished without a further word after that final decree. True to his word, Pan no longer saw any of the nymphs in the wooded area where they had been lingering. He no longer sensed them either. It was strange not being able to do so when he had always been able to before, yet he could still see Syrinx. It may have been because she had been human that morning. Or because she was dead. There were so many things Pan didn't understand, and he wasn't exactly sure he wanted to.

He lifted Syrinx into his arms and tried to flash to the stream, but it wouldn't work. He tried again. Nothing. Had he lost that power with the curse? Evidently it hadn't affected Dionysus at all.

Feeling like he'd been made mortal, Pan carried Syrinx on unsteady, hoofed feet through the trees and down the limestone landscape in the direction of the Asopos. After what seemed like ages of stumbling, he set her body into the water and watched her sink like a rock under the surface. Moments later, seven new water reeds popped up among the many others.

A sob caught in his throat, and he choked it down. He wouldn't cry; he had never done so in the past. It would solve nothing and would only make him more miserable. Pan sighed, startling himself when his breath made interesting sounds across the tops of the reeds—all that remained of an intriguing woman taken before her time.

Pan imagined a small dagger in his hand and was surprised when one appeared there. All of his powers hadn't been taken from him after all. He cut the reeds where they broke the surface and bound them together with long blades of the water plants nearby and sealed the fastening with magic. The reeds were different sizes, and he arranged them shortest to tallest.

He experimented by blowing lightly on the ends of the pipes, content to hear the sound was a pleasant one. Deciding he would move on in the morning, he laid back in the grass in the same spot he'd awakened that day to see her giggling at his nudity, and allowed himself to feel defeated.

The stars above him twinkled around the Satyr Moon in its final stages. Soon the moon would be as it was, and life would continue. Pan closed his eyes and played a tune with the instrument. His *syrinx*. He would name it after her, a tribute to the immortal life she'd been denied. That he could have given her, had she been his.

Pan's melody grew more frantic, darker, dripping with his despair. He wouldn't shed tears, but he bared his soul to the stars above, knowing they would allow him to mourn without judgment.

CHAPTER 11

As the water rippled and lightened before Kat's eyes, the images faded until only her reflection remained. Music filled the air until the final notes dissipated, but Pan didn't speak. She blinked and tried to clear her thoughts; unfortunately, her mind was in chaos as it processed what she'd just seen. Pan really was a god. Her boss really was *the* Dionysus, and it had been so strange seeing him in the memories looking so different, being so cruel. Those poor women...

She reached up and discovered moisture on her cheeks and lashes. She'd felt every emotion and sensation Pan had in the memories: the shock and confusion of becoming a satyr, the intense, sexual gratification when he'd had his way with those women. The pleasure had coursed through her loins, bringing her to orgasm as he climaxed.

She'd felt his utter despair when Syrinx had died in his arms, when he was powerless to save her. He'd believed he loved Syrinx though he'd only known her less than the course of one day. The statue at the center of the fountain captured a pretty accurate likeness from her clothing down to her hair and the shape of her face as she leaned down, sticking her fingers into the cool water below. He'd kept her memory alive for thousands of years.

Unsure how to comment after seeing such a painful memory, Kat quit staring at the spot in the water where the images had been. Fungus grew at the bottom of the pool and gave the liquid a pale green hue. Pan appeared just over her left shoulder in the reflection. He didn't have to say anything as his gaze met hers through their mirrored image, searching her expression.

It hadn't been a walk in the park, but to Kat's understanding of ancient Greece, the events that had occurred in the vision were not all that surprising. The tales of the gods alone were full of sex, incest, rape, and bastards being born to human mothers, but seeing Pan with other women affected her on a different level.

This confused her since she'd not expected him to have lived as a monk. It wasn't even so much the shock of having been privy to such intimate moments in his past, not really. How could she ever—*if* she decided to give him a go, and she wasn't saying she would—live up to the insatiable nymphs he'd once known? They were the only ones who could break his curse, and she was pretty damned sure she wasn't one. She'd know, wouldn't she? Kat had never turned into a tulip or a pussy willow or anything crazy like that.

As far as Pan's hand in what happened to Syrinx, Kat couldn't find it in her heart to blame him for being unable to stop the horror of that night. He'd tried to find the best way to spare Syrinx, not himself, and every option had been risky. Kat understood why he blamed himself, but she didn't think it was really his fault. Syrinx had tricked him into having sex with her, and that had been the catalyst for the whole disaster. Not that it was entirely Syrinx's fault, because she was a victim too, but she'd put Pan in the situation he'd been in because she'd deceived him.

There were too many people that could be blamed: Syrinx for her dishonesty, Silenus for offering his wife to Dionysus, Pavlo for using his sister to bargain with, and Dionysus for being a pig.

Sure, Pan could have done something more, but considering how Dionysus reacted, people would have been hurt regardless. And everyone who'd witnessed the proceedings that night could have acted as well. No one had stood up for Syrinx, and that had been the worst part of it all. Pan, who'd had the most cause to do it, had taken the responsibility of shouldering that guilt onto himself.

"Thank you for trusting me with that memory."

Pan's reflection inclined his head back at her.

"I have questions, though." Things had been nagging at Kat's thoughts since the water cleared.

"Ask." Pan betrayed no emotion behind the word. "If you *didn't* have any questions, I would have worried."

She turned to face him and paused to unstick her sleeve where sticky, sweet-scented pine sap remained from helping clear the fountain of branches. "Why was the dialect so modern?" Some of it had sounded like casual, present-day English. They'd had accents, but the dialect itself hadn't felt particularly old. She understood everything like it had been a movie she rented for the weekend, only set in Greece. *At least no one had a British accent.*

Pan smiled wryly. "Would you have preferred I kept it in the ancient Greek tongue?" He muttered something afterward in what she assumed was Greek.

"What?"

"I said, 'Can you hear me now?'"

Kat snorted. "You translated your memories for me?" She stretched out her scarred leg, which felt tight and achy, as she stood. That was very thoughtful of him and...sweet, in a way. Pan had considered how the best way of sharing his secrets should be presented to her, but it was pretty astounding he shared it at all. He had no reason to.

"It would defeat the purpose of showing you the memory if you couldn't decipher it. I could change the words to modern equivalents, but I couldn't produce subtitles. Cinema Pan can only do so much."

"That's sort of amazing. They didn't even look like they were originally speaking a different language, like in the old *Godzilla* movies." The way he could work illusion was fascinating. Kat eyed the panpipes in his hand, forgotten after the song had completed. They didn't look the same as the *syrinx* in the memory. These were made of some type of shoot, maybe bamboo, and they were slightly smaller. The color was darker and a leather cord tied them together. "You really *are* quite the musician."

"I tried to tell you before, but you didn't want to listen." One side of his mouth tipped up. He noted her gaze upon his instrument, "This isn't the *syrinx*." At her puzzled look, he added, "You think it's strange I don't have it on me, don't you? It's hidden away." He didn't offer any more information.

"One other question?"

"Of course."

"The curse itself, how did speaking it make it happen? You aren't, like, wizards or anything, are you?"

"No, we aren't wizards. But it's a fair assessment. In short, we do perform magic, in the sense that we can conjure items and create illusion, among other things. As to the curse, a decree from a god cannot be broken. Some call it the will of the gods, and that ability is part of the reason we were labeled as deities. Our word is law when we want it to be, and making the human race bow down and obey was made easy with this power. It's hard to explain how it works. Though, it is most often only accessible to us when we get really angry." He frowned. "At least, with me it is. I, uh, never took learning what I could do seriously. As you can see, I sort of screwed up the counter-curse."

"You did your best. You can't allow the past to rule your present."

"Says the woman who didn't accidently create a new race of creatures with sex addiction."

"Technically, Dionysus and Apollo assisted."

"Fuckers."

Kat snorted and thought about the explanation he'd given. It was more than a little frightening to know these beings wielded that kind of power. Dionysus and Apollo had been furious when they had spoken or passed their judgment, so anger very well could be key there, as Pan hypothesized. Kat found herself wondering if there was any truth to her God, the Christian God, if these beings that called themselves deities had such powers.

She was too afraid to ask though, unsure if the answer would be one she wanted to know. She supposed it was ironic that someone so skeptical about the unknown would believe in God. She'd been raised a Christian, and while she'd experienced doubt like any other person, she'd survived an animal attack that could have turned fatal. That sort of thing reaffirms faith.

"Like I said," Pan's voice dragged Kat from her thoughts. "It's hard to explain. Some of our abilities just kinda happen. I've only passed an edict upon two people. That I know of."

"That you know of?"

"I told you, it's unpredictable." He shrugged. "I might have blinded Homer."

"Might?"

"He made me mad."

"I'm sure he did. What did he do? Leave you out of his epics when he wrote them?"

"Actually, he was an oral storyteller. It was a long time before the well-known stories were ever written down. However, he had other stories to tell besides the ones you are familiar with. He told tales about me that weren't true. I may have objected."

"Okay, but isn't blinding the man a bit extreme?"

"No. I could have been far more creative."

Her stomach growled, and it was then she realized how late it was in the day. The sun was setting, and the half-moon glowed proudly over the top of the trees despite the fact it wasn't quite night yet. They'd been by the fountain the entire day and had missed lunch.

Pan held out his hand to her after an embarrassing gurgling made her hunger public. Kat hesitated, but if Pan was a threat to her, he'd not have opened himself up as he had and given her an up close and personal view of his deepest regret. He'd acted impulsively in taking her with him, sure, but he never truly intended to hurt anyone. And from what she'd discovered about him from his memories, he wasn't a psycho murderer. Of course, she'd not been privy to what had occurred after the *syrinx* had been made.

Kat slipped her palm into Pan's. His hand was warm, the grip gentle but strong. He led her back in the direction of the house.

"I meant what I said. You shouldn't blame yourself," Kat offered as they neared the front porch.

Pan's step faltered, and he frowned at her. "I should have hidden the nymphs from Dionysus and confessed my act. I was a coward and let her be violated and killed for my actions." He released his hold on her and then his steps became hurried. He moved on, done with the subject, and leaving her to rush after him.

Earlier she'd been dying to get away, but Kat found she wasn't ready to go back yet, not when there was so much to learn about Pan. Not when she knew he was hurting. A foolish thing, surely, but a horrible person wouldn't be the type to feel so strongly for his part in a tragedy such as Syrinx's last day on Earth. It didn't matter that he hadn't acted like a knight in shining armor and fought Dionysus to the death. Something told Kat that Syrinx's fate had been sealed long before he'd laid eyes on her, and if the myths about the Fates were true...Pan wouldn't have been able to do anything to prevent it.

Horrible thought that it was, Pan had actually saved Syrinx from suffering a public rape. She had still been pawed at, but she hadn't been completely assaulted in that way in front of witnesses. It didn't make it better, but Kat was glad she'd been spared some indignity.

Pan had mourned her loss even though he'd barely known her. Either creepy obsession or a poster child for the love-at-first-sight movement, either way he still suffered the loss.

Kat gasped, bringing a hand to her mouth.

He was infatuated, definitely, but not because of love. Pan had been charmed by Syrinx, had imagined a life with her, but then he'd realized who she was. She'd become a damsel in distress, and Pan had been consumed with the need to spare her from Dionysus' wrath.

It hadn't been love at all.

The idea of loving Syrinx, of what could have been if events had played out differently, was what he'd latched on to. His love was built on regret and a guilty conscience.

Guilt was one of the most terrible burdens—she knew it well, as her mistake with the cougar had nearly ended her life, and had flat-lined her career. It had also cost the cat its life and the cubs their freedom.

Kat ventured into the house after the retreating form ahead of her. Pan had built this place with the plans to start over in a new place, a new time, but had inevitably let it fade to ruin, never receiving guests, never throwing parties, or sheltering friends or family. A deep sadness consumed her.

Several feet ahead, Pan avoided her, but stayed near. He probably wouldn't admit to it, he seemed rather prideful despite the carefree air he let on, but he was a man, or god, who ached for companionship. In a way, he was living a Greek tragedy of his own making.

Uncertain why, Kat harbored an overwhelming desire to comfort him. He'd been a barbaric, manhandling caveman—with wings—who'd kidnapped her, forced her to sleep one of the most restful nights of sleep in her life, and cooked really delicious eggs over a fire. He'd also revealed himself to be an immortal god who'd had a hand in cursing a group of horny, voyeuristic jerks into an eternity of literal horniness. Yet he'd not taken advantage of her despite how evident it was at various moments that he wanted to. He was almost gentlemanly, aside from his bad manners with the kidnapping and public nakedness.

Thinking of it that way, being kidnapped by Pan really wasn't as bad as it all seemed. Although, Cindy and Rick must have been in hysterics back at the hotel, wondering if she was even still alive or not. Kat felt terrible she hadn't given them as much thought as she should have. Surely Pan wouldn't deny her the chance to let them know she was okay. Before, she'd feared Pan would balk at the idea because, if her friends knew she was alive for sure, they would never give up searching. Not that she believed they would anyway.

Perhaps she could bargain with him; she'd stay with him for as long as he'd like if he'd allow her to go back to let her friends know she was safe. She'd been stuck in a "research only" rut in a career that wouldn't miss her, and she would only have to inform her family she was on vacation. She'd quit the project and hope Mr. Bach, er, Dionysus, wasn't aware what was going on. Maybe he wasn't one hundred percent sure Pan was the Jersey Devil and wouldn't be suspicious.

She still had to wonder what Pan's feelings toward her were. Was her appearance just a ghost of Syrinx to him? The resemblance was there, even if he hadn't pointed it out to her. But she was not a nymph, and she didn't belong to Dionysus even if she'd signed a contract to do the documentary for him. Yet Pan could easily be filling a void, replacing one with a similar copy. Even more surprising of a thought was why it mattered. Why did she want him to want more from her than a one-night stand or to be seen as a mere replacement?

Stockholm syndrome. I so have it.

When Pan poked his head back out the doorway to see what was taking her so long, Kat decided it best to ask him about her friends in the morning. He'd opened his soul to her by sharing such a painful memory, and she didn't think bargaining with him was the best way to respond to it, despite the knot in her gut reminding her she was, yet again, extending her friends' distress. She'd make with the chitchat for the evening, let him have his way —but not in *that* way—and in the morning, the tables would turn.

～

"You knocked him out." Dion gaped as Melancton dropped an unconscious Silenus at his feet. The elder satyr groaned but didn't come to. "Why?"

"Pan and the woman are in a rundown house about a three-hour's walk from here. We would not have found them if Pan had not been playing his pipes for the girl. He was using the magic to show her something in a fountain. I can't say for sure what, as I did not wish to move too close and reveal our location."

Dion tried to mask his excitement, but he couldn't keep his grin tamped down. "Was it the *syrinx*?" The sentimental fool had named the instrument after the whore it was constructed out of. That he kept the instrument and continued to prance about—the Arcadians sporting identical copies of the pipes—irked him. The bitch should be dead in body and memory, but there was that part of her preserved eternally in the *syrinx*. It skeeved Dion out for some reason that the reeds, when bound together, resembled a rack of rib bones. *Ick.* Kind of morbid, really.

That didn't mean he disliked disemboweling humans and making hats out of their bones. He just didn't wear said rib bone hats himself. Dion usually made the person who previously had the bones connected to their spine wear them as their life faded away. He was considerate that way.

"No, sir." Melancton bowed his head. "It was one of the replicas, like the other Arcadians carry."

Shit. Either Pan had it hidden nearby, or he entrusted it to one of the other Arcadian fuckwits. It had been rumored Pan had done so, but Dion hoped it was a ruse. After those curly-horned satyrs followed Pan to his homeland in Arcadia, forming a bond much tighter than Dion had with his straight-horned Boeotian satyrs, Pan used the *syrinx* to magically imbue common panpipes with power. The rest of the satyrs remained throughout Boeotia or upon Kithairon with Dion. Ironically, most of the Boeotians had stayed with him throughout all the years, but Pan's friendly posse had dismantled long ago.

Perhaps to hide the syrinx? How had Dion not seen it?

Of course, Dion had also not realized just how powerful the *syrinx* was back then. If he had, he would have made a play for it long before. Once he had discovered how useful the *syrinx* would be to him, Pan had disappeared never to be seen for centuries upon centuries. It had been fool's luck that he'd made a connection to the fabled Jersey Devil, realizing the description of the beast resembled the image he'd had in mind when he'd cursed Pan in the first place. And there Pan was, hiding right under his nose.

Hindsight. The syrinx *will be mine, but first, I have to find it.*

"Let's return to the original subject at hand. Why is Silenus snoring at my feet?"

Melancton grinned and quickly resumed his blank expression. "I bashed him on top of the head with a heavy stick, sir. The imbecile was about to charge in and announce his presence by tearing into Pan. I thought—since you put so much forethought into this encounter by plying the human woman with your wine —you weren't ready to blow it all on a hotheaded act of vengeance."

Melancton removed the heavy, steel axe Silenus had convinced Hephaestus to forge from a leather sheath strapped across his back and placed it on the table. It was made years after Olympus had closed its gates to the world. Hephaestus still resided in his forge, locked out like Dion and Pan. It was rumored that Aphrodite, Hephaestus' wife, along with her lover Ares, took pleasure in keeping him out of their realm indefinitely. Silenus had used the ordeal with Syrinx to relate to the cuckolded god. Projecting his hatred of Ares onto Pan, Hephaestus forged the axe with pleasure.

Dion thought it foolish the Olympians had abandoned the only god able to create a weapon to slay an immortal on the mortal plane. But now Silenus had a weapon with the ability to kill Pan, and any other satyr, as though they were average humans. A weapon Silenus did not deserve and would not possess after his revenge was carried out.

Nevertheless, the image of Melancton cracking Silenus' skull amused Dion. The fool was unstable at best. Melancton was correct that if Silenus had killed Pan before they knew for sure he didn't have the *syrinx*, they could risk not ever knowing where it was hidden. They must wait, and watch, a little bit longer. Pan would die when Dion commanded it, not before.

"You did well. You always were the most level-headed of my Boeotians. But were you seen?" He didn't mean by Pan or the girl, because if he had been, Pan would have followed him back here, and Dion preferred to keep the mortals out of any upcoming confrontation. The hotel was located off a southern exit of the Garden State Parkway, which ran straight through the Pine Barrens. There was mostly wilderness around them, but a few businesses and neighborhoods as well. Any mortal presence was enough to be a problem.

"Doubtful. I cloaked us before exiting the woods." Melancton removed the leather sheath from across his torso. It shimmered and reformed into a *thyrsus*. The short, wooden staff had a pinecone-shaped ornament at the top and carved vines circling down the length of the shaft. Dion had once carried a *thyrsus* around as a method to fool mortals into thinking his power lay within it. Now for his satyrs, his power did reside within their *thyrsi*. Not all of it, but enough.

Thyrsi had been Dion's way of keeping the Boeotians from joining Pan in Arcadia once word spread of their magical panpipes. Pan had showed them how to play for illusions, to temporarily alter their appearance through notes of a song so they could appear human in the daytime. Even though Pan could hold his illusion with or without a melody as a god, he'd gone out of his way to help those other men, some of whom he'd only met the night of the curse. *Too bad they all deserted him in the end.*

Angered that Pan appeared to care more for his Arcadians than Dion did his Boeotians, and fearing the satyrs would abandon him, Dionysus gave them *thyrsi* to do all the panpipes could do, as well as taking the form of other objects such as the rings they wore to make carrying it around convenient. They were all linked to Dion's power, and in turn, they worked magic like a wizard's staff. Boeotians could give themselves mortal forms in the light of day—unfortunately, like with the Arcadian panpipes, they couldn't hold human form when the sun set. Dion suspected Apollo's hand in it somehow, though he'd never discovered the reason behind it. They could cloak themselves from the sight of mortals or create a sword, but they didn't need to play a song for it to work. They merely had to hold a *thyrsus* in their hand and will it to do whatever they wished. They also had to pledge their loyalty, and if their loyalty ever waned, the magic would abandon the wielder and return to Dion.

He had to ensure he had no traitors in his circle.

Melancton's *thyrsus* shimmered once more, shrinking back into the form of a silver ring. He slipped it on the ring finger of his left hand and excused himself. His glamour would fade soon, and Melancton had always preferred the company of trees when in his satyr form than being trapped indoors for the entire night.

Dion shut the door behind him, stepped over Silenus, and returned to his thoughts as he reclined in the soft, brown chair located in the living room portion of his hotel suite. The room smelled like the maids had emptied a can of Pledge on the furniture in preparation of his arrival. While not entirely unpleasant, Dion couldn't get used to the overpowering lemon scent.

To distract himself from the cleaners used in the room, he thought about the time when he was still considered a deity, before Olympus shut its gates and the entire pantheon became known to humans only through legends. Dion knew he'd acted rashly in the past by smiting those who dared to defy him. Doing so made him feel more in control. Amusing, given he was the Greeks' personification of drinking, fucking, and reckless abandon.

He thought back to the night, centuries ago, when he attempted to turn Pan into a hideous monster that would make the Chimera look like a puppy dog. It wasn't because he hadn't been the first to have sex with the beautiful woman-turned-nymph, but the fact she had chosen Pan over him. She had wanted Pan, but had been repulsed by him.

All the gods were guilty of their pride.

Pan had taken it further by turning the woman into a nymph. It doubly grated his nerves that Pan could do such a thing when Dion couldn't. He could be creating nymphs for his Arcadians, but instead he was fooling around in New Jersey.

Dion sneered at his reflection in the mirror and scratched at the cleft in his chin.

Then there was Apollo. What a prick. He could have a harem of nymphs, mortal women, and even a few mortal men at his beck and call. Dion could deliver them right to him, but he'd revoked Dion's key into Olympus over one pesky nymph who hadn't even wanted anything to do with Apollo from the start.

He couldn't go home. *Him. Dionysus.* The god of wine and excess, who was still celebrated through festivals of the present such as Mardi Gras. While Apollo, Zeus, and the others all lay, supposedly, in their gilded beds, snug and asleep, mocking Dion with their absence from the modern world. Dion snorted. It was such bull that they all slumbered in Olympus. Why they wanted anyone to believe that drabble was beyond him.

Furthermore, had Zeus done a thing to overrule Apollo when he'd denied Dion his right to go home? No. He'd agreed with Apollo's judgment. Said to learn from it and move on when Dion called out for help. His own father refused him entrance into his own home. His father, who had taken his shriveled fetus from his mortal mother's corpse and born Dion from his body to ensure he survived, making him full-blooded immortal. But it had meant nothing to Zeus. No, Apollo always got his way.

Screw Zeus, and screw Apollo. Dion would get his hands on the *syrinx* and show them all. It was more than just an instrument; it was an instrument created from a mystical being. The *syrinx* had been fashioned out of a nymph and in remorse by a god who had no idea how to work his powers. It was said to be usable by anyone, not only Pan, to do their bidding. While not one hundred percent sure what all the *syrinx* could do, Dion was convinced he could use it to go home. He could usurp Zeus, murder Apollo in his goddamned golden bed, and smite Pan once and for-fucking-all, for daring to meddle with his affairs.

But first, he had to be absolutely certain Pan had the *syrinx*. If he did, Dion would find a way to get his hands on it. If Pan didn't have it, Dion would need to figure out why he didn't, who had it, and where.

PAN KNOCKED ON THE BEDROOM DOOR, CAUSING KATERINA TO glance up from the book she was flipping through. She started to smile at his approach but quickly disguised it with a blank expression. He found it captivating. She'd ceased scowling at him at least, always catching herself as she attempted to appear nonchalant. Candlelight bounced over her face and the wall. The candles were unscented, but to his enhanced senses, the burning wax left a saccharine warmth in the air to overtake the musk of old wood and weatherworn walls.

"What are you reading?"

Katerina lifted the thick volume from her lap and revealed the shabby leather cover. It was one of his many mythology books. Pan could only guess which myth she was perusing.

"Learn anything interesting?"

"Yeah, that oral storytelling must have been one great, big game of telephone."

"Come again?"

"Telephone is a game we mortals play in school. One person whispers a sentence in another person's ear, and by the time it makes it through the whole class and to the original speaker it is a different sentence entirely. It's a game used to teach us how gossiping about people can result in false rumors. If the stories behind the myths were true, the written accounts of them are misconstrued by years and years of oral storytelling changing the details."

One of the reasons he kept mythology books was because he was often amused by the changes made due to the retellings Katerina alluded to. Yet sometimes, like with the book she held in her lap, he was saddened by their inaccuracies. Once more, he found himself curious about what she had been reading before he interrupted but was reluctant to ask again. He had a pretty good idea which it was.

Katerina scooted over to one side of the bed and patted the area beside her. When he stared at the spot and didn't move, didn't dare to breathe, she laughed.

"I'm not inviting you to sleep in the bed with me. I'm inviting you to sit and talk."

"Why?"

"Because it's hard to be at ease in a conversation with you while you stand there hovering."

He didn't hover. "No. What I meant was why do you want me

to sit next to you and not at the foot of the bed or on the other furniture?"

She turned the book over on her lap to keep her page and sat up a little straighter. "I'm not going to bite you, Pan. You're the one who brought me here, and I am trying to understand you. It doesn't help when you always seem to regard me differently every time we are in a room together."

"No, I don't." Pan shifted uncomfortably from hoof to hoof. It was strange how he could be wearing clothing but still feel naked in front of her observatory gaze. Even stranger when that bothered him.

"You do. When we first met, there was lust in your eyes. Curiosity too, I think. You wanted to know about me, but you were there for sex. A woman knows these things." She tilted her head. "Then when you brought me here, you were as unsure as you are now, but you disguised it by being bossy. Telling me not to run. Crossing your arms and being intimidating."

He didn't care for this conversation. He didn't want to dwell anymore on the past, of scaring her or intimidating her after he abducted her on impulse.

"The next morning was different yet again. You were a bit more hesitant. You saw to my comfort in finding a way to make the toilet work without insisting I had to use the bathroom in the woods, which wouldn't have bothered me. I've been out in the woods for days or weeks at a time before. I forgot what a toilet looked like when I was studying the leopard in the middle of Africa. I was actually surprised you went through the trouble."

His face felt hot. Pan didn't blush, ever. He refused to believe he was doing it then. He didn't know how to respond, so he focused on her riotous curls and the smirk that played across her lips.

"But then you got all defensive when I laughed at you and became the alpha male, with using the existence of your penis to bully me into submission, which I was not amused by." She arched a brow.

Then you threatened to bite it off, and gods help me, I wanted you more because of your defiance.

He cleared his throat. "Yeah...sorry about that..."

"I get it, though."

"You do?"

"You have the blood of the ancient gods in your veins. You're prideful. You're used to having your way when you want it."

"I rarely have things my way when I want them." He would not admit she had a point.

Katerina allowed herself to smile fully then. "Neither do I. So quit pouting and sit down." She patted the bed beside her once more.

He didn't even notice he'd moved toward her until he was standing there, looking down at the space she'd indicated. Pan felt as though sitting next to her would change things. He wanted them changed, yet he still wasn't sure if he really did or why. He wanted her, but if Dionysus had chosen her, there had to be a reason. The other god had to have known Pan would react this way, and giving in could have consequences. He just hadn't figured out what.

Pan sat down.

The area was warm from where she had been utilizing the center of the bed. Her citrusy smell wasn't as strong as the day before, but lingered still. His arm brushed hers, and she didn't flinch or seem repulsed. Instead, she looked up at him, her cheeks pinkened, and she peered back at the book in her lap.

Katerina flipped the book back around, and Pan's gut knotted. It was the myth of Syrinx. The one known to the world, as inaccurate as it was. It portrayed him as a would-be rapist and a murderer.

When Pan took a glimpse toward Katerina, he found her watching him, taking in his reaction. Feeling shamed by what had happened and the lies she held in her lap, he turned away. The crack in the wall above the door became incredibly interesting. *How long has that been there, though? Really.* He squinted at it. *Had to be the past five years, if that.*

"I know this isn't what happened. I saw the reality this morning."

"I'm not sure if that makes it better or worse."

She sighed. He heard a *thump* as the book shut. "The myth says you watched Syrinx bathing and wanted to have sex with her. You chased her around until she hid in the water as the reeds, then you cut the reads and formed the *syrinx* with them." She snorted. "It makes it sound rather silly in that version, don't you think?"

"I did chase her wanting to have sex with her. Got my way too. Then, because of it, she was murdered, and I did form the *syrinx* from the reeds that grew where her body returned to the water." The point was there—the events were different.

He felt a hand rest against his forearm, and he stared down at it. There was dirt under her nails, his fault for bringing her here to this house of filth and decay. He couldn't provide for her here. She should be clean and polished and surrounded by beauty at all times.

"It's been centuries. More than that, even. You need to let it go."

Pan considered her words before answering, "I can't."

"You won't. You hold on to it and use it as a reason to blame yourself for your current circumstances. There is nothing you can do about it now. It's past time you move on."

Pan bowed his head. "You're right. You must be a phenomenal zoologist because you see everything clearly."

Katerina snorted. "I'm a terrible zoologist. I can study and observe, sure. But I am always messing up and endangering myself. Look at me now."

"You think I'm a danger to you?" He searched her features for the answer.

"You're a satyr, Pan. A god. I am the delicate damsel lost in the woods. Yes, you are a danger to me. But I don't fear for my life, not anymore."

"Not even your virtue?" he asked.

She hesitated. "Not even that."

"I would never go further than you asked of me."

Even in the dull candlelight, he could tell Katerina blushed again. She pushed herself out of the bed and wandered over to the shelf to replace the book on the bottom with the other mythology tomes in order to retreat from the conversation. The one *she* had instigated. A gentleman would allow it, but Pan had never been considered a gentleman.

"Now you're hiding something you don't want me to know."

She turned back toward him as he spoke and then made a show of returning to the shelf to find another book.

"Katerina, if I know what I am doing that makes you uncomfortable around me, I can make a better effort not to do it."

He watched as her shoulders slumped. "It's nothing you are doing. At least, I don't think you are doing it."

"Doing what?"

She didn't reply. Pan rolled out of the bed, sidled up behind her, and then put his hands on her shoulders. He pulled her around to face him but didn't remove his grip.

"What's the problem?"

Katerina shrugged out of his hands. "It's embarrassing!"

"Vixen, I have hooves on my feet. Hooves. Like an animal should have. And horns on my head. I look like a cartoon devil. *That's* embarrassing. Do you think I'd make it two steps into a church like this?"

Katerina chuckled. "I don't suppose you would. They'd sling holy water at you and run for their lives."

Pan smiled. "Please tell me what is bothering you."

"You're not going to let this go, are you?"

He knew he should, but he couldn't. "Nope. You analyzed me and my actions. It's my turn to know something about you." He reached for her arm, meaning to draw her back to face him. She danced out of range.

"Fine. It's my reaction to you, okay. It's not...natural."

"Your reaction to...oh." He dropped his hand.

She turned and faced him once again. Still blushing profusely. "Yeah. Oh."

"Do I repulse you that much?"

"Repulse?" She laughed then. So much so, she had to take a seat on the floor and there was the sparkle of tears in her eyes. Pan didn't speak. He felt like the monster he sometimes looked like. He nauseated her so badly that repulse hadn't been a strong enough word for it.

Just when he thought he should remove his disgusting presence from her sight, she elucidated, "You don't repulse me at all, and that is the crux of the problem."

She didn't find him hideous then? Women needed a handbook or a decoder ring or something for the males of the world to decipher from.

Katerina cradled her arms around her knees from her spot on the floor, resting her chin on top of them. "I have never felt desire as strongly as I do in your presence."

Pan was sure he heard her wrong. She couldn't possibly want him, not as he was. Peter she had desired, but once he'd become a satyr in front of her, or the Jersey Devil? Then again, he had never attempted to sense her arousal again as he did at the hotel. He was too afraid he'd find it lacking and was content with not knowing for sure.

When he didn't reply, Katerina said, "It's overwhelming. Beyond reason. In the hotel room, I was still freaked out by the stunt in the woods, which I assume was your doing. I shouldn't have wanted to pounce on a complete stranger, but I did. Want to, that is. I feel it even now, though not as strongly as I did then. If I wasn't sure you hadn't drugged me, I would have thought something was influencing me somehow."

"Did you hear any music when you first felt it, like when I played you to sleep or showed you my memories?" It was doubtful he wouldn't have heard the music himself, but if something was influencing her to desire him, a set of Arcadian panpipes or the *syrinx* could do it.

The *syrinx*.

Had Dionysus found it? Was he using it to play with Katerina like she was a puppet?

"No? Why? Could your panpipes do that?" She stared at him then, eyes wide.

"To an extent, but I should have heard them too, if they were the influence. The ones we all carry were enhanced by the *syrinx*, so they hold magical properties as well. We can entice females to us, but it only works on women who are looking for a sexual encounter of some kind, on a subconscious level. It still allows for freewill, but they see the satyrs as the men they were, not as the satyr, and they make their choice. It's hard to explain it. But in short, it only works one time out of ten. For that particular purpose."

"What about the *syrinx*? Would it be capable of causing me to react this way?"

"Possibly." Pan sat on the floor as well, his back against the bookcase. "But in all honestly, I am not sure what all it can do. When I started to realize how powerful the instrument was, I knew it had to be hidden. I could influence people, their thoughts. Their dreams. I could gain entrance into buildings and realms I shouldn't."

Pan shook his head, dispelling the memory of Syrinx in the Elysian Fields. He hadn't approached her, and she hadn't seen him there. But Hades had not been pleased when he discovered he had an unwelcome visitor in the Underworld. No one enters or exits the Underworld without Hades' permission. No one but Pan, anyway.

"Why didn't you destroy it? Something like that could be used as a weapon."

"I tried to. I tried to crush it, to tear it apart. It was like it had been made of steel. I tried melting it, but the fire didn't work. When I removed it from the flames hours later, it was cool to the touch."

"How is such a thing possible?"

"Magic is unpredictable. The *syrinx* was created from the remains of a magical being, on the eve of her murder. Only the Fates truly know, and those bitches refuse to talk on the matter."

"But it is hidden away, isn't it?"

"It was. Hopefully that remains true." It may be time to track it down again. His brow furrowed.

Katerina shook her head. "If it isn't the *syrinx* influencing me, what is it?"

"Maybe I'm just sexy. Why can't that be the reason?" Pan grinned and hoped she couldn't tell he wasn't keen on the fact she believed her desire for him was unnatural.

"Well, yeah. But even if I was locked in a room with a naked Joe Manganiello after an invisible something was running around us in the woods, I would have appreciated the scenery but would not have wanted to go all erotica on him. At least not then. Maybe later..." She thought about it, eyes glossing over. Was she fantasizing about this other man?

Pan wasn't sure who this Manganiello person was, but he would regret it if he was ever naked in a room with Katerina. She did have a point, though. She'd reacted as strongly as he had at first sight. He had a curse he could blame, but her... Masturbation was an odd reaction for someone who'd been frightened, let alone experiencing an intense reaction to a stranger. Pan had never given it much of a thought before, too caught up in knowing he'd been the one who caused her arousal. Maybe, if he had let himself sense her arousal since that day, he would have realized there was a problem. Magic didn't work like a dog's sense of smell, where he would just know. He had to set his mind to it and push with his power to know. It was intrusive, so he didn't do it very often.

"The Boeotians, er, satyrs that follow Dionysus, don't use panpipes, but they have similar abilities. I don't think they can stimulate females without being present though..." Pan suddenly had a moment of clarity.

The wine!

"Something was in the wine Dionysus gave you." Pan stood to his feet. "I'm going to fucking murder that asshole." His body practically hummed in his fury.

Katerina scrambled to her feet as well. "I didn't even consider it, but it does make perfect sense. How observant am I? I even thought how peculiar it was that my boss was sending me wine, but I drank it anyway like a dumbass. If this had been a horror movie, I would have been the first big-boobed bimbo to bite it."

His gaze immediately zoned in on her breasts, and he had to snap himself out of his lecherous thought process. "I'm sorry for everything that has happened to you. There was no reason Dionysus needed to bring you into this. His issues are with me."

"I know you had nothing to do with it." Katerina took a few steps away from him. "But we'll talk about it more in the morning. Right now, I need sleep."

Sighing, he nodded his head and crossed the room, stopping in the doorway to take a final glance at Katerina before he closed the door. "Good night, vixen."

CHAPTER 12

Pan was as nervous as a teenage boy with the aspirations of getting laid for the first time. Not that he was about to get laid, unfortunately. His nervousness stemmed from the fact he had no idea how to act around Katerina after sharing so much of his past with her. Then of course there was the wine Dionysus had spiked to make her horny in his presence. It would be unfair to take advantage of her when she couldn't distinguish if her arousal was genuine or not.

He'd never felt so awkward, which was saying a lot because he was old as hell. He paced back and forth in the courtyard of his home, hands folded behind his back, head bent as he meandered from one side of the unkempt lawn to the other. The grass was high but had ceased growing at about mid-calf. He should probably cut it.

You're thinking about cutting the grass? He had it bad.

It no longer mattered that Dionysus planted Katerina Silverton in New Jersey to entice Pan for whatever nefarious purpose. The pull of desire gripped him every time he looked at her. His groin tightened with need, desperate for release. But he couldn't have her, and he needed to take her back to her friends.

Even if it meant he had to let Katerina leave him. Actually, if Dionysus had anything up his sleeve, it would be better if she did.

If he could have one night with her, one, well...maybe it would be enough to hold on to. He was just too damned nervous to make a move based on how much he had screwed up since that first moment he laid eyes on her. Pan ran his hands through his mess of dark hair. What would be the best approach?

Sorry for kidnapping you. Let me help you remove your clothes now?

He didn't think that one would go over really well. Gods weren't supposed to care about things like human emotions and fear. Zeus would have been like, "Knees. You. Now." *Ah, such a lady's man, Zeus.* Why Hera hadn't castrated him in his sleep was a miracle in itself. Pan shook his head sadly. Not his style.

Pan wasn't Zeus, but he wasn't exactly a saint either. He'd had sexual encounters with women since the curse—thanks to Apollo's addition to it, it had been impossible not to—but after the deed was done, Pan had never desired to remain in those women's company. Katerina wasn't going to be a notch in the metaphorical bedpost, and Pan had come to the conclusion that he had absolutely no idea how to handle a modern woman without the intent of sleeping with them and then bailing.

Katerina seemed calmer since Pan had showed her the memories. It was like she'd accepted him as a human without letting the god or satyr factors define him. He'd expected her to despise him, to not be able to handle the truth of his existence. But no. Instead, she had spoken to him like an old friend, with gentleness and an understanding Pan couldn't quite comprehend. While she explored the inside of his embarrassment of a home, there he was, circling the yard like an agitated animal.

The diminishing sunlight left the sky above awash in coral and pink. Pan blinked in surprise to have come to a stop in front of the fountain, having not been fully aware he'd ceased his pacing. While the sculpture of Syrinx was an accurate likeness, it wasn't exact. Regret washed over him in waves, swirling within was everything caught in the current: the sorrow for the lives lost and the men cursed into sharing his punishment.

Hatred seethed inside him for Silenus. Pan would have slaughtered that wretched cur if Ariston, Iakovos, and Xanto hadn't held him back and talked sense into him. He'd been ready to kill the three of them as well for denying him vengeance, but he came to his senses before he acted on the impulse. Killing his friends would have made him no better than Dionysus.

Dionysus.

What was the god up to? Why had he practically gift-wrapped Katerina and dropped her on his doorstep? Pan was missing something about this whole ordeal, and it would be wise to figure it out before Dionysus acted. He turned and sat on the ground with his back against the fountain. He rested his forehead against his knees.

Was Dionysus merely wishing to settle an old score by repeating history, or did he have a bigger play in motion? Was it possible he sought the *syrinx*? If so, the god would be sorely disappointed when he discovered Pan didn't have it in his possession. He'd entrusted its care into the Arcadians when he realized it should be kept out of the hands of those who would abuse its abilities. With no way to destroy it, he couldn't chance trying to bury it somewhere, and he worried one day he would be too tempted by it to keep it. So the Arcadians had devised a plan.

Swearing their allegiance to Pan, the Arcadians had decided to seek out one of their own every hundred years or so to ensure the *syrinx* passed to a new satyr for protection, or at least they hoped to. Pan had no idea who would have it presently or if it had been passed on. Only two satyrs would know: the satyr who possessed it, and the one who had handed it off.

I haven't thought about its location in far too long. Where is it? The Fates must have been deep in their cups the day the thread of his life was fashioned. He was not cut out for godhood. He wanted peace to enjoy his life without the constant drama. Nonetheless, if

Dionysus was making a play for the *syrinx*, Pan needed to locate it before he did.

"What are you thinking about so solemnly out here?"

Pan turned and waited as Katerina approached him. Her hands were in her pockets, which subtly made him notice the dirt smudges on her sweater. Darting his gaze upward, he observed that her hair was wilder than he'd seen it before, but then, he hadn't exactly brought her there with beauty supplies or clean clothing. Yeah, he needed to take her back to civilization. While he didn't mind dirt and tangles, he wanted her to have every luxury. She shouldn't be forced to rough it with him.

"The past, the future"—he let his gaze sweep over her curves —"the present."

Katerina faltered, and she attempted to play it off by looking around and ceasing her stride toward him. "Oh, um, sorry for bothering you then." She toed a rock around in the grass with her left sneaker-encased foot.

"What's on your mind?" Pan asked. There was no point in beating around the proverbial bush. He had a pretty good idea what it would be. She'd want to leave, go home, away from the likes of him for good. *Can't blame her.* It was wrong for him to keep her against her will. It'd been selfish of him to do so.

"I..." Katerina met his gaze and sighed, her shoulders slumping. She took a few steps to the right and sat on the ledge of the fountain pool. "I need to go back to the hotel."

Pan smiled, yet it felt thin. There were some occasions where he really hated being right, but this was foreseeable. His past wasn't pretty, and he would have worried if she'd accepted it at face value.

"I see."

"Wait. That didn't come out how I intended it to. There are things I need to do at the hotel. For one, I need to ensure my friends know I'm okay. I hope they didn't call my mother, and if they haven't, they will soon if I don't show up. I don't want my family involved in this. They will have half the nation in an uproar over my disappearance because my mother is as stubborn as I am."

Katerina blew a stray curl out of her face. "I also need a shower like you just don't know; my hair is all oily, and I need my lotion and toothpaste to feel clean. I'm girly. If I am not working, I need shampoo and things. Not to mention, if I don't shave my legs soon, they'll look like yours. Where it works for the whole satyr thing, yeti legs on women are unattractive."

He lifted his brows toward his hairline. "Hairy legs, you say? Yes, I could see how that could be a deal breaker," he said dryly. "You are aware women did not shave their legs back when I was not yet a satyr, aren't you?"

She made a show of shuddering. "Yes. I saw the hairy armpits in your memory too. I was trying to forget them. Speaking of which, I have a date with my razor, and I think I shouldn't miss it. If I start looking like a werewolf, I might develop a hostile attitude to go with it."

Pan threw back his head and laughed. "I am terribly inept in taking care of humans. Please forgive me for not having the bathrooms in better working order before I abducted you." He'd hoped she wouldn't need more than him, but he was ever a fool. Katerina laid a hand upon his shoulder as he looked away. She sought to comfort him? Surely not.

"Pan, I didn't say I was leaving for good. I just have to get my things and make sure Cindy and Rick know I am okay. I should have demanded it sooner, but I was afraid you wouldn't allow it." She bit her lip. "I should probably quit my current job as well, as I won't have any results to turn in. Well, I will...but I won't be doing any reporting on you that would lead to your identification."

He loved hearing her call him by his name. It'd been far too long since a woman knew it, let alone called him by it. He all but trembled with the need for her to stay with him after gathering her belongings, and her vow not to reveal his identity to Dionysus or to the public warmed him. But he was sure the god already knew; otherwise, Katerina wouldn't have been sent to the Pine Barrens.

"I'm not sure quitting is wise. If Dionysus sent you here as a lure, he will know something is up as soon as you resign." Pan helped Katerina to her feet. "Trust me when I say you don't want to tempt his anger or his curiosity."

He stripped off his T-shirt, feeling smug when Katerina visibly swallowed as she watched the cotton slide over his abs. Perhaps it was wrong to make a show of it instead of magically making the shirt vanish. So worth it, though. His arousal strained against his jeans, and he saw her notice that too. Before he had any more crazy ideas, like kissing that stunned look off her face, he summoned his wings, and then stretched. He held his hand out to her.

"I grant you permission to board, my lady." He wiggled his brows.

"I don't know if that is the best mode of travel..."

"It's the *only* way to travel."

～

KAT KNOCKED ON CINDY AND RICK'S DOOR. WHEN IT OPENED A crack, she heard a startled gasp moments before a five-foot-four brunette woman flew out and attacked her with a vice-like embrace.

"Kat! Oh, my God, I am so glad you're alive. We've been so worried! We thought for sure you were dead. Mr. Bach even came out here to get the police off their asses to search for you."

Kat stiffened. Dionysus was here? What did that mean for Pan? She couldn't help but worry the whole thing really was set up from the beginning to lead him straight to Pan, and she'd fallen right into the role as bait.

Rick came running out of the room next, also attaching himself to Kat in a giant bear hug, or as much as he could manage of one because Cindy was still clinging to her for dear life.

"Did it hurt you?" Rick asked, letting her go and looking her over. "Did it let you go, or did you kick its ass and escape?"

"Can we go inside please?" Kat had an inescapable feeling of being watched, and not in the way Pan would. The sensation didn't feel observatory. It was malicious, leaving a cold dread in its wake that iced her veins. She glanced around uneasily. She knew Pan waited for her in his commandeered hotel room—she'd seen him go inside herself, mentally picking the lock and all—so who would be watching her? Dionysus?

Cindy ushered them in the room, and Rick shut the door. A quick scraping of metal on metal signaled the chain latch sliding into place. Not caring how filthy she was, Kat collapsed on the bed and exhaled loudly. "I think I'm a freaking magnet for things that aren't supposed to be there. Maybe I should be a cryptozoologist after all. I keep finding everything. I'm the Indiana Jones of cryptids."

"How long were you wandering around out there without water?" Rick filled a plastic cup at the sink and handed it to her, not backing down until Kat drank it. What a mother hen.

"For a while. I actually wasn't that far away," she fibbed.

She couldn't say, "Hey, the Jersey Devil is really the Greek god, Pan, and he flew me back here so I can take a shower and assure you I'm alive." No, they'd check her temperature and call the doctor. Even though they'd seen the Jersey Devil with their own eyes, Greek myths in the modern world would still be too difficult to accept.

"It didn't...hurt you, did it? That thing had a...a...weenie," Cindy whispered the childish word like it was profanity. Kat snickered. There was nothing "wee" about it.

"Nothing like that happened. I think he wanted a friend. He let me go."

"You must be starving," Rick interrupted as he flipped through the room service menu. Kat shook her head at his antics, wishing she could share everything with them. She would tell them eventually, after Dionysus was no longer a danger to them all.

"I'm fine. Really. I wanted you guys to know I'm okay. I really just want a shower and a good night's sleep."

Escaping their clutches proved more difficult than she'd expected, with Cindy offering to stay in the room with her and feeling betrayed that Kat wanted to be alone. Finally, with the promise of room service being delivered—that Rick—she'd finally convinced them that she would be fine.

CHAPTER 13

I f vanity was a terrible sin, Kat was a ginormous sinner. She sat on the closed toilet seat, foot propped on the lip of the tub as she lotioned her freshly clean and shaved legs. The tropical coconut scented cream made them even silkier to the touch, and she sighed from contentment due to the warm, sultry aroma. Pan was next door, but she was primping like she was getting ready for prom or something equally silly. She shrugged it off, telling herself that she always felt more feminine after shaving. It wasn't anything out of the ordinary.

Liar.

Although, it wasn't completely a lie since when she'd peeled off her jeans and gotten a good look at her hairy ape legs, she couldn't hop in the shower fast enough. The hot water had felt so nice, and her skin was still a little pink from the lengthy amount of time she spent under the scorching stream. The mirror had clouded up, and the white tile floor was damp from where the steam dissipated.

Wrapping a towel around herself, Kat opened the door to find her suitcase and clean clothes. Unfortunately, she didn't make it more than five feet out of the bathroom before stopping dead in her tracks and temporarily losing control over her bottom jaw as it hung open. The intruder upon the double bed farthest from her waved cheerily as he gained amusement from her reaction.

Pan reclined in nothing but a pair of black slacks, hands behind his head, watching her with a devious expression. He fixated his gaze on her bare legs. How long had he been in her room? The tray of food that room service had sent was on the table next to him.

"Someone had to answer the door for you. You were so lost in your singing that you didn't hear the knocking." He grinned wider while holding up a wadded five dollar bill. "I didn't even have to tip the boy that brought the food. He tipped *you* for your singing. Said you had the voice of an angel, and even Adele herself would envy it."

Her face was on fire. "H-how long were you here?" Kat winced at the shrillness of *here*.

"Since about five songs ago. I must say, you are like a karaoke master's reason for living. Just what are you so chipper about this evening, vixen? *Hmm?* You sounded oh, so...passionate."

Kat's face was going to become permanently affixed to her palm in his presence. She hid behind her hand to avoid eye contact. She would have to look at him eventually, but not while she was half-naked. Grabbing some items from her suitcase, she stomped back into the bathroom and then slammed the door shut behind her. It barely muffled his laughter.

He sounded way too pleased with himself.

When she returned, she was dressed in a light gray T-shirt and sky blue pajama pants with little white stars all over them. She had on a bra too, mostly to avoid any extra jiggle that could draw attention to her breasts. She had a feeling kicking him out of her room wouldn't be an option.

Pan rolled over to his side, rested his head against his fist, and smiled. He was in human form at the moment. She could almost believe he was some ordinary, albeit sexy, man lying in her bed. As edible as he appeared, Kat only wanted one thing in her mouth at the moment.

She stalked past him to the cheeseburger and fries room service had brought her. It smelled delicious, the spices it had been marinated in tangy and appetizing, and prompted another growl from her stomach. She was going to tear that burger up.

And she did, Pan watching her the whole time. It wasn't the unnerving sensation she'd experienced earlier while waiting for Cindy to open the door. When Pan watched her, she felt like she was standing in a desert on a summer day, but it was pleasant. She enjoyed the heat of it, but she didn't know how to handle or react to it.

"Feel better?"

She nodded. She had skipped lunch two days in a row, and from what she saw out the window, it was well past dinner. Back in her own environment, away from his creepy mansion in the woods, Kat had her hackles back down, and it left her a bit shy. Kat was never shy.

"Why are you so nervous?" Pan called her on it.

"Me? I'm not nervous." She quickly shoved a ketchup-laden fry into her mouth.

"You are. You can barely look at me all of a sudden. You're using your meal as a security blanket to hide behind."

"*Pfft*. Am not." Yeah, she was really mature. Pan's grin widened knowingly, and his green eyes sparkled in the lamplight. That man was so fine and looked every bit the trickster he was. *Ugh, blasted hormones!*

Kat wiped her hands on a napkin and then loaded everything onto the room service tray, placing it back on the cart. She did it all slowly, taking her time, stalling the inevitable. She then moved the cart outside the door so the hotel employees could collect it when they came by.

Shuffling and bedsprings groaning made her glance over her shoulder as she closed the door. Pan was no longer on the bed.

She started to turn around when his hands scooped her up under her arms. He spun her slowly toward him, and he was every bit a satyr of legend. His horns were a solid black, jutting out from his dark brown hair. It was hard not to stare at them. She wanted to reach out and touch one, but didn't know if that would be considered weird or rude. Kat knew, without looking down, he was naked. His feet would be hoofed.

It was wrong. It was *so* wrong to desire someone who had hooves and horns. They were traits given to depictions of Satan and his demons; therefore, the satyr was surely a manifestation of sin and lust sculpted into an exquisite male body with perfectly formed abs. The ultimate temptation.

Kat had told herself she wouldn't have sex with him. He'd kidnapped her! If she kept reminding herself of it, she could resist him. Trying to keep that in the back of her mind, she lifted her chin and defiantly stared him down. His emerald eyes were dark, reminding her of the forest and the pine trees growing in abundance nearby. His gaze was riveted on her mouth, and she could barely breathe with the desire for him to claim it, to claim her. Nevertheless, she couldn't give in so easily. She had to stay strong.

"Such challenge in your eyes, vixen. Every instinct within me screams to tame your spirit, but to do so would be tragic." His breath tickled her lips with its nearness, and he didn't have to move far to take them if he wished. "I can't be denied any further in this. You fear giving in to me, but it's meant to happen. I know you feel it too."

With scarcely enough time to take a breath, Pan's lips crashed against hers. They were warm, inviting...impatient. Kat whimpered as her thoughts were stomped out by the weight of her desire—her need. She kissed him back, trembling as he claimed her mouth as his. Kat clung to his shoulders, gasping at the feel of his hot tongue against hers.

She very nearly failed to acknowledge being led in the

direction of the bed, befuddled as she was. His kisses were intoxicating, and the warmth of them traveled downward until her whole body was flushed. She'd never been more ready for a man than she was in that moment. Her hands traveled his strong back, groped at his ass, his...her hands brushed the hair thickening halfway down his thighs and she stilled. "I can't do this."

Pan sighed. "I'm not an animal, Katerina. I have only been altered. I was not born the cub of some strange union of man and beast."

She knew that, she did. It was just...not right. Kat repelled the thought of being with something—she cringed—someone...that had hooves. Ashamed of herself for offending him, it was too late to hide her reaction. It bordered too close to fetish lines she would never cross.

Pan placed one of Kat's hands on his thigh and dragged it down to his knee where the hair was more fur-like and continued until her fingertips brushed his hoof. He raised her other hand to cup a horn. It was cool to the touch, smooth, solid. The fur, in contrast, was coarse but thin. Contrary to the images she'd seen of satyrs in the mythology book she'd flipped through, Pan's legs didn't taper into scrawny appendages. They were thick structures that were capable of supporting his weight, closer in size to a horse's hooves than a goat's, which made them more proportional to his body and weight.

"These things," Pan said, "these things were done to me. I didn't ask for them. I was not born with them. I'm a god, yes, but the gods are merely a superior bloodline to humans. One with magic and immortality. Many believe in the purity of this bloodline, and they would commit incest again and again to keep it so. But we were made compatible to mate with humans. Why else would we be given the same body structures? Why else would our reproductive organs fit with those of humans and create offspring that in turn could mate with each other, populate the globe, and outnumber the immortals a thousand to one?"

He broke their connection and sat on the bed. He raised a leg, offering her a view of his ankle and hoof. "Look closely, Katerina." He brought her hand down again to his ankle, where the fur was thicker and slightly tufted, but the width was no different than any other man's. My leg does not grow this pelt until mid-thigh; above them, my body is normal. My knees bend the same as that of a human, but it is the ankle where the true distortion begins. My feet are perpetually locked as though I'm walking on tiptoes. Imagine, if you will, that you were forced to wear high-heeled shoes for the rest of your life and couldn't take them off. Then imagine the heels broke off, but the only way to keep your balance in those shoes was to walk on only the balls of your feet, for all eternity."

He ran her hand over his heel, which jutted out, forming the backward bend in his leg, and down to the cloven hoof, where the ball of his foot and toes once were. "This is how my legs have been reformed. Granted, it doesn't feel like I am tiptoeing about, at least not any longer. At first it did. It was difficult to balance my weight this way, but I have learned to bend my knees ever so slightly to even it out."

Pan stood. He was suddenly in human form, dressed once more in black slacks. He didn't face her, but his head was bowed, his expression haunted.

"Your mind sees what is done to me, and you think, like the descriptions in mythology, 'he is part animal, and so it must be like laying with a goat, not a man.' But I assure you. I am a man. At the root of all I am, I'm a man. A man with a disfigurement. And I hope one day you can see that. I wish beyond wishes I could keep this form for you, but even if I could, it would be a lie. An illusion."

Pan stormed past her, opened the door, and left.

Shaking, Kat sank down on the bed. She felt like the lowest of the low. She'd been stuck on his "half-animal" state, it was true. It had stopped her, and Pan knew it. Judging by the memories he'd shared with her, that precise reaction had been the purpose of the curse: to make him unattractive so women no longer wanted him sexually. A punishment made more extreme by the insatiable lust.

Perhaps that is why satyrs were so sinfully arousing in stories and art. The idea of the lascivious beast-man taking his pleasure from an unsuspecting delicate female he comes across as he wanders through the wilderness. The opportunity to be wanton and free in sexuality with that creature was seductive in its own merit, not for what he was physically, but what he stood for. And what did Kat do when given the opportunity to participate in what was sure to be one of the most erotic experiences of her life, with a freaking god? She'd freaked out because he had a few alterations to his structure. Because his body wasn't to her preference.

Kat felt like an idiot. She raced to the door he'd left open and spotted him entering the line of trees across the street. She looked both ways, saw no people or cars, and chased after him.

DION WATCHED FROM HIS WINDOW AS KATERINA SILVERTON RAN across the street after Pan. He'd been informed of her miraculous reappearance earlier by both Silenus and the Martinezes, but had promised not to confront the woman until the morning. The police were relieved, of course, to be free of a potential missing person's case, but they were irritated at the same time. Law enforcement believed the lot of them were attempting a Jersey Devil hoax, and Dion had to promise the group would not cause any more of a commotion while in the state.

Silenus had witnessed Pan's return to the hotel that afternoon and had wanted to act. It was too soon, and Dion had gone through too much trouble to end it so quickly. Besides, there were witnesses at the hotel. Humans. The elder satyr was turning out to be more trouble than he was worth.

Nonetheless, Dion hadn't thought Pan would bring the girl

back after such a short time. It meant things were working far too well. The god cared for the human, and if they hadn't fucked yet, they would soon. No doubt they were heading out to do just that.

Dion let the curtain fall back into place. He needed to finish up the formalities and move on with his plan. If Pan had the *syrinx*, it would be at the house Melancton had found. He could send Pavlo out tonight to search for the *syrinx* while Pan was occupied with the human. Hopefully it was found, and quickly, as Dion's patience was waning, and so was his control over Silenus.

CHAPTER 14

"Pan, wait!"

He kept going.

"Damn you, I know you hear me."

Pan stopped, waiting for her to catch up to him. "What do you want, Katerina?"

They were well into the Pine Barrens and out of sight from the hotel and the road. Katerina panted as she caught her breath from chasing him. Her red hair cascaded over her shoulders, the ends were drying and wild, but most of it was still damp from her shower. Her light-colored pajamas looked positively bright in the dark forest. It was then he realized she was wincing. He glanced down at her bare feet.

"No shoes? You could have stepped on something and cut yourself." He kneeled and inspected her feet. A few scrapes but nothing serious.

"I couldn't waste time on a stupid pair of shoes when you were stomping away. You might not have come back, and I'd never see you again."

Rising slowly to his feet, Pan studied her. She was sincere. She'd been afraid he'd never return, but he'd only wanted to blow off steam until his erection went away. He almost laughed at the notion it could go away, given his curse. However, he didn't want Katerina to think he was making fun of her. Could it be his beautiful vixen truly desired him?

"Oh? And why would it matter if you didn't?"

"I'm sorry. I just wanted you to know I didn't mean to offend you with my petty human fears." She flung her arms around his neck and hugged him to her. He was unsure what to do. His arms remained at his sides, as he was too afraid wrapping them around her would scare her off again. He could smell the citrusy shampoo she'd used and wondered how apparent his hard-on was against her belly.

Katerina backed up and removed her shirt, tossing it on the bush beside her. His eyes widened. She couldn't be insinuating what he thought she was. When her bra followed suit, he swallowed and held his breath. Her breasts were perfect. Not too big, but they weren't small by any means. The nipples were pebbled and begging for him to run his hands and tongue over them.

She stepped forward and unfastened his pants, kneeling as she pushed them down his hips and met his gaze. "Be yourself with me."

"Are you sure you know what you're asking?"

She hesitated a moment, but then ran the tip of her tongue across the sensitive head of his penis where it hovered in her face, seeking attention. He shuddered at her teasing.

"I don't want to make love to an illusion. I don't want the lie, Pan. I want you."

He trembled a little. He'd seen the dawning of so many civilizations and had hidden in nature through most of the last centuries. He couldn't even remember how long he'd been alive. But he had never, not even once, felt as desired as he did that moment. Not even Syrinx had wanted him as much; she'd just wanted a gentle lover to take her virginity. Katerina, he wagered, wasn't a virgin. She'd known desire and the pleasure it could bring. And she wanted him, *all* of him.

Pan dropped the glamour, and the pants she had pushed to his thighs dissolved to nothing in her hands. It was a handy skill to have.

"Take off your clothes, vixen."

"Before I do, you should know I'm imperfect too." She troubled her lower lip with her teeth. Pan didn't see anything she should be insecure about. Then he realized she'd positioned herself so her left side had been obscured by the shadows ever since she'd removed her top.

"Show me."

Katerina stood, took a deep breath, and then pushed her pants and panties down her legs to step out of them. She raised her chin and moved into the sliver of moonlight cutting through the canopy of treetops above them.

The pale light cast her in a bluish hue, and so distracted was he by her natural beauty that he didn't see her scars right away. The puckered flesh traveled her left thigh and hip, coming just to her waist and across her stomach, and likely her back as well. The crisscrossing scar tissue was the only imperfection on her soft, otherwise flawless, skin.

"Oh, vixen," He dropped to his knees and drew her closer. "What did this to you?" He ran his hand over the markings.

"A cougar. I wasn't as cautious as I should've been and was too close to its den where it had cubs. I moved as it attacked, which is why I'm lucky the cat only got my hip and not my throat. The group with me scared it away by firing a gun."

He kissed the area where the scars were the largest, left behind by the feline's massive jaws. The beast had attempted to steal her from him before she'd even met him. But she'd survived. His Katerina was fierce and strong.

"I think I only agreed to Mr. Bach's—Dionysus'—project because I was still shaken from the attack. I love the big cats, but maybe it was a sign I was in the wrong field. This was my first actual job aside from at-home research and lab work since the accident." She started to laugh nervously. "What's funny is the cat that tried to kill me wasn't supposed to be in the area we found her in. Then I come here to look for something else that isn't supposed to exist, and I found you. Do you think, if I jumped into Loch Ness, Nessie would rise from the depths to finish me off?"

Pan stood and pulled Katerina closer, rubbing a hand lightly over her scarred flesh. "These are battle wounds. They may not make you feel beautiful when you look at them, but they are badges of survival. You're a warrior. They make you far sexier to me than you were before, which is saying a hell of a lot. Call it imperfection if you please, but I don't see anything less than perfect about you. You're the most beautiful woman I've ever seen."

"That's bull. You grew up with Aphrodite and all those gorgeous nymphs. I saw some of them in your memory, even Syr—"

"Syrinx was a beauty, yes. I was young, well...younger. I believed I was in love with her when I simply wanted what I couldn't have. Back then, I confused love for lust. Since I'm related to Aphrodite, I really didn't look twice at her as anyone but a family member. I stand by my previous comment. You really are a great beauty. You know what else?"

Katerina shook her head.

"You're *mine*."

She started to protest, and he cut her off with a kiss.

Though Pan was irritated he couldn't give her the comfort of a soft bed for this first time, he couldn't help but be pleased they would come together in the forest. This was his home, his territory. He belonged here, and nothing had ever felt more right.

He glanced around when he broke the kiss and smiled when he saw the low hanging branches of a white oak tree. He scooped Katerina up and carried her over to the bottommost bough. It was sturdy, but Katerina seemed a bit wary about why she was placed there.

"Ah, this will do nicely." He fit himself between her thighs. The branch was at a perfect height. She held on to his shoulders for balance. "Grab the limb above you, both hands. Yes, like that. Now hold on to it like your life depends on it. I'll catch you if you start to fall."

Pan wanted to take his time with her, but he was on the edge already from the feel of her naked body against his. He caressed her breasts, and then he leaned and took the left one in his mouth, suckling, nipping, and licking it. With each flick of his tongue, Katerina shuddered in his grasp. He trailed his hands down her torso as he turned his attention on the other nipple, and spread her legs as wide as he could without toppling her off the tree.

With one hand against the small of her back as added support, he ran a hand over her sex. She was hot and wet, and she moaned at the contact of his skin to hers. He lightly pinched her clitoris, and she sucked in a breath. He didn't have the willpower to go slowly this time. He would give her foreplay later, but for now, he had to have her. He'd been waiting too damn long to be inside her to be patient.

His voice sounded hoarse when he spoke. "Gods, I hope you're ready for me."

KATERINA WASN'T GIVEN TIME TO RESPOND TO HIS COMMENT before Pan entered her, hesitantly at first. At her gasp, he pulled back and thrust in again, all the way to the base. Her fingers dug into the smooth bark of the limb above her. She could feel chunks of the wood gathering beneath her nails. Pan didn't move, but leaned in to kiss her, muffling her moan of pleasure. He was so big, much bigger than the lovers she'd had before him, and he seemed to realize that once he was snuggly sheathed within her.

He had his hands on her hips, holding her steady as he pulled back and thrust inside slowly, allowing her body to get used to his size.

The cool night breeze was welcome on her bare skin, and her nipples were chilled where Pan's tongue had licked before. The rough branch where she perched contrasted with the feel of Pan's body heat against her and the wet flesh sliding between her legs.

It seemed as though she was suspended in the air, barely aware of holding onto the tree for support. Slivers of moonlight danced over Pan's features. His gaze locked with hers, determined. A smile of triumph plastered on his beautiful face. He had her right where he wanted her, and she could only hold on for dear life as he thrusted into her because the movement could topple her. She had no control, but she liked how he staked his claim, forcing her to feel the way he ruined her for any other man after their night together.

They were shaking the tree with each movement, and she became vaguely aware of the leaves raining down on them. She wrapped her legs tighter around Pan's waist, squeezing him closer. She elicited a nip on the side of her neck from him in response. If the branch cracked and they tumbled to the ground, she didn't think his momentum would change. Kat didn't want it to.

Each thrust increased the friction against her clit as he slid in and out. She was so close that her body shook and trembled, ready for a release that hovered beyond her reach. Pan would randomly mumble something in Greek in that deep timbre of his, but she couldn't understand the words. Kat could only feel what he did to her, and she loved it.

When she tried to get closer to him, she felt the branch shift and groan beneath her. Was that a snap she heard? Pan thrusted, harder this time, holding Kat in place. One hand splayed across her hip, and the other gripped the bough beside her.

As she was about to come, Pan moved his palms across her flesh, gripping her thighs and spreading them wide once more. He kept his hands positioned there, and she was unable to move. She could only take what he provided, and he provided everything. A few more well-placed strokes had her screaming. Kat clawed the bark on the limb above her. Pan's pace grew faster, frenzied at the feel of her release, drawing out her bliss until he came as well. The burst of hot semen caused her to shudder as a louder *snap* made the world collapse.

Pan held her, keeping her impaled upon his shaft as the tortured branch fell to the dirt. She moved her arms around his neck and clung to him, breathing heavily. The branch had snapped at the base, broken. Kat breathed heavily, afraid her legs would be worthless if she tried to stand. Pan kissed her deeply, cradling her to his chest. He sat down with his back against the tree trunk. Then he positioned her to where she could comfortably move herself over his still-hard erection. She stared at him in shock. He didn't intend to start again this soon?

As though he were amused by her surprise, he arched his hips. No, they were definitely not done. She braced her legs on either side of his thighs, using her knees as leverage as she lifted up and dropped back down again and again to the gentle coaxing of his guiding hands. Pan let his head *thump* against the tree but held her gaze as she pleasured him to her own rhythm. Kat realized she could never return to an ordinary life after this night with him in the woods.

She *was* his. She didn't want it any other way. But what if Pan didn't want her anymore after they were finished and he'd gotten what he wanted? She couldn't allow herself these thoughts.

Kat squeezed her inner muscles as she slid down Pan's shaft, and he groaned. She laughed, becoming more turned on when he kissed her hard, taking in her mirth and turning it to a searing passion. She came again, but Pan still wasn't done with her.

He rolled her over onto her hands and her knees and thrust into her wet heat from behind. Sex with a god was entirely different than with human males. Their stamina was apparently as immortal as they were, and his arousal seemed to trigger hers.

The moon was low in the sky, dawn threatening its appearance on the horizon, when they finally dressed and returned to her hotel room for a few hours of sleep.

CHAPTER 15

I f Pan didn't know any better, he would think Katerina was a nymph. He began to wonder if somehow he'd triggered a change in her like with Syrinx. Perhaps it was possible he somehow altered his vixen as well. She'd had the stamina to match his, which, in an ordinary human, was impossible. Her body would have had a limit to the activity, the amount of friction, but didn't. When they'd made it back to her hotel room in the wee hours of the morning, Katerina had promptly fallen asleep, but she should have tired hours earlier. In truth, she shouldn't have been able to walk after all they'd done.

Smiling, Pan recalled when he first saw her in the woods, and he'd imagined they'd leave a crater in the Earth in the wake of their lovemaking. They'd left deep indentions in the ground last night, proving him right. He'd tried to let her rest several times throughout the night, but every time he did, she'd be willing and ready for him again, and he couldn't resist her.

Just thinking about the events from the night before had him hard and ready for her, but she had to deal with her friends in a few hours. Not only that, but she had to face Dionysus in a meeting Rick and Cindy had set up. Pan wasn't eager to allow Katerina within the other god's sight.

Katerina rolled over and snuggled against him, sleeping with her mouth wide open. He figured she'd be embarrassed by that and didn't plan to tell her. Instead, he wrapped his arm around her, drawing her closer, and then kissed the top of her head.

He'd deluded himself in thinking he could keep her, thinking the night they'd shared was proof they were meant for each other. If Katerina was smart, she'd leave here and get as far away as she could. What future could he provide for her? Sure, he could fix up the house, buy her pretty things, and make love to her so hard the ground quaked, but how long would it last?

Katerina was mortal, and regardless of how it perplexed him that her stamina far outlasted a normal human's, she wasn't a nymph—but not even they were immortal, unless their mother or father had been a god. If Katerina had been a nymph, they'd ruined any chance of removing his curse because they hadn't waited until a lunar eclipse to have sex. It still wouldn't have mattered because Pan was immortal and wouldn't revert to a human form to live out his remaining years. In short, Katerina's mortality mocked him.

Completely lost in his thoughts, Pan hadn't noticed her waking. She was currently studying his somber expression. "What's up?" She wiped at her cheek, and her skin grew flushed. "Oh God, I drooled on you, didn't I? I'm sorry."

How could he not love this woman?

He blinked, momentarily taken aback by the direction of his thoughts. Looking down at her, he smiled. "You didn't drool on me, vixen. Though I can't say the same for last night when your tongue was acquainted with a certain part of me." He chuckled as she turned redder.

No. He hadn't misthought before. He did love Katerina. Syrinx, he'd desired, idolized even, but since he'd made such a mess of things, her place in his heart was more a tribute to his failure to protect her more than anything else. Sometimes Pan imagined all the different ways he could have saved her. With Katerina, he lived for every smile, every blush—even when her random spurts of shyness were completely uncalled for—and he even looked forward to her smart-ass little remarks. She was his equal in so many ways.

Too bad he couldn't keep her.

"You're frowning again."

"Do you think you could convince your friends to sneak out of here with you? Without Dionysus knowing you left."

"What?" She shuffled around until she was on her back and could see him without straining her neck.

"Meeting with Dionysus isn't a good idea. He's up to something, and I know there is at least one satyr here with him. I heard Rick and Cindy mention Pavlo. I don't want to make the same mistake twice."

"He's not going to kill me. Why go through all the trouble of putting this together if that was the goal? Why not make a move on you before now? Anyway, by the time I could actually convince them to get packed and leave with me he'd be knocking on the door wondering why I'm late. Not to mention, the van is in the shop. You tossed it on its side like it was discarded trash, remember?"

He'd been living in the moment perhaps a little too well. "Oops."

"'Oops,' he says. Typical man." Katerina pried herself from his grasp.

"Where are you going?" He tried to pull her back in bed, but she wouldn't have it.

"I need to shower." She didn't have to explain why. She still had leaves in her hair and dirt smudges all over. She glared at him. "How did you get so clean?"

"One of the perks of being a god."

She rolled her eyes and sauntered off to the bathroom. No

reason why he couldn't join her. It would be unkind not to help her with those hard-to-reach places. He stretched and sat up, a smile on his lips. He'd slept in human form despite Katerina's assurances she didn't mind him as a satyr, that she'd overcome her issue with his feet. He didn't want to accidently kick her with a hoof or jab her with a horn while she slept.

Remaining in human form, he strolled into the bathroom, yanking the curtain back, and eliciting a squeak of surprise from her.

"Oh, no you don't." She pushed at his chest when he crowded her space. "We have to meet with the others in less than an hour."

"That's plenty of time. I have skills." He flashed his most smoldering smile and took smug satisfaction when she made a sexy little noise without realizing she had.

Deciding to draw out the seduction a little while longer, Pan snagged the pink loofa from her hands and poured her coconut-mango scented body wash on it, replacing the bottle on the side of the tub where he'd retrieved it. She eyed the loofa suspiciously and backed up a step.

"I'm perfectly capable of washing myself, thanks."

"Undoubtedly, but what kind of person would I be to not help those in need? Besides, taking care of dirty, dirty women is a specialty of mine."

She snorted. "I'm not that dirty."

"Absolutely filthy. Now, turn around and put your hands on the wall."

"What's with the macho alpha male posturing? I didn't mind it last night, but damn you're bossy." She crossed her arms, making her bared breasts lift and press together. His gaze was glued.

"If you turn around and put your hands on the wall, I'll reward you."

She seemed to consider his offer before she rolled her eyes and turned around. "Fine, but not because you want me to do it. I'm just curious about the reward."

He laughed as he began scrubbing her back, slowly, making her body arch in response to the sensation. "You know what they say about curiosity, don't you?" Pan didn't give her a chance to respond before he lifted one of her feet to rest it on the side of the tub and entered her, finding her clit with his free hand. The loofa dropped, forgotten as it rolled under the spray of the water.

Curiosity killed Kat or almost did anyway. Five consecutive orgasms in a row, all in less than ten minutes, had been her reward. He hadn't lied about being quick. She shifted around on the sofa in Dionysus' suite, wishing she'd had time for a nap to recover from the shower. Cindy and Rick sat on either side of her, and they both kept giving her strange looks. Did they know what she'd been doing all night and all morning in the shower? Was it written all over her face?

She tried really hard not to blush, but knew she failed. Pan was in the woods, keeping his appearance cloaked. He would wait for her to finish her business with Dionysus and her friends as he stood by in case she needed him. *"One scream, just one, and I will rip his fucking head off,"* was the last thing he'd said before she finally convinced him not to come with her. There was still hope the other god didn't know Pan was near. Granted, it was a really small chance.

Dionysus—Mr. Bach, she had to remember not to call him by his real name—had to take a very important phone call, or so Pavlo told them when they arrived. Kat found herself staring at the man. His hair was much shorter than it had been in ancient times. He fidgeted a bit under her close inspection, but if he knew what she was thinking about, he didn't make it obvious. Pavlo flitted around, bringing them all bottles of water and chitchatting about the weather and every other common topic of small talk while they waited.

Feeling a gaze on her, she turned to the right and faced Cindy. Kat raised a brow, questioning without speaking. They'd been friends long enough that words weren't always necessary.

Cindy raised both her brows in response. It was a sarcastic, *Really? You're going to play coy with me?*

Kat shrugged with a slight frown and shake of her head. *Whatever do you mean?*

Cindy glared. She was not dropping this conversation or lack thereof. Luckily, Dionysus chose that opportunity to stroll in from the closed-off bedroom. To avoid staring and making it obvious she knew the truth about him, Kat took in the surroundings again. The suite was awash in the same maroons and greens with dark brown furniture as the smaller rooms. It had a separate bedroom that connected to the living room they were in, with a small kitchen area beside the front door. It smelled like lemons.

"Dr. Silverton, I'm relieved you are well. Your crew, myself included, was so terribly worried something bad had happened to you."

Kat stood to shake his hand. "Thank you. It was only a scare— no harm was done. Everyone is okay. I would like to forget about it and move on."

He nodded in greeting to the Martinezes and took a seat in the armchair across from them, crossing his right ankle over his left knee. "Let's cut the shit, shall we?"

Kat frowned. She had to have misheard. "Excuse me?" To her left, she felt Rick stiffen, clearly taking offense to the man's tone and use of language.

Dionysus continued as though he hadn't heard her, "I know you've learned the truth about the Jersey Devil. I must confess, he moved in on you much sooner than expected."

Kat gaped. She snapped her mouth shut again.

"What is the meaning of th—" Rick began.

"Shut it, young man." Dionysus waved a hand at Rick

181

dismissively. Too baffled to protest, Rick complied. "Where were we? Oh, yes. The Jersey Devil. I felt quite foolish once I heard of him a few years back, as I should have known after he first appeared in the area and revealed himself to humans. You see, some of the others have the bad habit of being spotted, and then they become urban legends around the areas they were sighted. I shouldn't have been surprised. If I had thought to look for him that way sooner, I would have."

"Mr. Bach, why are you—" Kat began, but she was cut off as well.

"Dr. Silverton, I know you know who I am. The speculative gleam in your eyes when I entered the room said as much. Furthermore, you've been staring at Pavlo as though you've seen a ghost and don't quite believe what's in front of you."

Pavlo sheepishly peered at his feet. Cindy and Rick seemed to be too bewildered to comment at the outlandish turn in the conversation. All they did was gawk.

"Call me Dion, would you? It's my name, or at least the short version I have started using the past few centuries. Less conspicuous." He'd pronounced his name *Die-on*.

Rick gave Kat and Cindy a concerned glance. He obviously believed *Dion* to be a few screws loose.

"Um, Dion, then. Why go through the ruse of sending a film crew here if you knew the truth about the Jersey Devil? Why not make contact yourself?" What Kat really wanted to know was why she had to be involved at all.

Dionysus made a great show of bowing his head and looking forlorn. "He wouldn't have welcomed my visit. I made a great mess of things in the past." He met her gaze, "If you know about Pavlo and who I am, you know what transpired." He straightened in his chair, resting his forearms on the armrests, and met her gaze. He seemed to have forgotten the Martinezes were present at all and was talking only to her. "You don't understand what it was like in Greece in the old days. Men and women devoted their lives to appeasing the gods. They gave us sacrifices of meat, of jewels, of virginity and women..." Dionysus glanced at Pavlo.

"After a while, we *expected* these things rather than appreciated them. Power corrupts more than any sin. When you have it, you think you are invincible and stop thinking about your actions, let alone the consequences of those actions. You take the power for granted and cease considering who is harmed by your actions and your demands."

He inclined his head ever so slightly. "I was one of the worst because I was so well-loved by the citizens of Greece, but ended up becoming the very thing I didn't wish to be. I provided wine, merriment, and entertainment. I left Olympus and celebrated *with* them. I didn't sit upon my pretty throne, hidden in another realm, only to come down to plant my seed into the belly of a woman and leave her to raise the brat on her own. I associated with my followers. I provided for any bastards I begot upon them. After..." A haunted look entered his eyes and he shook himself to dispel the ghosts of his earlier life. "Events of my past I do not discuss, ever, I forgot why I did these things. I became Olympian more than I ever was before."

As Kat contemplated what events could have changed his demeanor, a knock at the door sounded. Dionysus nodded at Pavlo, who in turn made his way to the door and opened it. A tall, gorgeous man with long black hair came in. It was Melancton. Kat recognized him right away. The only difference from the man she'd seen in Pan's memory was in his clothing. His hair was the same length as it had been, stopping slightly above his hips. The short sleeves of his shirt displayed the scars she'd glimpsed through Pan's memories. Pan ambled in after him, dressed as he had been the day she met him.

Cindy leaned in and whispered, "Why is Peter involved in this nonsense?"

At the same time, Rick muttered, "I knew he was up to no good. Can you please explain what is going on here?"

Kat exhaled in a rush and braced herself for their reactions. "I'm sorry, but I wasn't completely honest with you. It is hard to believe either way, but the short version is that Peter is really the Jersey Devil, and he is also the god, Pan. Dion Bach is Dionysus, and the two other men are satyrs. I'll explain it more as soon as we get out of here."

Her friends stared at her, blinking.

"Perhaps you were out in the woods too long," Rick stated after a few long moments that felt like hours. "Do you need more water? Are you feeling dehydrated?"

Cindy shook her head. "I don't know, Rick. Either she is overly tired and imaginative, or the whole lot of us are crazy. We saw the Jersey Devil with our own eyes. Maybe we should believe what she is saying."

"I was going to tell you after this was all over. I know it's a lot to take in on words alone." She chewed on the edge of her lip under her friends' scrutiny. Soon they began bickering amongst themselves and, thankfully, forgot her for the time being.

Pan's gaze settled on her, assessing. Then he glared at Dionysus who had risen from his chair as Melancton ushered him into the room. Dionysus had the good grace to look abashed, but Kat didn't believe he was genuine. The whole ordeal seemed off to her. Like he was putting on a show. She didn't believe he regretted his past actions regardless of the sob story he'd been putting on for her benefit before.

"It's good to see you again, Pan. It's been a long time."

"Not long enough." Pan moved to stand behind Kat, and his hands landed on her shoulders, squeezing lightly. She pretended she didn't see the speculative look from Cindy or the confused glower Rick was transferring between Kat and Pan. "I found Melancton roaming around the hotel. He wouldn't be here for you to hide behind unless you feared I'd come after you. I'm here. You and I have words to exchange, but whatever you have to say to me doesn't merit the involvement of the humans. Let them leave."

Why *was* Dionysus involving Cindy and Rick? It didn't make sense.

In fact, Dionysus acted as though he'd only just realized the Martinezes were present. He glanced at them and frowned. "They insisted on being here when I spoke to the girl. I grow weary of pretending to be a human, albeit a wealthy, powerful, and incredibly handsome one."

Kat rolled her eyes.

Dionysus wasn't finished droning on, "I don't have the patience to pretend Katerina doesn't know who I am or who you are, and I believe she isn't keen on pretending the same. I'm sure she would have told the other two eventually."

So she was Katerina to him now, was she? It was the first time he hadn't referred to her by her title. The entire facade had collapsed.

"You know, I've gone through a lot with you in the past, Kat, but everything being discussed here isn't possible or rational." Rick looked from Pan to Dionysus after his outburst, beseeching some sort of confirmation that they were talking crazy.

Dionysus sighed. "I miss ancient times. People had faith in the unknown. They didn't require demonstrations." He snapped his fingers and the glamour fell away from Melancton, who stood behind Dionysus as a sentry. Perhaps in case Pan acted on any notion of revenge.

Melancton was exquisite, even as a satyr. His legs were covered in black hair, thin at the top like Pan's, thicker closer to his dark hooves. Matching horns arched upward, stopping at sharp points above his head. He was fully naked, revealing an abundance of scars on various parts of his body, and impressive. Showing no sign of discomfort due to his sudden exposure, Melancton regarded those who studied him. He glanced at Kat briefly before turning his lavender eyes away.

Cindy sucked in a breath, and she covered her mouth. Rick

stood slowly, slack-jawed. He stumbled over to Cindy's side of the couch and covered her eyes with his hand.

Yeah, Kat had been there. She yawned. A strange world it was when she was no longer surprised at witnessing a man go from fully dressed human one minute to naked mythological creature the next.

"What is the point, Dionysus?" Pan gritted out. His skin flushed with fury, he grasped her shoulders tightly. She wiggled a bit, and he loosened his hold on her. Beside her, Cindy peeked over the top of Rick's hand at Melancton. He noticed, giving her a wink. Rick was too distracted by Pan's outburst to see it.

"Yes, the point," Dionysus said, relaxing in his chair. "I wanted to make contact with you, and I knew you would not welcome a visit from an old friend." He snapped his fingers again, and Melancton was in human form, wearing jeans and a gray shirt.

Pan snorted. "After your hissy fit because you didn't get to have sex with a virgin? No thanks. I prefer keeping the company of people who don't behave like spoiled children and kill people when they don't get their way. Most of the men you cursed along with me were innocent and didn't deserve what happened to them."

Dionysus shot to his feet. "Innocent? Innocent! A fascinating way to refer to the lot of debauchers who were there that night, is it not? They may have been humans, who weren't necessarily involved in what you or I did, but they were anything but innocent. Let's examine the facts, shall we?"

He held up his index finger. "Pavlo here wanted to be welcomed into my circle because he was too shy to go out and find a wife. Instead of manning up and winning a woman over, he threw his one and only sister into the hands of Silenus; the man who turned around and offered his future bride to me on a silver platter."

Pavlo's face paled considerably.

186

Dionysus held up a second finger. "Secondly, Adonis was there because he'd been snubbed by a goddess and wanted to make her jealous. Pride is a bitch, is it not?" A third finger came up. "Melancton abandoned his post as a soldier in preference of wine and women. Cowardice isn't listed as a sin, but I think it very well should be."

Melancton's eyes narrowed, the only sign he was affected by the words spoken about him. Dionysus' raised a fourth finger, "Ariston—"

"Enough!" Pan leaped over the couch and those sitting there, shielding them from the others in the room. "So they weren't pure white lambs of innocence. So what? They weren't guilty of any crimes worth being made into monsters over—Silenus aside. I'm not stupid. I long ago figured out that the form of the Jersey Devil was what you tried to curse me with. If I hadn't attempted to counter it as I had, what would have happened if it still reverberated and all of us were turned into mutated abominations? The Greeks would have hunted us down like the Chimera. Like Medusa. Do I need to mention Hydra or Scylla, many of which were made the way they were by the fury of the gods?"

Kat wondered how many of the Greek "monsters" had started off in human form. There were so many in the Greek legends. Heroes were worshipped for defeating them. Hell, movies were made glorifying the defeat of those very creatures.

"How else could the gods prove to the ever-prideful humans that their wrath should be feared?" Dionysus shot back. "If you hadn't botched your attempt to send the curse back at me, none of them would have been cursed. It's your fault they were pulled into this mess, not mine."

"You initiated the first curse, so it falls on you. As to your comment about the gods, they shouldn't have sought fear. They should have sought respect!" Pan ran his hands through his hair, mussing it. "It's why people lost their faith," he said more calmly. "I saw it then while the beliefs faded. As new religions surfaced and people chose to convert to a less wrathful power."

Dionysus considered it for a moment and then shook his head. "If you are referring to the Christian deity, keep in mind he threw a tantrum and flooded the entire Earth in the process. He's been just as vengeful in the past as any of our family or ancestors."

Kat eyes widened. If she'd heard right, they'd insinuated the Christian God did exist. But regardless of all the questions that revelation brought to her mind, she decided, almost immediately, knowing was enough.

Dionysus was still speaking, "The Greeks and Romans lost their faith because the gods holed up in Olympus and left them to their own devices. They were forsaken and went elsewhere for guidance."

Pan growled. He turned to Kat and the Martinezes and nodded toward the door. "We're out of here."

"Not so fast." Dionysus stood directly in front of Pan before Kat could blink. "I didn't come here to argue theology with you or to rehash old times. I came here to offer peace."

Pan crossed his arms. Alpha male posturing at its finest. "Why would I want it? I've been quite peaceful without your presence to sully my mood."

Dionysus rolled his eyes. "Quit being the ungrateful child your father claims you are and listen to me, damn you."

At mention of his father, Pan stiffened. Kat thought he'd been mad before, but he was positively livid now. However, he didn't respond to it. Dionysus seemed pleased and strolled over to the refrigerator. He extracted a wine bottle without a label, which contained a deep red liquid and brought it to Pan, holding it toward him.

"I don't want your wine, Dionysus. I didn't really want it then, and I never want to know the taste of it again."

"Insulting me does not disprove my last comment. Besides, this isn't for you to consume. It's for her." He nodded at Kat, and all eyes turned toward her.

"Me?" Why did he have to bring her into this? "After the last bottle you sent screwed with my mind? No thanks."

"Do you care for this...ingrate?" Dionysus ignored the growl from Pan.

"Y-yes, but the last time—"

Dionysus acted as though she hadn't spoken. "Then you are aware he will never age. He will never die unless struck down by a certain type of weapon or dismembered in a certain fashion." Kat assumed he didn't elaborate because it was the same weakness he had, being gods and all.

Pan huffed. "Why does this concern her?"

"Why are all of you so fucking defensive?" Dionysus shoved the bottle into Pan's hands. "You love the woman. I can smell it on you. It's different from the desire you had for Syrinx, or any of the nymphs I've seen you with in the past. This is pure."

When he didn't reply, Dionysus gritted out, "She's going to age and die, you moron."

Pan flinched and looked back at Kat. She couldn't breathe. Pan loved her? He didn't just want her, but he *loved* her? Could this be true?

The look in his eyes confirmed it for her. She felt her chest tighten. He loved her. She wasn't sure if she could call her own feelings love, at least not yet, but she had grown to care for him. Hell, she was hoping to send her friends packing so she could stay and explore her feelings with the satyr some more.

Pan snapped out of it and turned back to Dionysus. "Then why are you giving us a bottle of wine? It's not something to celebrate if we can't be together. What did you do to it?"

"That accusation hurts. As I was telling Katerina before you rudely interrupted a meeting you weren't invited to, I am letting bygones be bygones and turning over a new leaf. Consider it a gesture of good faith. Besides, I already told you it was for her, not you. It's not merely wine, idiot. It's ambrosia."

Pan's skin turned pasty. Kat had heard several myths about ambrosia over the years, but she always fell back on imagining her grandmother's ambrosia salad, which was a fruit salad with marshmallows mixed in it. Her stomach usually rumbled at the thought, but she had a feeling Pan's ashen complexion meant something she wouldn't like.

"I sent her a bit of it before. To test if she could handle it in its diluted form mixed with wine. As she drank it, and lived through it, without any of the sometimes regrettable side effects, we know she is eligible for immortality. This is the real deal."

Pan shook his head as if he didn't believe what he'd heard. "You risked her life with your little ambrosia experiment? What the fuck, Dionysus! You had her thinking there was something wrong with her because it affected her libido."

"Oh, don't act all offended." Dionysus smirked. "She drank it before ever starting to film in the woods. If it hadn't worked, I would have allowed her to finish her job here, found a replacement, and tried again. I'm trying to make things right between us. Consider her to be my gift to you, a peace offering."

"You can't just tie a bow on someone and give them as gifts!"

"If you don't want her, she can go home."

Pan glanced at the bottle of red liquid. "There's got to be a better way. I don't trust that there is nothing in this for you to gain if it goes wrong. I've seen what happens to humans when this doesn't work the way it should."

Dionysus sighed. "Believe what you want. I find New Jersey doesn't agree with me, and I'm taking my Boeotians and leaving. Don't come crying to me if you dispose of that bottle and then want my help. I won't be supplying a replacement." He dismissed them all and disappeared into his bedroom with a comment to Pavlo and Melancton about preparing for their departure.

When Pavlo shooed them all out the door, shutting it behind

them, Katerina couldn't hold in her question any longer. She cleared her throat, regaining Pan's attention. "Okay, I know ambrosia is what makes mortals immortal. What is it? Why did you freak out?"

"We shouldn't discuss it in the open, Katerina." Cindy and Rick were watching them.

"Tell me."

"It's blood, vixen. Before, he gave you wine with his blood mixed into it. Now it's one hundred percent pure Olympian blood."

CHAPTER 16

Katerina helped Cindy pack her clothes, which were strewn about the hotel room. Rick had thrown the suitcase at the wall when they made their way inside. The zipper hadn't been closed, and the contents had rained down all over the place. He continued to shout at them because he couldn't handle the truth of why Kat was sent to the Pine Barrens.

"Satyrs? Gods? What the fuck, Kat? You drank some rich dude's blood? His fucking blood!" Rick placed his head in his hands and sat on the side of the bed.

"Hey, don't speak to her in that tone," Pan warned.

Rick raised his head and glared.

"Stop it." Kat stood and tossed rolled up socks into the suitcase on the floor. "I didn't know about the blood. I didn't tell you about Pan when I came back because I didn't think you'd believe me."

"We watched the Jersey Devil fly off with you, but you didn't think we would believe he was actually Peter...who was actually Pan." Rick shot him another dirty look. "Dude, really? Peter Pan?"

"Humor. Get some." Pan shrugged.

"Boys," Cindy interjected, "put the rulers away, please. It doesn't matter now, does it? It happened. A freaking Greek god

192

used us in his little game. We lived through it. Time to pick up the pieces, or in this case, our shit that *you* threw, Rick."

"That doesn't mean Kat has to stay here with this thing."

Kat placed herself between them when Pan stepped toward her friend. "Whoa. Cut it out. He's not a thing. What's the matter with you?"

"It's not safe for you here, Kat. I refuse to go home and leave you here with mythological creatures and pretend it's normal."

Kat was starting to regret breaking the news that she was staying with Pan when she'd given them the whole story. Rick wasn't handling the situation well at all, but Cindy seemed to know someone needed to stay calm and took the task upon herself. Her lack of criticism worried Kat, and from experience it meant she'd be hearing about it for years at the drop of a dime.

"You don't have a choice. This is what I want, and I want to stay. Pan's not forcing me. Dionysus isn't forcing me. I made this decision on my own."

Rick scowled, but Kat thought it looked more like he was pouting. He had the bad habit of being a bit melodramatic when riled. Cindy was always telling her how he threw more temper tantrums than a two-year-old when he didn't get his way. And, bless the man, he only wanted to keep the two women in the room safe from anything he considered a threat, including Pan.

"Doesn't make it the right decision."

"Ricardo Martinez." Cindy stood up with her hands on her hips. "Obviously she cares for Pe...Pan. She was glowing earlier. You saw. A fling in the woods might be good for her. Do you remember how Kat wasn't very happy to learn we were dating, but she didn't stand in our way?"

"That's different."

"Oh, yeah? How is it different?"

"He has hooves. Freaking hooves!"

Pan's eyes were starting to glow red. If this didn't stop soon, he might shift into the Jersey Devil again and frighten Rick so badly that he'd sling both Cindy and herself over his shoulders and run off with them. Kat laid her palm against Pan's arm. Her touch seemed to placate him, and the red faded from his irises as he looked at her. She offered him a weak smile.

Cindy wasn't backing down against her husband. "So the man has hooves. He's not an animal. He's just different. Some babies are born with a pronounced tailbone and it has to be surgically removed. Does that make them an animal?"

"That's different," Rick repeated.

"You're being a bigot and incredibly rude. He's standing eight feet away from you. Not to mention, he's a god. Do you want him to turn you into a toad? Because I promise you this, Rick Martinez, I do *not* kiss toads."

Kat almost laughed at the disconcerted look on Rick's face, except the situation wasn't remotely funny. Rick excused himself and went outside, slamming the door behind him.

"I apologize for my husband," Cindy told Pan. "He means well. He's always been a bit overprotective, though. He'll come around. Just let the shock of it all wear off."

"What about you?" Kat asked, leaning against Pan for support. She couldn't bear it if both her friends were repelled by the idea of her staying with Pan.

Cindy sighed warily. "It's not my decision. I know you wouldn't stay unless you really wanted to. I worry Mr. Bach— Dionysus—isn't being entirely truthful about wanting to make amends. I don't like the idea of you staying and possibly playing into some grand scheme neither of you know about, but I respect that you need to be sure if you have feelings for each other or not. Spending time with Pan is the best way to do it. But I don't like it, Kat. I wish you would have told us sooner." Her eyes watered and she rubbed them before tears spilled over. "We were really worried about you. If Mr...Dionysus hadn't sent that stupid gag order, we'd have had your mom and your whole family in an uproar."

Not that Kat didn't love her family, but she was definitely glad no one else had known about her disappearance and made a spectacle of it. She didn't particularly want her name in the news a second time for being caught unaware by a creature that wasn't supposed to be there.

"Thank you," Pan offered when Kat didn't reply.

Cindy turned toward him. "Know if any harm comes to her, I'm going to take Rick's shotgun and go satyr hunting. I will bury buckshot so deep into your ass, you will be shitting gunpowder for a month."

When the Martinezes' white van—good as new—left the hotel parking lot an hour later, Pan cleared his throat. "Vixen, your friend is kind of frightening."

～

TWO WEEKS HAD PASSED, AND PAN WALKED INTO THE DINING AREA to find Katerina staring at the bottle of ambrosia on the table in front of her. She hadn't touched it, but she couldn't stop staring at it. She had repeated this process nearly every night since they'd taken it from Dionysus. Not that she was mesmerized by it, but he suspected it had something to do with the fact that the more they got along, the more her mortality weighed on her.

Pan washed his hands in the kitchen's new stainless steel sink. Since departing from the hotel, he had been steadily working on restorations to the house in the Pine Barrens. He'd created documentation making him the legal owner by today's standards, and replaced the downstairs bathtub, toilet, and the kitchen appliances. He had even brought in a washer and dryer. The repairs to the grand staircase were his current mission. He could bring in help, but he didn't want strangers in his home. Having to call the utility companies to come out and hook the place up to modernize it with cable and Internet had been enough trespassers for his liking.

He dried his hands on a dishtowel. The house was slowly starting to look like a home again, at least from the inside out. It would take months, perhaps years to do it all. He ambled to the table and lightly kissed the top of Katerina's coppery head. She jumped at the contact, torn from her thoughts.

"I didn't mean to scare you."

She smiled and rose to her feet, then hugged him around his shoulders. "It's okay."

"Oh?" He wrapped his arms around her waist, drawing her close enough to feel the hard ridge in the front of his jeans. Because of the utility workers coming and going, he felt it better if he stayed disguised during the daylight hours, until things settled down enough that he could cloak the house from human view once more. The last thing he needed was to stir another panic about cryptids, as Katerina called them, in the Pine Barrens.

"I can't stop thinking about our conversation with Dionysus."

Pan extracted himself from her arms and fell into his restless routine of pacing. He seemed to do so a lot lately. "I know you want to think the best about the situation, Katerina, but I don't trust his motives. Why would he randomly decide, 'Hey, Pan seems lonely, I'll find him a mate?' No. There is a catch somewhere. A god that selfish does not wake up one morning playing matchmaker."

"I know. It doesn't make a whole lot of sense. Although, he did make explaining things to Cindy and Rick a little easier."

Pan snorted. Rick had calmed down enough to go home, but only Cindy seemed to think his feelings for Katerina were genuine. Even though he didn't particularly care for the idea, he'd promised once the house was in better condition that they could invite the Martinezes back to visit. Katerina called Cindy every day to assure her she was alive. She hadn't made a decision, but every conversation ended in an argument with Rick on the line. He'd noticed the disagreements had become shorter recently, and he wanted to believe the other man might be coming around.

She hasn't made a decision.

Pan couldn't quite understand how he could know he loved her, but Katerina wasn't sure she loved him back. To be fair, she had a lot to consider at the moment. She'd been utterly repulsed when she learned she'd been drinking Dionysus' blood—who could blame her? She'd called herself a vampire, said Buffy should slay her and be done with it. It was meant as a joke, but Pan couldn't help but wonder if she regretted her decision to stay with him and was hoping for an easy out.

"I've been thinking about the blood in the wine," she said suddenly. "Why couldn't I just drink yours to become immortal? Why does he think it has to be his?" Katerina scrunched up her nose and made a show of shuddering. The diluted blood hadn't been enough for a human to turn immortal, but it had given her some of the effects, such as her increased stamina. It had passed from her bloodstream already. She was once more entirely human, unless she drank the undiluted substance. True ambrosia of the gods was blood straight from the veins of an immortal, of a specific bloodline of Olympians.

"It's only been proven to work by those sharing Zeus' bloodline directly: his siblings and his children. Dionysus is his son. Since Zeus is my grandfather rather than my father, I am one generation shy of being able to successfully create an immortal that way. My blood would have repercussions or may not work. It's not worth the risk to find out."

"I didn't realize you were Zeus' grandson." Katerina raised a brow, looking him over with renewed curiosity. "I had forgotten how, um, close the gods' family tree was."

Pan snorted. "Don't look at *me*. I never slept with a goddess. I wasn't one of the culprits."

"What happens if you share your blood?" She'd asked him many times before, but he'd suddenly become interested in her breasts in order to distract her. Discussing ambrosia was a subject he'd rather not dwell on, and he wished to the gods Dionysus never brought up the topic.

"Well? You said there were repercussions, and you've been dancing around the subject for weeks now." He heard her foot tapping against the wooden floor.

"I've never shared my blood. As I haven't needed to create an immortal, I've never seen it done firsthand."

"But you know someone who has?"

"I do." He sighed and decided he might as well tell her. "Any time a god or goddess who didn't directly share Zeus' bloodline attempted it, disaster arrived in its wake. Sometimes it didn't do anything at all. Other times it made the drinker deathly ill. While I have not seen this occurrence, the blood could make the drinker...dependent. Some developed a taste for it, and blood became the fruit of which they survived."

"That sounds remarkably like vampires."

Pan lips twitched.

"Oh, God. They were vampires, weren't they?"

"They were. In a sense. Though the Greeks called them *vrykolakas* and had their own theories as to their existence. They were rare though."

Katerina put her head in her hands. "I'm not even going to attempt to pronounce that, let alone spell it. But...were they like Dracula? With fangs, widow's peaks, and swooshy capes?" She looked up expectantly.

Somebody has seen way too many horror films. Pan decided he dare not mention that King Lycaon had been the first lycanthrope and that werewolves existed as well. The world harbored a great deal of monsters of legends, but humans couldn't handle the truth of it. "No, well, I hear their canines were longer, but I can definitely say no to the capes. I never met one, and in some circles they were considered a cautionary tale not to give mortals ambrosia if you were not of the right bloodline. Supposedly they looked like normal humans as long as they fed regularly, yet they became immortal as the ambrosia intended. They only experienced extreme side effects. Like replacing ice cream with immortal blood as their favorite snack. They drink human blood too but prefer the other." Immortal blood sustained them for longer periods of time.

Kat seemed to digest the information rather well. "Did they start creating legions of vampires to do their evil bidding?"

Her imagination was going overboard. "No. They couldn't create new vampires with their blood."

"Was becoming a vampire the side effect Dionysus alluded to?"

"No," Pan said warily. "Ambrosia given by any god other than Zeus has a fifty-fifty chance of working. Magical beings, like nymphs, often have no reaction at all. But human genes cannot always support the changes. If the mortal is not susceptible to immortality, they become ill and can die. Sometimes death is only a catalyst to changing them into one of the *letum*. Living corpses."

"Zombies are real!"

He laughed. "You're so excitable." Then he became serious. "Which is why I was pissed off when he admitted to risking you like that. *Letum* actually *do* create more of themselves with their bite. The so-called zombie apocalypse humans are obsessed with lately is a very likely event. Luckily, it's always been prevented any time one almost occurs."

Katerina stared at him, mouth agape. "Remind me to tell Rick he may need the zombie apocalypse survival kit he has in his basement after all. Was there a close call any time recently?"

"The last one was in the colony of Roanoke, Virginia."

"Holy shit! Croa-freakin'-toan. The crazy nerd theories are actually true."

Pan started to walk away when Kat grabbed his arm and said, "Let's go outside. You've been cooped up all day. I've noticed you seem more at peace out in the open with the trees around you."

It was true. Being indoors felt unnatural to him. He figured it was part of the reason he'd never fit in on Olympus. Even though it was a realm with its own sky and land, he'd always felt trapped there when the mortal realm was so much bigger and just beyond the gates.

Kat held Pan's hand as they neared the front door. The fountain had become their favorite place to sit, and they often sat beside it at night and discussed anything and everything, catching up on years of not knowing one another.

"Do you think he put different blood in the bottle, and I would become a vamp or a zombie if I drank it?"

He stopped in his tracks. "You're not drinking it. Pour it down the drain when we come back inside. I hadn't even thought him capable of doing such a thing, but now...I don't know. I thought..." His jaw clenched.

"Pan." Katerina rested her free hand on his cheek. "You've been keeping something else from me. Every time ambrosia comes up, you look away and change the subject, or you try to distract me with sex. What is it you don't want me to know? If you didn't think he'd trick me into becoming a walking corpse, what were you worried about?"

"If you drink it, you will be tied to Dionysus. It is rumored that should he choose to, he could call you to his side and could locate you whenever he wished. I'm not sure if that is entirely true." He hesitated. "And, um...I have heard some stories about those Dionysus has given blood to. It drove those people mad. That is, sadly, fact."

"What! Do you know how close I was to drinking that blood tonight?"

∽

"YOU WERE REALLY GOING TO DRINK IT?" PAN PAUSED, HAND hovering above the doorknob. He didn't even blink. It was like his life depended on the answer.

"I was."

"What does that mean?"

She bit her bottom lip. *What did it mean?* She knew she'd been so terribly close to chugging some type immortal-O and throwing caution in the wind for this man. She didn't even notice when he was in his satyr form or his human one anymore. It didn't matter what he looked like, as long as it was him.

"It means... Pan? What is it?"

He was standing in the doorway, gawking at something in the yard. Kat followed his gaze and gasped. The fountain had been destroyed. Syrinx's likeness was shattered into dozens of pieces. Who could have done it, and how had they not heard something like that happening? The statue had been whole a few hours ago. She'd seen it from the front window.

Pan didn't say anything, but he moved toward the wreckage as though pulled to it. Kat followed, searching around warily but could find nothing suspicious. When they reached the debris, Pan picked up a chunk of marble and stared at it. Syrinx's face.

Kat folded her arms and looked away. She'd suspected Pan hadn't really loved Syrinx, but seeing him there looking so miserable... Tragedy surrounded the nymph, even in death.

He stiffened suddenly and returned to his feet. "We have a problem."

"What? Why?"

"Hoof prints. Recent. Made by a satyr, not an animal." He pointed. There were clear depressions in the soft dirt where something had left a trail coming from the woods, passing the fountain and continuing to the right side of the house.

"How do you know they aren't yours?" Kat thought it was a reasonable question as they had seen no other satyrs besides Pavlo and Melancton, both of whom left with Dionysus weeks ago. But she knew Pan wouldn't return to his house until he found the source of them.

"I don't leave footprints where I tread."

Kat stared down at his feet. He shifted to satyr form and

hopped around the other tracks. Nothing, not even a slight indention.

"Whoa, that's totally eerie." She'd never noticed. Hard to focus on footprints when she couldn't tear her gaze away from the man. It explained why the Jersey Devil could remain so elusive. Nobody could track a creature that left no sign of his presence.

"Yet another perk of being a god." He grinned, but it didn't last long. Pan began scanning the area. "Stay here. Maybe the satyr who did this is still hanging around." He was there one minute and gone the next. Invisible. Even though she knew he could do that, it still took her by surprise.

Pan would find the satyr, remove the threat, and they could resume their happy getting-to-know-each-other stage without further distraction. She would be fine where she was, in the open, with no discernable threat in sight. Kat narrowed her eyes at the tracks.

The extremely obvious tracks.

All delusions of safety promptly vanished. She didn't know why she didn't think of it before, but these were purposely left in the open. Whoever put them there wanted them discovered. They had to have used magic to tear the fountain to pieces since there hadn't been a sound from the act. So whoever did it must have left a trail knowing Pan would follow it. They'd probably circled around behind the house, out of view, and doubled back. To the spot where she stood, alone.

Kat had just opened her mouth to cry out when a hand clamped over it. She felt the cool metallic press of a blade under her throat and knew if she were to struggle, she'd die. She wasn't ready to die. She hadn't even had the chance to tell Pan that she loved him.

CHAPTER 17

"Don't make a sound, or I'll slice you open from neck to navel," a man with a rough voice gritted out. Hot, stale breath whisked across her cheek. She'd heard the voice before. Her assailant lifted his hand off her mouth and moved it to hold her steady around her waist. She prayed she was imagining the semi-hard erection poking into her hip, but she knew from experience that satyrs were ever-horny.

"Who are you?" she squeaked, determined not to ask *why* he was there. That was obvious: he wanted to hurt Pan. If this satyr knew Pan cared for her, she'd become leverage.

"I'm the one who's going to save you from your lover. You know everything he touches falls to ruin." It wasn't a question. He made it sound like plain fact. Kat couldn't see what he was holding to her throat, but she could make out that it was long and heavy at one end, and the handle was between his arm and across her chest.

An axe? Who in their right mind holds people hostage with an axe? Duh, an axe murderer.

She was so screwed. Her captor dragged her into the thicket of trees. Kat had to move her feet quickly to keep up with his long strides. If she were to slip, she'd slit her own throat.

"Saving me?" she gasped out when he paused, giving her a brief reprieve. "Funny way of showing it. Pan never held a blade to my neck to get me to comply."

"Perhaps not, but he did abduct you. You only think you want to be with him now because he plays the *syrinx* to you while you sleep and controls your thoughts."

Kat's blood ran cold. Could he do that? Her panic was short-lived. Pan told her he didn't have the *syrinx* in his possession anymore. Claimed the instrument had been too powerful and tempting to keep with him. He'd been so understanding the past two weeks by letting Kat spend time getting to know him, letting her fall in love with him on her own. He'd been adamant she decide her own future. He'd never keep her there against her will...at least not since the first time he took her to his home.

"This is about the *syrinx*? Is that why you destroyed the fountain?" She realized a statue of Syrinx would have been a great hiding place, a little obvious, but she saw the logic in looking for it there. "Pan doesn't have it."

"Pity," the satyr said, "but regardless, Pan and I have a score to settle. The *syrinx* would have been a great trophy to remind me of my revenge. Guess I will have to settle on his pretty female instead."

"Silenus! Let the girl go." A new voice came from her left. She saw movement in her peripheral vision, but it wasn't Pan. It was Pavlo.

The same Pavlo who'd supposedly left with Dionysus. Did the wine god want the *syrinx*? Kat wouldn't put it past him. Maybe they'd intended to kill Pan all along, but why go through the trouble of making her immortal? Something didn't add up.

"You again?" Silenus sneered from behind her. "Come to witness justice being served? Pan will die by my blade this night, and nothing you do will stop it."

Pavlo approached them, hands raised. He wore only jeans and was in his satyr form. His horns weren't as long as Melancton's, but they were straight as the Boeotians' were. Kat hoped Pavlo and Silenus' hostility toward each other meant they weren't working together.

Only one way to find out.

"Pavlo, help me." Kat felt the blade bite into her flesh with a burning sting.

"Nuh uh, little human. No one will be saving you, so do as you're told, so I don't have to slit that pretty throat of yours."

Pavlo scowled. "Do you think I will stand by and watch you kill another innocent female? This wasn't the plan. I should have killed you that night for what you did to my sister."

The plan? There was a plan? One they both know about?

"Like you could have. You were such a simpering, little fool, longing for a god to notice you and make you worthy in the eyes of women. Come to think of it, the whole problem didn't start with Pan as I have believed all this time. If *you* hadn't been such a weakling, you never would have promised me your whore of a sister, who went off to fuck someone else as soon as she could."

Pavlo's face turned molten. "You're the one who drove her into Pan's arms. Syrinx was a sweet girl. She would never hurt a fly. But you wanted to whore her out to Dionysus before marrying her."

Silenus removed the blade from Kat's neck and pushed her to the ground. Stunned, she raised a hand to her throat and felt the sticky wetness from where the axe had scraped the skin. She looked up in time to witness Silenus swinging the weapon into Pavlo's gut. After it connected, Silenus yanked it to the side, ripping his stomach open. Kat screamed.

Blood dripped from the sharp edge of the axe blade. The entire weapon was steel, the handle included. It had some sort of writing on it, but Kat couldn't tell what kind from that distance. The blade itself was small at the base and widened into a half circle. Pieces in the middle were cut out in an elaborate pattern resembling what looked like the horned head of a goat or a ram.

Silenus' eyes were wild. The salt-and-pepper colored hair upon his head and legs was matted, as though he'd ceased grooming long ago. His manhood waved about as he turned back to face her. *Would it kill a satyr to wear some pants? Pavlo had the decency to do it at least.* The smile across Silenus' face was cold and cruel when he took in her horrified expression. Kat glanced at Pavlo. He was still alive, but barely. Even in the moonlight, she could see his insides were extracted from the hole in his torso. Kat felt sick looking at it.

Silenus took a step toward her, his sinister smirk promising malicious deeds. Then a terrible crashing sounded through the treetops. With a roar, Pan—no, the Jersey Devil in all of his fearsome glory—landed between Kat and the other satyr. Silenus gaped. Evidently, he hadn't expected to face such a fearsome beast, and it worked in intimidating the satyr enough that he took several steps backward.

Silenus quickly recovered from his shock, once he gathered that the monster was Pan, and swung his axe. Pan leaped to the side, barely escaping the slash of cold steel aimed at his heart. He roared, loudly, and the ground around them quaked with the reverberation. Birds took flight from the surrounding trees with frightened squawks, going in every direction to escape. When silence fell once more, Silenus, like the coward he was, retreated through the trees.

Pan turned to her and noticed the small cut left from the sharp blade. The sound he made could only be likened to an attacking wolf about to defend his territory. Within the blink of an eye, he was on Silenus' trail, and soon they were both out of sight.

Kat stumbled to Pavlo. He cracked his eyes open and gazed up at her face. She wanted to cry; he'd gotten hurt because of her. If Pavlo hadn't tried to rescue her, he would be fine. She'd never watched someone die before. "Is there anything I can do?"

Pavlo shook his head and winced. His breathing grew sporadic.

"N-no. It's just a scratch." He grasped for her hand. "Tell Pan. T-tell him Syrinx's mother was not the same as m-mine. D-Dionys-sus didn't even know. He t-thought I took after m-my father." He groaned and coughed. He spat blood to the ground beside him. He explained as best he could how Syrinx's mother was a water nymph, and Pan had triggered the gene, though even Dionysus hadn't been able to figure out exactly how.

Why does it matter? Kat merely nodded, she'd tell him, but she didn't understand why Pavlo thought it was important after so long.

"P-pan has more p-power than he knows. Dion-nyyysus believes the nymphs no longer realize they're nymphs. Or the gene has gone dormant. No one has f-found one in over a thousand years. Pan is the on-only one w-who..." Pavlo's eyes closed and his breathing stopped.

"Pavlo?" She shook him gently. "You're immortal, right? You shouldn't be able to die from a little flesh wound." The wound was not little, but she attempted to downplay it for him as best she could.

"Technically, he cannot die from a flesh wound," a new voice said. "But Silenus wields a weapon forged of Hephaestusian steel. It was designed to eradicate a god, Pan specifically, and therefore can kill anyone or anything of equal or lesser power."

Kat glanced up. Melancton stood by a tall pine tree. His hair was wet and matted on the right side, and he had blood on his face. She didn't know how long he'd been standing there.

"What happened to you?"

"I attempted to keep Silenus reined in, but the psychotic fuck sucker-punched me with the hilt of his weapon." He bared his teeth and tenderly touched the side of his head, wincing. His hand came away stained.

"He's going to try to kill Pan." Kat's stomach knotted.

"Yes." Melancton's hooves clip-clopped as he strode closer to her. *Hey, he remembered pants* and *a shirt.* "Let's get you back to Pan's home and away from Silenus, if he succeeds." He held out a hand to her.

"If it's all the same to you, I'm not going anywhere with anyone but Pan. I don't trust you. And if you cared about my safety, you would go help him."

He expelled a breath and dropped his gaze. "Unfortunately, I cannot do that."

"Then you are working against him. Dionysus didn't want peace, did he? He wanted to use me to bait Pan so Silenus could kill him and steal the *syrinx.*"

Melancton hesitated. "I do not know if that is entirely true. I was charged to keep Silenus from Pan while he was in town. Though I tried to keep him from coming after either of you, I cannot break my vow now that events are in motion."

He hadn't denied Dionysus gave him those orders. Or that she was bait. And obviously the taxi that had transported them from the hotel hadn't made it to the airport. For all she knew, Dionysus was still here, munching on popcorn as the chaos unfolded. "Why can't you break them? Dionysus said you were present the night of the curse because you disobeyed orders. Is he here too, watching us?"

The reminder of what Dionysus said seemed to anger him, but he quickly disguised it. "Dionysus left weeks ago. Pavlo and I stayed only to keep Silenus restrained. Not very well, apparently. As for my past, I was to go to battle, yes, but after a bout of wine and thinking too much about things I could not have, I abandoned my people. That night I was cursed into a beastly form. Then my spear was used to murder a woman right before my eyes, and other...events kept me from atoning. Tell me I am not being punished for my actions."

"Awful things happen, Melancton. It doesn't mean you have to suffer for them the rest of your life, especially not for eternity. Make amends. Save Pan."

"I am sorry, Katerina, but I cannot."

~

PAN WAS GOING TO KILL HIM. HE WOULD RIP SILENUS' HEAD FROM his disgusting body and stomp on it like a pumpkin.

His target ran ahead like a frightened rabbit, knowing he stood no chance. However, Silenus still clutched his weapon in his hands, which kept Pan on guard. The satyr would play dirty. Perhaps Silenus played him, hoping Pan would strike so he could turn and bury the blade into his neck.

Pan's first goal was to disarm him. He unfurled his wings and took to the air, but he couldn't maneuver as swiftly as he'd like because of the branches. Flight saved him from having to watch his footing and dodging all the obstacles of the forest floor. Also, he'd have a better trajectory for striking once he got a clean break through the trees. As Silenus leaped over the small plants and upraised roots, Pan tired of the chase. At the first opportunity, he dove for the axe.

Just as he anticipated, Silenus twisted as he hopped over a fallen tree and swung the axe toward him. Pan spun out of the way, knocking into a tree with a *thud*. Wrongly assuming the hit would take Pan out of the fight, Silenus closed in. Gripping the axe handle with both hands, he brought the weapon up again. Pan growled and crouched down, set to attack. He flexed his fingers, letting the ends morph into claws, ready for Silenus to make his move.

Silenus pounced, swinging the axe downward while leaping, intending to cleave Pan's chest open. Throwing himself to the side, the axe planted into the tree where he'd been. Pan smiled, knowing animalistic features in that form made the motion unsettling. "You always did blow your load too fast. At least, that's what the nymphs told me." He slashed at Silenus with razor-tipped claws, cutting him down the side of his face and across his chest.

Silenus abandoned the axe and resorted to brute strength. Pan used his tail as a whip, slapping the man's face and knocking him over. The hit broke the skin down the satyr's other cheek. While Silenus was down, Pan pulled the weapon from the tree and tossed it into the woods where it couldn't be used against him. He wasn't ready to end the fight yet. No, he wanted Silenus to suffer. Pan tackled him, intending to rip the elder man's heart out with his bare hands.

The attack came from the left. Neither of them had time to react when it occurred. Pan was struck and he toppled. When he glanced up, Silenus stood there stunned. He vanished a moment later. Pan looked left and right, shifting back to his satyr form.

There. Silenus lay about twenty feet away. Headless, with a huge hole in the center of his chest.

"What the fuck?"

"Language, son."

No. This is not happening.

There was a slight blur in his peripheral, and then Hermes was there. He held Silenus' axe in one hand with the severed head dangling beside it by its hair. In the other hand, Hermes carried the satyr's dripping heart.

His father was dressed in swim trunks with white, Hawaiian flowers on them. The trunks themselves might have been blue or green, but in the evening's fading light it was difficult to discern. Hermes wore black flip-flops, and his black hair was tangled, slightly damp, cut to his shoulders. The pairs of tiny white wings on each ankle folded around his legs. They dissolved into what looked like wing tattoos. Cool trick. He must have picked it up to blend in with the humans. Hard to be inconspicuous when it looked like doves had flown through his heels and gotten stuck there.

210

"Were you at the beach?" Pan was appalled. Hermes was supposed to be in Olympus. Asleep!

Hermes raised a brow. "Will you dress yourself like someone civilized, or did you go Neanderthal when you were cursed? No one wants to see all that. Seriously. Why do the lot of you run around with your dicks swinging?"

Pan rolled his eyes, but reverted to his human glamour. He completed the illusion by dressing himself in jeans and a black T-shirt. "Tell me how you really feel, *Dad*."

"I will!" Hermes tossed Silenus' non-beating heart over his shoulder like it was a simple apple core. It hit a stump with a sickeningly wet slap. He then dropped the severed head and kicked it away from him, making a noise of disgust when the blood remained on his flip-flop.

Hermes waved the axe around to draw Pan's attention. "You see this?" He pointed at the goat headed emblem in the center. "Hephaestusian steel. The inscription denotes it is specifically designed to kill 'the first of the satyrs.' This asshole is running around carrying one of the only things in existence that can kill you, and you're going to dive-bomb him? You're not a mockingbird chasing a housecat, you're a god. Act like it. Next time, conjure something sharp and stab him in the face. At least blast him with a laser beam or something cool."

Hermes knew full well none of the gods had laser beams. Zeus had lightning, but that was different. Though Pan supposed he could've had the tree roots rise up and capture Silenus. *Ugh!* It pissed him off when he had good ideas after all was said and done.

"I had this," Pan said. "Silenus was as good as dead until you showed up and got in my way. Why the fuck are you even here?" He snatched the axe from his father, not trusting the prick not to use it. "I thought you were hibernating."

"Does it look like I want to be here right now? I was in Malibu, chillaxing in my beachside hot tub when suddenly my phone rang. It was Zeus letting me know my son was possibly about to be beheaded by an idiot, and if I had any sense, I'd drop what I was doing because he was anticipating meeting his new granddaughter-in-law and great-grandson."

Pan's mouth dropped open. "Wait. Run that past me again."

"*Mazel tov*. It's a boy." Hermes couldn't sound less excited.

"That's not possible." He thought he was sterile. Other gods knocked up women left and right where he never had, and furthermore, no satyrs had ever sired young. It was part of the curse he supposed. "I have never impregnated anyone, so why now?"

"That's exactly what I said when I knocked up your mother. Oh, she was *maaaaad...*" His eyes glazed over. After staring at nothing for a few moments, he shook himself. "Anyway, if we don't get your woman immortalized soon, your son will be mortal. Zeus doesn't like watching his family die unless he smites them himself." Hermes glanced around. "Where is the ole lady anyhow?"

"You didn't answer my question. Why aren't you, and Zeus for that matter, sleeping like everyone locked outside of Olympus was told?"

"Oh, that." Hermes waved a hand dismissively. "We only told people that so they'd leave us alone. Got tired of answering all their cries for help. Pushed them off on newer deities. The gods who didn't want change and wanted to be all-powerful all the time were booted out, the rest we forgot to tell. Sorry, son. Your memo was lost in the mail. Well, it was all a bit need-to-know, anyway, and we didn't have cell phones back then. To be fair, you were a bit busy crying over dead nymphs and didn't need anything else to worry about. You weren't exactly speaking to me anyway."

Pan gritted his teeth so hard his jaw began to tic. He lunged at his father, wanting to throttle him, but Hermes was too quick and hovered in midair a few feet away, wings at his ankles fluttering at a rapid pace. Pan wondered how he kept his flip-flops on when he skyrocketed about like a hummingbird. *The random shit I think about.*

"Now, now. Patricide does not become you. And here I was helping you so you didn't become a murderer like some of the rest of us. I know how much it means to you to not be like us." His tone softened and Pan could almost believe Hermes' was sad.

"I didn't need your help!"

Hermes crossed his arms as he landed on a branch out of Pan's reach...for the moment. "Of course you did. You've never killed anyone in all your years on this world. Zeus and I agreed we didn't want you to start now. It was the obvious choice that I save you from such dark deeds, and I haven't gotten to do Zeus' smiting for so long." He appeared positively euphoric at that thought.

"Whatever. You helped. Go back to your hot tub." Pan turned his back and walked off.

"Not so fast." Hermes appeared in front of him.

"Oh, you're still here?" Pan brushed past him as he headed in the direction he'd left Katerina. She had a small cut he needed to attend to. It didn't look serious, but that bastard had marred her skin. He wanted to kill Silenus all over again. And fucking Hermes had denied him the vengeance that had been his by right.

"I know about the ambrosia Dionysus gave you, and you need to know he cannot be trusted. You cannot accept any handouts he gives you."

"No shit, Sherlock."

"Dionysus is seeking the *syrinx*. Apollo has a spy on the inside of the Boeotian satyr clan or herd or flock or whatever the hell they are called? Gaggle maybe? A gaggle of satyrs? No? Anyway, you don't want to do anything that will tie your chick up with that yahoo."

Pan wondered who the spy was, but he'd have plenty of time to consider it once he made Hermes leave. "That's very interesting; color me intrigued. Why are you here again?"

"To make your woman immortal so you can stop being a dick and get an attitude adjustment."

Yeah, okay. Pan was the dick. Of course he was. As much as he wanted to tell his father to fuck off for abandoning him when he'd been cursed, Pan wanted to keep Katerina too much to continue the argument. And even if Hermes made Pan's life miserable, he was a god who could be trusted in the long run. He was just annoying. "Fine. But when it's done, you're leaving."

"*Pfft.* Like I'd stay in the dump you call a home anyway. I might get attacked by a killer dust bunny or something equally disgusting." He looked back down at the severed head. "Hey, ever seen a three-headed dog play fetch with a decapitated head?"

CHAPTER 18

The sound of crunched pinecones and footsteps over dried leaves pulled Kat from her thoughts. She rose to her feet as Pan came into her line of sight, but she halted as she was about to run toward him. A dark-haired man in shorts appeared behind Pan—hovering above the ground. And he looked very similar to Pan. So similar, in fact, that he could have been his brother.

Okay...

But if Pan was the Jersey Devil *and* a satyr *and* a god, then it wasn't even remotely strange that half-naked men could float. Her life really had taken the most unlikely turn.

The floating man seemed to appear directly in front of her without having moved. He kissed her hand even though Kat hadn't even offered it to him.

"So you must be Katerina. My son told me all about you." He winked at her, and he smiled, displaying a set of dimples.

"Son?" She couldn't help it. She immediately dropped her gaze to his ankles as he floated down to the ground and the little white wings stopped fluttering. "Hermes."

He bowed dramatically, and then rewarded her with a wide grin. "In the flesh."

215

"I told you nothing about her. Quit lying," Pan interrupted. He didn't seem pleased. But he did have possession of the axe Silenus had wanted to kill him with, which had to be a good sign.

"I'm so glad you're alive." Kat removed her hand from Hermes' grip and flung herself at Pan. She hugged him tightly.

Pan kissed her then, claiming her mouth as his reward for making it back to her alive. Kat stepped back and took the axe from him, noting absently the blade stained with blood. Amazingly, she didn't care. She tossed it aside and then kissed him back like her life depended on it. She almost forgot they had an audience until Hermes cleared his throat behind them.

Kat reluctantly pulled away. "Later." She winked at Pan and glanced back at his father. The same dark wavy hair and eyes, similar facial structure...yeah, Kat could see it.

"What happened?" she asked finally, bending to collect the axe she had dropped. It *did* have a goat head in the middle, with curled horns like Pan's, slanted eyes, and a goatee. Strange lettering appeared here or there. Greek? It was really a remarkable weapon with its slightly curvy handle and semicircular blade. It looked like a combination of a battle axe and movie relic. The sticky red-brown smear along the sharp edge chilled her as she finally let herself think about the implications.

Silenus had to be dead, and she should be upset. But...she wasn't. She gripped the axe handle tightly, her knuckles turning white.

"Be careful with that." Pan gently took the blade away from her. "You could have cut your stomach." He stared at her midsection with a frown. Then he squinted as though trying to see through her shirt or something. She started to feel self-conscious about it. Was she getting fat? Kat glanced down.

"What happened to Pavlo?" Pan asked suddenly, bringing her back to her senses.

"Melancton showed up after you and Silenus disappeared. He

took Pavlo's body with him." Though she suspected he left some internal organs in the leaves.

"Which way?" Pan clenched his fists around the axe handle.

"Just leave it, Pan. Melancton said we shouldn't be bothered again. *He* didn't mean us harm."

"That's what Dionysus said before Silenus tried to kill me, and possibly you. Sorry, but I don't believe a word either has to say. Melancton is loyal to Dionysus."

"Is he?" Hermes asked suddenly, but it had sounded rhetorical. The Olympian studied his fingernails. "Hmm. I guess he is, if you say so." He motioned for them to leave. "Go converse whilst I give Hades a call. He'll send Cerberus to collect Silenus while I personally escort his filthy soul to the Underworld. The last thing you need is him haunting the woods." As an afterthought, he said, "Should probably take Pavlo too while I'm at it."

"How is a dog going to col—never mind. I don't want to know." Kat's mind was on overload with processing all that had happened. When Hermes left them, she whispered, "He takes souls to the Underworld?"

Pan shook his head. "It's not his primary job, but he has been known to do so in the past. He's right though, Silenus' soul doesn't need to be wandering around until someone comes to collect it."

As they traipsed through the trees, Pan told her about his fight with Silenus, and how Hermes showed up to deliver the deathblow. He seemed irritated about it, and Kat wondered if he felt he'd needed to prove himself. But Hermes taking the decision from him may have been for the best. She was relieved he'd not killed anyone. One day she hoped Pan would be too.

"Did you really want his death on your conscience?" Kat caught him staring at her stomach again. He looked away quickly. *Okay, no more cheeseburgers for her.*

"I hadn't ever killed anyone before." Pan seemed to ponder it. "Which is being remarkably well behaved, if you know your

Greek legends." He snorted. "I'm accused of murdering all kinds of women in the stories. That's me, rapey, murdery, ugly Pan."

"You know you're *none* of those things. I know you aren't. But why are you so upset that Hermes saved you from changing one of those traits that make you so unique?"

"Pride mostly. Silenus killed Syrinx. He hurt you. Letting him live was no longer an option. How am I supposed to keep you safe if others fight my battles for me? If I can't protect you myself, staying with me is a risk."

"The battle is far from over. You said Dionysus is after the *syrinx*? I gathered as much from Silenus' destruction of her likeness. He must have thought you'd hidden it there. So let's deal with one crisis at a time, and be glad this one is over. You may not have killed Silenus, but the deed was accomplished. Your hands don't have blood on them."

Pan shook his head. "They do have blood on them, though. It's my fault Syrinx and Klytie died that night. I may not have delivered the blow, but it was because of me. Silenus was here to kill me, so his death was my fault. Pavlo's as well."

"You're going to be stubborn about this, aren't you?"

"Sorry. I know you're trying to help, it's just...I don't know... *Ugh.* I had him right there and then Hermes took the choice from me. I *had him*, vixen."

Kat dragged Pan to a stop. She turned his face toward her and held it there with both hands. "Stubborn man. Hermes was trying to help, not hinder you. And you did keep me safe today. You chased him away from where I was. Whether or not you killed him or let him go, you got him away from me. I was safe."

"Yeah, but—" He tried to pull away, yet Kat didn't let him.

"There is no, 'but.' He had a weapon that could kill you. He'd already killed Pavlo, and they were working for the same team. You were fearless. You can't possibly think because you didn't kill him you are less of a man. In fact, it's because you didn't kill him that makes you more of one to me."

He shut his eyes and leaned into her touch. "I would have gone through with it. Killing him, I mean." It was no more than a whisper.

"I know. But you didn't have to. Be grateful."

Loud barking reverberated through the forest, like a pack of wild dogs had appeared out of thin air. Kat tensed, but didn't see any nearby.

"Don't worry. It's just Cerberus. Let's get out of here."

Kat nodded in agreement, not particularly keen on meeting a giant hound from hell. *Just Cerberus, indeed. Like it's no big deal.* She'd had her fair share of cryptids for a lifetime.

"I don't deserve you," Pan said a short time later, keeping pace beside her. "If you had any sense at all, you would have run screaming weeks ago."

"I tried that. You kidnapped me and locked me in your bedroom."

He had the decency to look sheepish. "Oh, yeah. Sorry about that." He hesitated before he continued his thoughts. "You still could escape, you know. Return to a boring life without gods and satyrs and cryptids."

"I don't want to leave. Quit trying to chase me away."

"Foolish."

"I love you."

Pan tripped over a root, and his glamour vanished. His curled horns popped out from the sides of his head. He looked every bit a nature deity. So his legs ended in hooves and were exceptionally hairy. So what? There was no greater man than him, and the forest, whether it was the Pine Barrens or Arcadia or somewhere new, was his kingdom.

His appearance might have been shocking at first glance, but he was compassionate and gentle. He had his own alpha streak, but he didn't let it rule him. And there was no one else she'd want to spend the rest of her life with.

To spend eternity with.

"What did you say?" Pan straightened.

"I said, I love you, you silly satyr." She pulled him down by his horns and kissed him.

"I should tell you something," Pan began as he started to undress her.

"I probably should too. I almost forgot because of Hermes being here." She told him what Pavlo said before he died and Pan frowned, his brows creasing narrower with each bit.

"So Pavlo believes I inadvertently triggered something genetic in Syrinx and made her nymph gene awaken? I'd always wondered how the change happened. Interesting."

"But don't you see?" She backed away from his hold on her. "If the nymphs of this age don't know they're nymphs, you can have Hermes or another god help you find one and break the curse with her. Or trigger her nymph-ness or whatever you did with Syrinx. I can't help you. You have to remain cursed to be with me." She hung her head, ashamed. "You'll have to be a satyr forever."

"Two problems with your theory. The first being I had to have sex with Syrinx to make her a nymph, and I can't have sex with a nymph until a lunar eclipse, *if* I wanted to not be a satyr. If she isn't a nymph until after the sex, the window of time will have passed, and if it doesn't void the no-nymphs-'til-the-eclipse rule since she wouldn't be a nymph *at the time*, I would have to find another nymph. Vicious cycle."

Kat hadn't thought it through as he clearly had before, and she wasn't sure she appreciated that he'd given it consideration. In fairness though, he'd had a lot of time before meeting her to deliberate if such a thing was at all possible.

"The second, and most important problem, is you are wrong. You did break my curse."

She opened her mouth to call him some form of ridiculous when he held a finger to her lips to stall her.

"Hear me out, Katerina. You went through all that earlier about how I was trying to get rid of you, yet here you are trying to boot me away. Stop being fickle."

She attempted to bite his finger, but he was too quick for her.

"Before I met you, I existed, but I wasn't truly alive anymore. After I got the lust under control, I'd only blow off steam with women when I had to. I amused myself by scaring humans with their local superstitions. Then you appeared, and I wanted to be alive again. I wanted to put on a human glamour and sweep you off your feet."

He grinned. "Of course, that wasn't what happened. However, I did sweep you off your feet when I flew away with you. It was unfortunate I wasn't able to have my wicked way with you for several nights." He winked. "I love you, Katerina. You brought me out of the darkness I was living in for centuries. I don't mind being a satyr forever as long as you are by my side through all of it."

She wiped at her face as her eyes misted up. "Damn, I think I have dirt in my eye."

As Pan made another move to unbutton her jeans, she halted him. "Wait, what was it you were going to tell me?"

He kissed her, and she realized he was avoiding the subject. Well, Kat had some news for him: she was on to his little trick. She only let the thought get away from her because her body was on fire. So alive, electric with lust and warm with the knowledge her love for him was truly reciprocated.

"I'll tell you after." He licked her neck, and his tongue left little goosebumps in its wake. Her toes curled. She kicked her shoes off so she could shimmy out of her pants and panties. Pan ripped her shirt down the middle, and her bra followed in the same fashion. *Aww, I liked that bra.* When she pouted her bottom lip, he tugged at it with his teeth, causing her to open for his kisses once more.

He brought her onto his lap as he lay on the ground, and Kat lowered herself on top of him. She needed him inside her more than she needed to breathe. Pan guided her hips as he thrust upward, and she met him in the middle, moving downward. She knew it turned him on, so she fondled her breasts as she undulated, and he began to thrust more erratically.

When her orgasm hit, she cried out and laughed as he spilled his seed inside and ripples of aftershocks shook her to the core.

Pan sat up and kissed her, their bodies still joined as he cradled her against him.

"That Cerberus. You should have seen how excited he was when he chased down Silenus' head. Though the one on the right was greedy and swallowed it whole..." Hermes came to an abrupt stop and gawked at them. "Oh, come on, really? In the dirt like animals? Get a fucking room." He covered his eyes, and then peeked through his fingers.

Pan growled and conjured a blanket around them. "You were supposed to go to the house when you were done, not linger around the forest."

"I told you, I wanted to know the mother of my grandchild. Hard to do that when you won't take her to the house because you don't want her to talk to me."

Grandchild! Kat looked at Pan and back at Hermes. Then she recalled Pan's observation of her stomach from earlier. His reluctance to tell her what else had been plaguing his thoughts. *He'd known!*

"Wha—" The world spun.

"Oops. You didn't tell her, did you?"

Pan glared at his father. "I was about to tell her before you showed up bragging about your morbidity."

The world went dark.

CHAPTER 19

Melancton had retrieved Pavlo's body from the Pine Barrens, and since Silenus hadn't been heard from, it would seem Pan had triumphed after all. The elder satyr was dead. Good riddance to that nuisance. Dion stared at himself in the mirror. His plan had failed, but that only meant he could act on one of the backup plans he had in place. Still, Silenus had contained so much rage that it was a shame he couldn't follow through.

Silenus had been his most devoted member of his favored circle of humans in the old days. Back before Pavlo sought entrance and Syrinx came into the picture. Just like a woman to ruin a good thing. They were good for sex, but not much else. Dion had learned that they were more trouble and heartbreak than they were worth long ago and had no aspirations of ever going down that route again. His only mistress now was Power, and he courted her with everything he was worth.

The reflection in his bedroom mirror glared back at him—his true reflection, thanks to that meddlesome idiot of a god, Pan. The horns protruding from his head were huge, solid thorns of ebony. So thick at the base he couldn't wrap a hand completely around one. They curved out from his temples and then narrowed up vertically as they reached the sharp, dangerous points. His irises glowed with unnatural red light. He didn't need to look down at the tawny, tufted legs with cloven hooves to know how hideous he was.

When Pan had countered the curse meant to deform him, Dion hadn't anticipated he would have succeeded. True, Pan was cursed, but not in the way he should have been. While he, Dionysus, was supposed to be beautiful and perfect in form, but wasn't anymore, not since that night. No, he had to expend perfectly good energy on glamour like the rest of the *Satyroi*. It was exhausting. He'd been reborn after death, the only full-blooded god to ever have a mortal mother. Since Dion was better than Pan, he should never have had to share a curse with him. Especially one Dion had devised.

He wasn't going to share this burden much longer. He'd get his hands on the *syrinx* and then would have the power necessary to stamp down the curse without diminishing his god powers. Truthfully, Pavlo and Silenus' deaths had improved his strength greatly as the magic he'd placed in their *thyrsi* diverted back to the source: Dion himself. They didn't have to die for it to happen, but he did prefer to tie up loose ends. He could, in theory, slaughter the other Boeotians to retrieve the rest of the magic he'd shared with them. But Dion needed the satyrs. Once he had the *syrinx*, their usefulness would run out. And power, well...power would never be a problem again.

With the *syrinx,* he could return to Olympus and gain access to the prison of the Titans. The location of their prison varied in legend. Some said the Titans were locked in the middle of the ocean. Some would say Hades kept an eye on them within Tartarus. But the prison was underneath that forsaken mountain named Olympus. Where better to hide their dungeon than underneath the gates to the realm that housed the Olympian's own asses?

The Titans had far greater powers than the Olympians, almost as potent as the Primordials had been, and once Dion restored them, they would be forthcoming. Rhea had saved him once; it had been she who'd returned life to his body when he'd been murdered by Hera's hired assassins. If Dion returned the favor to Rhea, she was sure to grant him a boon. A Titan could lift the curse, he hoped.

Dion took a long swig from his wineglass. The vintage soothed him. Soon Pan's woman would be tied to him, and, like the maenads, she would go bat-shit crazy under his direct influence. He would use her to maneuver Pan however he saw fit, but he didn't *want* to go that route, at least not yet. He'd already underestimated Pan far too much, and at the moment, he only wanted the *syrinx*.

How dare he think to kill two of my servants! The mirror before him shattered within its frame, obscuring his reflection and creating a mosaic of tiny slivers of himself. Dion sighed. He had to rein this rage in. It seemed to worsen as the years progressed. Almost as though he lost control of his own mind momentarily, ever since...

He didn't want to think about *that*. Not now.

He refocused on the meeting with the Boeotians he was due to attend shortly. Silenus had killed Pavlo, not Pan. But...the Boeotians didn't need to know that. Melancton would keep his mouth shut, Dion could count on it. Perhaps the deaths of two of their own would be the catalyst to bring the Boeotians together against the Arcadians in this hunt for the *syrinx*. The Boeotians would aid in his return to power.

Dion took a deep breath and concentrated on his energy, creating the flawless, imperceptible illusion. The horns and the hooves detracted, and he appeared as humanesque as a god could. Clothing himself in a crisp black suit, he straightened his favorite burgundy tie as the finishing touch on what he considered perfection. It was rude to keep company waiting.

The loss of Silenus wouldn't upset anyone. The satyr had been useless for the most part, complaining constantly. But Pavlo, despite his dislike of Dion, had been useful and likable. A loss the others would surely feel, and damned if he didn't realize he was back to needing a personal assistant again. He'd worry about it later.

Dion traversed through the upstairs corridor with its richly furnished carpeting and elaborate candelabras that left the smell of beeswax permeating in the air. The stairs were marble, padded with a red carpeted strip down the middle. The banister was solid gold. Why should he live in less than exquisite comfort and style because the doors to Olympus had shut so long ago? No, the Olympians were not slumbering. They hid away and mocked them all, Apollo especially. His death would be one of the first Dion saw to.

The ground floor foyer displayed a huge, ceiling-to-floor portrait of himself—or rather a classical depiction that was fairly accurate that he'd taken a liking to. Many artistic interpretations amused Dion, especially the ones which portrayed him wearing a crown of grapes off the vine. As though he ever wore grapes in his hair. Humans had such imaginations.

The formal dining room had a long, solid oak table which seated twenty diners easily. There were only nine men present. Except they weren't men, not anymore. They were all satyrs. The Boeotians. Not one among his guests knew Dion shared their curse. As far as anyone was concerned, the curse hadn't worked on him. The misdirection and display of his power kept them in check.

The satyrs ceased conversing amongst themselves as he entered the room and took his place at the head of the table. His guests were dressed formally, as Dion always demanded for a seat at his table. And what a table it was!

The cook had prepared a succulent meal of ham with several appetizing side dishes of vegetables and pastas. The mouthwatering aroma held a hint of spices and roasted meat. His stomach clenched in anticipation, even though he didn't have an appetite that demanded he consume food often. A smorgasbord was a thing to desire regardless.

"Gentlemen," Dion began as a courtesy. The men at the table were not gentlemanly in the least, with the exception of Melancton perhaps. "I have gathered you here today because the *Satyroi* are on the brink of a crisis." He clasped his hands in front of him on the table, keeping his posture and doing his best to appear concerned when what he really wanted to do was tear into that baked ham.

A few of the satyrs looked nervous while others seemed intrigued. Adonis appeared simply bored, his head leaning against his fist. Melancton displayed no reaction, which wasn't surprising.

"It's come to my attention that Pan has murdered your brethren, Pavlo and Silenus." Dion took a sip of his wine as he let the news sink in. Melancton raised a brow. Dion negated his silent question with a tilt of his head. Perhaps Dion would give him Pavlo's old job to ensure he stayed quiet.

A satyr with light brown hair and a crooked nose spoke up. "Why would Pan do that? I understand why he'd have a grudge against Silenus, but Pavlo?"

"I wish I knew, Theron. I wish I knew. Syrinx was Pavlo's sister. Maybe he decided to take revenge on both of them for what happened. Or maybe he's finally snapped. No one's seen him in so long, it is quite possible he's gone insane from solitude."

Theron contemplated it further. "What are we supposed to do about it?"

"Punish him." Dion had to force himself not to smile. "Unfortunately, we cannot act on Pan without the *syrinx* or Hephaestusian steel. It is rumored Pan has such a weapon, but he has entrusted one of the Arcadians with the *syrinx*. We need the instrument to disarm him. Otherwise, he will pick us off, one by one." Luckily Silenus had never been fool enough to bring the weapon around the few times Dion insisted he be present, making the lie possible as it slid silkily off his tongue.

He was pleased to see the reactions going in the direction he wanted. Looks of shock, horror, even disbelief met his gaze. Well, other than Melancton and his eternally blank expression. He disapproved though. That satyr was eternally too good for his own wellbeing. It almost made Dion regret doing what he had. Almost.

"Let's start our hunt with Pan's closest friend, as he was the most trusted of the Arcadians. Rumor has it he'd left Greece with the instrument, but I dismissed it, believing Pan would never hand such an item to a non-Olympian for safe keeping. Furthermore, after much research, I believe I know where Ariston is hiding." Dion watched Adonis from the corner of his eye. "I would like one of you to find out if he has the *syrinx* in his possession. I already have a strategy in motion to distract him. Through careful heredity tracking, I believe I've found a nymph."

Having money in the present era meant resources. With the Internet and connections, anything could be tracked down if the time and money allowed. Unfortunately, Lily Anders was the only lead that panned out, and once he settled on a way to bring her into Bach Industries, it would be time to move onto phase two. Ariston was the strongest contender to have the *syrinx*. He and Pan were closer than Ariston was with his own brother, Adonis.

Whispers erupted around the table. Eneas stood abruptly. "Why waste her on an Arcadian? Wouldn't it please you more to give her to one of us?" Several heads nodded, agreeing with his suggestion. Dion had expected the uproar. A nymph was their only hope of breaking the curse, and none had been found. If any of the *Satyroi* deserved a chance to be rewarded, it was his own followers. Not one of Pan's. But a beautiful woman, and one that promised freedom, was the best way to distract an enemy, and since he couldn't feel Katerina Silverton's life force coursing through his blood, he knew she'd not yet taken the ambrosia he'd left her. If she refused to drink it, she wouldn't be controllable, and was officially a lost cause. Of course, ambrosia wasn't guaranteed to work the way he'd intended. Apollo was only able to find someone he'd given blood to if they were outside in sunlight, just like anyone else he needed to locate. *Served him right.* If anything though, at least Katerina would keep Pan preoccupied and out of the way.

"You haven't let me explain myself," Dion said patiently. "The nymph is merely to be a distraction. Dear gods, I don't mean for Ariston to keep her. A Satyr Moon is on the horizon, or it will be at the time this play goes into motion. The one to take on this duty may keep the nymph to himself when he's done, or give her to another if he desires."

Adonis gulped down his wine, straightened up, and cleared his throat. "Ariston is my brother. I would like this task, sir."

Around him, the Boeotians all started complaining at once. All of them wanted their curse removed, and Adonis had never been that friendly to them.

Dion pretended to contemplate the offer even though he'd been counting on Adonis' cooperation. "I'm not sure if that's wise. What if your brother is hostile and you have to harm him?"

"I harbor no feelings of love or compassion toward him. He brought this curse upon me, and I will never forgive him." Ariston was the reason Adonis had been present that night. Hatred would serve its purpose in completing the task.

"Stay around this evening, Adonis. I will fill you in on the details, and we will begin to plan our course of action."

Adonis nodded in acknowledgement.

"On that note, let's eat." Dion smiled at his guests and stabbed a fork into a slice of pork.

CHAPTER 20

K at was pregnant. She hadn't seen it coming, at least not anytime soon. She woke up in the bed she shared with Pan, dressed in a pair of pajama shorts and a tank top and glared at the ceiling. How long had he known and not told her? Masculine voices alerted her that Pan and Hermes were downstairs.

With an exasperated huff, Kat kicked the covers away and pulled herself out of the bed. Her head was a bit foggy, but she managed. She padded quietly out the room and down the stairs where she found the two of them thick as thieves in the kitchen. Hermes waved at her from his perch on the island countertop, and Pan ceased pacing when he heard her approach.

"Katerina." He bounded toward her. "Are you okay?"

She brushed him off, eyeing Hermes warily. She didn't know what to make of him as he sat on the edge of the counter, kicking his winged feet. "I'm fine. I was a bit shocked is all."

Understatement.

"Well, I'm glad you're awake," Hermes called from behind Pan. He lifted the bottle of ambrosia Dionysus had left and popped the cork. It struck the ceiling before landing on the floor with a barely audible *thud*.

"Um...you might not want to drink that," Kat offered.

"Don't worry. I know full well what this is." He examined the bottle in the light. "Ambrosia, literally the essence of eternal life. It is almost poetic that what gives eternal life isn't water from a mysterious fountain no one will ever find, a grail hidden by Templar knights, or a glass of the most delicious wine to ever pass one's lips, but blood itself. The very source of life within any being. I can understand how the sharing of immortal blood is a method of sharing immortality. It makes such perfect sense, it's almost painful. However, when things are so easy there is usually a reason."

Hermes hopped off the counter and carried the bottle to the sink. He proceeded to pour Dionysus' blood down the drain. "Bottoms up."

Kat gasped. "What are you doing?" Her eternity with Pan was being washed away before her eyes.

"Oh, this? I am getting rid of Dionysus' blood. What does it look like? Trust me when I say I'm doing you a huge favor." He winked at her, flashing his dimples as he grinned mischievously. "All those who have become immortal by his blood have been put down. Violently."

"But...I..." What could she say? She'd had some of his blood already, and she didn't want Pan to witness her die, which she would without the ambrosia. She could take Pan's blood, but she didn't want to be a vampire or zombie or whatever else could happen. Maybe Hermes didn't think those options were horrible. There was always the possibility he assumed she wanted to drink it just because it resulted in immortality. That she was using his son for personal gain.

Pan wrapped his arms around Kat's stomach, pulling her against him. Comforting her, keeping her close. She needed his strength, his warmth to guide as well as anchor her.

Hermes said, "My son is worried Dionysus plans to tie you to him for malicious purposes. He also told me you worried the blood may not be the wine god's at all. And since the world wouldn't welcome new *vrykolakas* or *letum*...or gods know what else it could have resulted in, it seems the best course of action is to avoid the what-if scenarios and find a new approach."

"Like what?"

Hermes rested the empty wine bottle on the counter. "Zeus is my father too. You could take of my blood, and both you and your unborn son will become immortal. Zeus has consulted the Fates in this. If you take from me, the ambrosia will work as it should."

Everyone wanted her to drink their blood lately. *Gross.*

"That all sounds very convenient." Kat always believed if something was too good to be true, it was. That was one of the factors keeping her from drinking Dionysus' blood sooner. She broke away from Pan's hold and pivoted so she could see them both as she spoke, "My baby's going to be a demigod." She had a hard time processing it. "He's not going to be born fully grown, is he? I've heard some pretty crazy birth stories about the Greek gods and goddesses. There's one where Aphrodite was the result of a castrated penis landing in sea foam."

Hermes threw his head back and laughed. "That one was embellished to irritate Aphrodite. Kinda like I told everyone Pan's mother was different people to confuse them all. When really his mother was Hybris."

Pan did a double take at Hermes while sputtering. "Excuse me? Did you say the goddess of excessive pride, arrogance, and just about every other terrible attribute known of man, is my mother?"

Hermes was by his side in a flash and patted his shoulder. "But, hey...you didn't turn out so bad, did ya?" And in the lighting of the kitchen, it was remarkable how alike the two looked. They could be twins, other than the wings versus horns and what not. Well, and Hermes' face was slightly narrower. Pan was taller. *Oh, God, I can't stop staring.*

Pan was at a total loss for words as he gawked at his father like Hermes had grown additional heads. Kat couldn't fault him. There was something a bit dumbfounding about learning important information from a passing comment. *At least Pan didn't faint like I did.*

"I never heard of a goddess named Hubris." Kat frowned.

"*Hy*bris," Hermes corrected. "She's the goddess of hubris, but it isn't her name. It pisses her off if you get it wrong—in case you ever meet her."

"Oh. Um, thanks. I guess."

Not seeming to be concerned about rendering his son speechless, Hermes clapped his hands together. "So, let's do this, shall we?" He returned to the counter where he'd been sitting before and produced a glass pitcher from the cabinet underneath. Kat had used it to make lemonade a few days before.

Hermes held his wrist over the opening at the top, and a small dagger appeared in his opposite hand. He slit the skin from his wrist up to the midpoint between his palm and elbow. The blood poured out and into the glass like a dense, red, watered-down milkshake or syrup. It was thicker than what could be mistaken as wine. Her stomach churned, and she had to turn away to keep from being sick.

"It'll be okay." Pan drew her attention away from the bloodletting in the kitchen as her stomach jerked irritably and she choked on a retch. He'd finally recovered from the mystery of his parentage being revealed when she'd started to dry heave. It shouldn't warm her heart that her nearly vomiting outweighed his shock, yet it did.

"You don't have to drink all of it at once," Pan said, rubbing her back.

She gagged again. "Not. Helpful."

"Besides," Hermes added, "I've heard ambrosia tastes sweet. It's not coppery like normal blood. Or maybe I'm thinking I heard that because I believe I taste delicious. You'll have to let me know."

"I don't think I can do this," Kat whispered. She tried to calm herself, but she felt her breaths coming faster than before, deeper. She was panicking.

Pan kissed her, and her world faded away. The sound of the blood dripping as Hermes' wound began to heal itself became white noise in the background. All she knew in that moment was Pan. He was rather distracting, and her disgust vanished, leaving only the throbbing need of desire.

Kat pulled away before they accidentally showed Hermes a repeat of their earlier performance. A glance back at the counter revealed the pitcher of blood was half-full, and she managed to observe it without the urge to vomit from the sight. Maybe it was a pregnancy thing, considering she'd seen leopards and lions tearing into gazelles and never was grossed out by the blood.

Wiping his arm with a paper towel, Hermes said, "The amount in here should make about six cups. It's more than what is usually required, because you have to ensure the immortality of the baby as well as yourself. Do not dilute it with water or wine, or else it will pass from your system and won't hold. Drink one cup in the morning and one at night for three days. Start tomorrow because you're looking a bit pale."

Kat returned her gaze to the pitcher and noticed the liquid had changed color and consistency. It now looked like a rich burgundy wine rather than syrupy blood. *What the hell?*

Hermes noticed it. "Hey, look at that. It almost looks appetizing now." He put it in the refrigerator and then handed Pan a scrap of paper with three phone numbers on it. There was a smear of blood. Kat saw that Hermes' wrist was completely healed. Only a light smudge of crimson proved something had happened there.

"The top number is mine, and the second is Zeus. Hybris is the third; although, I do warn you, she lives up to her title. She's too proud and arrogant to admit to motherhood. I'm only giving you this because she may, despite any excuse she gives you, wish to know her grandchild. She visited you often when you were a baby, even if she didn't tell anyone she was doing it. Give her a chance. I only kept it from you because she asked me to."

With his parting words, Hermes' wings spread out from his ankles, and then flapped a few times to warm up for their rapid little flutters, and he was gone. The door slammed a second later.

"Snap, he's fast."

"It's annoying, isn't it?" Pan angled his head to the side as if he was listening for something.

"He wasn't as bad as you'd led me to believe." He was actually pretty amusing to be around, if not sickening when you just wanted to have alone time with his super-hot son.

"Try living with him constantly dropping in to harp at you. You'd change your opinion. Fast."

"Are you going to call your mother?"

He lifted one shoulder and dropped it again. "Maybe. Not like she ever tried to contact me. And why do gods have cell phones anyway? This is weird as hell." He made a face.

"Give it some thought. Perhaps wait until after the baby is born and give yourself time to think about what you want to say to her." She rubbed her belly and smiled up at Pan. Kat never really gave motherhood much thought, but she was surprisingly happier about it than she would have believed.

"I really love you," he told her.

Her smile turned into a wide grin. "And I love you."

"Get naked." His voice became deeper and huskier. How could one ever say no to that?

"Make me."

She sprinted up the stairs and made it to the landing before he caught her, lifting her into his arms where she kicked her feet and squealed with delight as he marched her toward their room. He yanked the shirt over her head as he dropped her onto the bed. Pan hadn't bothered dressing Kat with a bra before putting her to bed earlier. Panties either, she realized as she shimmied out of her shorts. He'd been anticipating this. Truth be told, she was anticipating an eternity of this. And if the immortality came with the increased stamina she'd experienced that first night, it would be amazing if they ever came up for air at all.

"I thought Hermes would never leave," Pan said as he leaned over her. Kat was caged between his body and his arms, which rested on either side of her head. He kissed her with such ferocity that she groaned from it. Free from his glamour and clothing, his hard length brushed against her stomach. She trembled with eagerness.

Pan slid a hand between them until it brushed up against her sensitive folds and rubbed the hidden nub there, making her gasp. "You like that, vixen?"

She answered him by arching up, begging for more with movements and sighs. He licked a trail down her body and explored her with his tongue. He assaulted her with his mouth until she screamed and shook from it. He lapped the evidence greedily and crawled up her body, kissing her once more as he entered her. Pan teased her with his length and thickness until he was to the hilt.

Kat whimpered and wriggled to create delicious friction. Finally, Pan slid back out, almost completely. Each thrust afterward came quicker than the last until both were so lost in the sensations, in the rhythm, that everything ceased to exist outside of the act.

The second orgasm swept her away. And as she flew high, he continued to thrust, keeping her grounded to this world. Keeping her tied to him. He kissed her with a passion that shook her to the core, matching his tongue with the speed of his movements. Kat could hardly breathe, but that was okay. It felt too good to worry about oxygen.

The third orgasm had her spouting off pretty words of love and a colorful vocabulary she would have been embarrassed by had she not been out of her head with pleasure. Her cheeks were damp, and her whole body alive like an electric wire.

Pan jerked against her. He groaned, biting gently on the tendon between her neck and shoulder, drawing out her orgasm as he spilled into her. He rolled to the side, pulling her close to him as he did. His hand rested on her stomach, comforting the tiny life beginning to develop there.

Kat snuggled against him, aware she hadn't just found the love of her life, but a family as well. Contentment washed over her as she opened her eyes and caught a glimpse of the night sky through the window. The stars Pan held so dear watched over them from above the Pine Barrens, witnesses to the happiness they both felt from lying in each other's arms.

BONUS SCENE

Olympus, 1123 B.C.

"You will never believe what your offspring has done now."
Hermes landed lightly on his feet in front of Zeus' throne and lifted a brow. Considering Pan had shunned his family, left Olympus, and had little control over his magic, there was absolutely no telling what he'd done. "I shudder to think."

Zeus stroked his clean-shaven chin and narrowed his eyes, the dark eyebrows plummeting toward the bridge of his nose in his annoyance. "Where to begin? Oh, yes, he defiled a virgin sacrifice meant for Dionysus, which then caused Dionysus to seek vengeance. Pan fought back and now all the human males present have become a new breed of monsters. Apollo named them the *Satyroi*."

Hermes had zeroed in on one aspect: Pan had fought back. *Good for him!* It wasn't in his blood to lie down and take that shit, not from the likes of Dionysus. "So some female chose Pan over Dionysus and everyone lost their minds? He looks like me, so can we really blame her for having exceptional taste in men?"

"That is all you have to say? Hermes, this is a serious matter. Pan must be punished for making a mess of things. Had he stayed in Olympus—"

"Had he stayed in Olympus he would be miserable and bored. His powers are centered on nature. Like Demeter, he needs to be close to things that grow. Which is why she only lives here during the half a year she has Persephone, and even then, she has to seclude the two of them to her garden."

Zeus grunted and waved a hand, brushing a dark lock of hair from his eye. "If he had stayed to learn his powers, he would not have cursed those poor mortals. What do you have to say about that?" There was a glint in his eye. His father thought he'd pointed out the crux of the issue.

Hermes, however, was not convinced his son did anything to warrant a punishment. "If a group of mortals stood around to watch two gods cursing each other, it serves them right that they were affected. Fools." He bit his lip to hide his pleasure when Zeus' smile faltered. Always these games between them. None of the other gods dared debate an issue with Zeus without fearing retribution. Hermes was too quick to be smited, so he'd tell Zeus every piece of his mind if he felt it necessary. "Where is Pan now?"

Zeus closed his eyes and concentrated, searching the mortal plain. "Beside the Asopos. Kithairon. The woman he defiled, the nymph. She has died. He blames himself and mourns her." Zeus sighed. "I suppose you should go to him, but hear me now, Hermes. He is not to be brought back into Olympus, not in the state he put himself in. If you know what is best for you, you will cease contact with him. This is his punishment. He didn't want to be Olympian, and now he isn't. He's *Satyroi*."

"He is my son."

Zeus dipped his head, sadly. "And my grandson. It matters not in times like these."

"What if I don't obey this order?"

"He will be punished in...different ways. Go to him. Say your farewells."

Glaring at his father, Hermes turned his back on the King of Olympus and stormed out of the temple. Fluttering down the paths through the city, Hermes passed a multitude of gods and goddesses, all giving him looks out the corners of their eyes. Whispers built in volume until he heard bits and pieces of their chatter.

"He brought upon her death."

"Nobody is fool enough to anger Dionysus; he's not stable."

"Apollo settled *that* issue."

Why had Apollo stepped in? He'd only made things much worse. Hermes took flight, the wings on his ankles beating quickly with his haste. He shot through the gates of Olympus, exiting the realm of the immortals and cascaded down the path of the mountain. Cities and wilderness passed beneath him like dust caught in the breeze, and within moments he was beside his son on the bank of the Asopos.

"Pan, I... Gods, what happened to you?" Hermes took several steps back in surprise as Pan faced him. He was nude, in the throes of lust, but doing nothing to relieve it. He had grown horns from upon his head which resembled the curled appendages of a ram, and his legs had been reshaped and covered in hair. His hooves were the most surprising, though Hermes had seen such before. The Minotaur of Crete came to mind.

Except, Hermes wasn't looking at a Minotaur. There were some similarities, but he remained mostly a man in form. *Satyroi...* His son was a *Satyros*. Satyr.

"Go away!" Pan shouted and covered himself, wincing at the contact.

"I do not wish to offend you," Hermes said softly, "but you really need to take care of *that*."

Pan roared at him, and then thrashed into the cold waters of the river and dove in. "Do you think I haven't tried! Nothing is working."

"Well. I can find a woman for you, if you wish."

"I do not need my father picking out my women for me. A woman got me into this mess."

"I heard what happened. Do you want to talk about it?" Hermes sat himself on the ground, frowning at the strange instrument beside him, hidden by the tall blades of grass. It seemed to be composed of water reeds, seven in all, bound together shortest to tallest. "What is this?"

Splashing and cursing exploded from the river, and Pan exited the water to snatch the instrument away. "I call it the *syrinx*. I made it from the reeds that marked her body's passing. It's all that is left of her."

Hermes remained quiet and stared from the instrument to Pan and back. Objects made from beings of magic by those with power were often dangerous when in the wrong hands. Zeus was right in one regard: Pan did not know the limits of his magic. What he created could do fantastical things, but it could also bring destruction.

"Why are you staring at me like that?" Pan asked.

"Because I worry what these changes will bring to your future."

Pan scowled. "You don't care about me. You won't even tell me who my mother is."

Pain lacerated Hermes' heart. Hybris had made him swear not to tell. It was nothing against Pan. "One day I will tell you, but not today. Tell me about Syrinx, the nymph?"

"She was a human when we were together. Somehow, something I did changed her."

His eyebrows lifted. "You turned a woman into a nymph? Really?"

Obviously it hadn't been the right thing to say. "Why do you act like it is so surprising?"

"Because no one has done such a thing before."

"So you're saying I am even more of an abomination than before with the horns and hooves? Wonderful."

Hermes stood once more. He tried to approach his son, but Pan kept a distance between them. A shiver ran through the skin above his hip. The mark of the caduceus had settled there this week. It was a staff with two snakes entwined around it that gave Hermes his wings and was the symbol of his messenger status to Zeus. The shiver was letting him know Zeus was calling him back. His time was up.

Hermes opened his mouth to say his goodbyes when Pan spoke first.

"I wanted her. If I had been thinking clearly, I would have put it together who she was and why touching her was a bad idea. She'd been promised to Dionysus, but had chosen me."

He probably shouldn't repeat his quip about her good taste in men, so he nodded instead. "I understand. Not every choice we make will be the right one, but we can only strive to do the best we can. She wanted you, and you wanted her. And that is why they call it temptation, my son. It's everything we think we want, what we think we need, and the consequences fail to make themselves known until it is too late."

Pan nodded. "The consequences were a bit harsh, I think."

Hermes laughed, and Pan cracked a hint of a smile. But then the caduceus shivered again and he sobered.

"I have to go. Zeus is calling me back to Olympus."

Pan's scowl returned. "Leave then. I'm fine on my own. I need to go find the others and see how bad this curse is. If the lust is this excruciating for me, it's going to be worse on former mortals. I can't let them leave the mountain and wander into the villages below."

Even the pride he felt in his son's responsibility for the others couldn't diminish the heartbreak of having to leave him now, when he needed Hermes the most. This punishment wasn't so much for Pan, but for him. A reminder of who was in control, and who was merely the messenger.

Message received.

"Pan, I—"

"Go!" Pan gritted out, turning his back.

Hermes watched him leave, emotions gripping him hard. One day he'd be able to make it up to Pan. One day.

ABOUT THE AUTHOR

Rebekah Lewis has always been captivated by fictional worlds. An avid reader and lover of cinema, it was only a matter of time before she started writing her own stories and immersing herself in her imagination. Rebekah's most popular series, The Cursed Satyroi, is paranormal romance based on Greek mythology. She also writes Fantasy and Time Travel. When satyrs, white rabbits, and stubborn heroes aren't keeping her busy, she may be found putting her creativity to use as an award-winning cover artist. Rebekah holds a Bachelor of Arts in English Literature and lives in Savannah, GA with her cat, Bagheera.

www.Rebekah-Lewis.com

facebook.com/RebekahLewisAuthor

twitter.com/RebekahLLewis

instagram.com/rebekahlewisauthor

bookbub.com/authors/rebekah-lewis

goodreads.com/RebekahLewis

BOOKS BY REBEKAH LEWIS

-The Cursed Satyroi Series-
Wicked Satyr Nights
Midnight at the Satyr Inn
Under the Satyr Moon
Mercury Rising
Satyr from the Shadows
The Satyr Prince
Pride Before the Fall

-London Mythos-
Rescued by a Sea Nymph

-Wonderland-
The Vanishing
The Unraveling

-Other Books-
Through the Maelstrom
Hela Takes a Holiday
Monsters in the Dark

Made in the USA
Columbia, SC
01 May 2024

34753192R00141